WOMEN AND WHISKEY

WOMEN AND WHISKEY

A NOVEL

ERIC MAUS

Highball Press
New York

Library of Congress Control Number: 2025922484
Maus, Eric
Women and Whiskey / Eric Maus
290 Pages
ISBN: 979-8-9935228-6-9 (ebook)
ISBN: 979-8-9935228-0-7 (Paperback)
ISBN: 979-8-9935228-1-4 (Hardcover)

Front cover image by Joni Wildman
Book design by Joni Wildman @JoniWildart
Author Photo by Amanda at Sub/Urban Photography

Second printing edition 2026.

Eric Maus
767 Broadway Ave #1398
Manhattan, NY 10003
USA

To all the women I ever lied to

WOMEN AND WHISKEY

ONE:

AT THE OTHER END OF THE BAR, the woman in a cardinal dress perches atop a stool amongst the usual line of crows.

High cheekbones painted to perfection, a plunging neckline drapes over her slender frame, and the wedding ring on her left hand presses against her half-melted vodka tonic. She's a vision of Venus and just as lifeless.

Shoulders hunched, she taps at her phone, sighs, and flips it face down on the bar. Burying her face in her hands, she wants to cry, but she can't—there's nothing left to cry about. All she needs to do is sign the divorce papers.

A light glows beneath her phone. Unable to stop herself, she picks it up and reads the message. Shaking her head, her grin turns into a grimace. She drops her phone onto the bar. Whatever was said, she's leaving on read.

Her fingers find the straw again.

She ducks her head to suck down her cocktail. Her smoky green eyes discover mine and linger as she empties her drink.

She turns away, showing off her backless dress, and watches the small wooden stage by the door, where two men with beards play the guitar and the washboard.

Their relentless rattles and strums fill the sultry room with a carnival-like atmosphere. Freckles march up her spine. The muscles of her shoulder ripple as she twirls the ends of her espresso brown hair.

I swirl my glass and come up with only ice water.

Casually, I get up from my stool, tighten my burgundy tie, and tuck the rumpled ends of my white button-up into my tailored trousers. I remember I'm wearing my nametag. I unclip it and slip it into my vest pocket.

It's Tuesday night. I just got off the evening shift at my job and I'm on the next shift tomorrow morning. Sophie texts, wondering where I am, but I'm not ready to go home yet. My mood is ripe—a combination of strung-out and devil-may-care.

Weaving through the crowded tables, I pass a white-haired couple watching the musicians. The man taps his foot to the beat, his hand wrapping the palm of the woman he met when he was my age. That's the dream, I think—to be that old and still be holding onto each other for dear life.

Too bad it's boring as hell.

You see, I've got women all figured out. It's a blessing and a curse. To be able to approach any woman with poise and charm, like I do, doesn't take luck, it's a skill honed from years of practice. There's an art to love. A language to saying all the right things. I'm a connoisseur with a taste for all varieties and subtleties.

The married woman pretends not to notice when I step into the bar space next to her. My whole routine relies upon the moment between making my drink order and speaking to her. This is where I prepare. I decide how she is the prettiest woman in the bar. This is vital. Even if she isn't

the best looking around, to sound the least bit convincing, I must believe she is a goddess amongst mortals. I glance her once up and down—I suppose I could worship her.

Her diamond-studded earrings glint in the bar light, but I can tell those have been complimented before, to no avail. The laser precision of her make-up says she's either a fashionista or self-conscious, neither the territory for stimulating conversation. She flits her hair.

A sweet, floral perfume wafts over to me. It's *Unmistakable*. It's the same fragrance as Sophie's. I bought it for her on a Tuesday some years ago. She hasn't changed since.

I lean over the bar and give the bartender my drink order: a whiskey-soda. The difference between men and boys doesn't start with what's in their glass. It starts when they begin a conversation with a woman.

The first words mark a transcendent moment between the past and future. When I meet a woman, the weight of these words entwines our lives for the next few seconds, to the next few minutes, to the next few days, maybe for the next few weeks, to months, to the years that follow. If I don't wear a condom, life itself can hinge upon what I'm about to say, but let's not get ahead of ourselves.

"Excuse me," I say over my shoulder, interrupting her dissection of her fingernails. "Are you wearing *Unmistakable?*"

Then, there's the moment after my first line. It's a stretched amount of silence where my words hang upon a metal wire—ready to be snipped or electrified.

A current of surprise overtakes her. She reacts, "How did you know?"

This is connection.

From here on out, she'll be judging my every word. She'll be guessing whether I had sisters or an overbearing mother or if my girlfriend's love steeps my soul. Or she'll think my question is a clever ploy. Am I a snake wound around a barstool?

That is why I must read for moments like these. Wisdom doesn't grow on trees. I don't read just books or magazines. I read gazes, smiles, and most importantly, the words coursing out of her mouth. One must be well-read to read well. I'm reading her look—

She'll give me one chance. She knows the type of man who greets women at bars. She endures that type well, but she doesn't know me. That is why my response matters—my words separate me from the others. She doesn't know my story yet, but I'll make her want to. My silver tongue aims to please.

She's alone for a reason. I don't need to know why, but I do want to make her mine. I can be ruthless. I can be direct. I want her. I can say that. It isn't smart, but it's the truth. Yet, the truth doesn't win a game of poker; the notion of the truth does.

Humor.

That's what I see she needs beneath the veneer of her downcast eyes, a slight twist of light, like the tonic in her glass of vodka.

I imitate the ad, *"It's your signature, sealed in a scent. Unmistakable."* I drop back into myself. "If I'm not mistaken, it feels like I'm standing next to a field of wildflowers."

"Glad to hear." She smirks. "A store on State Street gave me a free sample."

"Oh yeah? Where did you go?" I ask, gripping the backrest of the empty seat next to her.

She crinkles her nose, amused. "Aren't I a bit old for you?"

Sure, the fine lines of age weave creases across her brow, mark ravines in her cheeks, and give her that deep look of someone no longer in their twenties. It's an objection. She is testing my commitment. I could back out now, but this is where the fun begins.

Most men will say something stupid and leave tongue-tied, but I'm not like most men. I'm willing to lose it all on my only chance. "What do they say about wine? It only gets better with age?"

My assured breath disappears. My ego, a limp balloon, waits to be blown up or blown away.

A breath of laughter escapes her, she says, "Rachel." It's enough air to start a true conversation.

"Pleasure to meet you. I'm Danny." I lean in. "What brings you here tonight?"

"Bored."

"Bored?" I say, knowing a few ways to cure such an affliction. "You're in luck, you just so happened to meet Madison's finest poet."

She arches her brow and says, "And what kind of poetry do you write?" Her voice is as smooth as a cold shower first thing in the morning.

I squint in well-practiced thought, an aloof artist's look, the reminiscing of life's work, "I've written love poems, hate poems, poems of star-crossed lovers, two silhouettes passing in the night, you know, the kind of things that make you wonder what if you could do it all over again."

"Sounds romantic." Her eyes roll. "Is there any money in that?"

"Why do you ask?" I smile.

Rachel sighs, resting her elbows on the bar. She uncrosses her hands. The ring sparkles openly in front of her. It's a telltale sign she's taken, but then again, why is she alone? "Just because you call yourself a poet, doesn't mean you're a poet."

As if I haven't heard that before, I clear my throat and give my voice a low grovel—

> *There's no true way to woo.*
> *When fire ignites between a lonesome two,*
> *then it's a law, one must pursue.*

I bounce my gaze to hers, her lips tremble ever so slightly—

> *By hell or heaven above,*
> *it is lust that begets love.*
> *It's desire that forgets romance,*
> *and a well-timed approach*
> *that starts the first dance.*

The music pulses with a yo-yoing rhythm of strings and thumps. Rachel lingers on me, her mouth a smooth line. Warmth swells in my cheeks, and I clench my jaw, keeping my face as serious as I can despite the absurdity. She's never met a man who recited a poem to her. And a good poem at that—I know because I wrote it.

Her lips part as a white flag creases between. "How long did it take you to memorize that one?"

"If I told you, I think our conversation would be over."

"Would that be so bad?"

"It depends." I place my foot on the bar's footrest and lean forward getting closer to her, "Are you trying to have a good night?"

"I could use one."

My response is a look, not words. It is patience, not actions. It is her examining me now. Words would ruin this moment. There must always be room for silence in seduction, but silence doesn't mean nothing happens. I look at her, into her, and she does the same to me. It is brief, but heavy, this silence.

Love springs into my thoughts again. The quest of my heart and the drug of my mind. Whether it's one night or a lifetime, there's no other feeling like it. Despite being committed to someone else, this woman could love me. Like I could love her, just for tonight. A passion that lives and dies by the morning light, a quick hit of something new to remind us how much we truly care about our significant others.

In her stare, there is pain. She knows it. She tries to hide it with mascara, with lipstick, with liquor. Yet it remains, dull and unrelenting. I cannot help wanting to relieve it, wanting to love it, wanting her to love me. I stay quiet and wait. I can't tread on someone unready to let go. It doesn't matter how pretty or desperate they are.

She breaks the silence. "What do you want?"

I laugh. "To get to know you."

She gives a multi-syllabic, "Please!"

I shoot the bartender a look and he comes over. "Another whiskey-soda for me and a vodka-tonic for her," I say. He nods and gets to it. I turn back to Rachel.

She pretends not to notice me, which is fine. I prefer attention though. I think over my words. I was forward, perhaps too forward; if I draw back, I'll draw her back into conversation. Then again, I don't want to waste our time getting to know each other.

I look once around the bar to see if there are any other possibilities tonight. Even if there was another woman to try, I know I'd leave here regretting Rachel.

Alright, I'll risk this line anyway, I say, "You know what's attractive about you?"

She looks back at me over her shoulder. No one can resist a compliment.

"You try so hard to be beautiful." Her stare stays on mine. "But what you don't realize is your eyes can kill a man with just one look."

"Is this enough of a look for you?" Her brow creases and she kind of growls at me.

"Ow." I clutch my chest.

"You're terrible," she shakes her head. "Does that actually work on women?"

"You tell me," I leer. It's up to her to decide what kind of night she wants. She knows the type of man who greets women at bars.

The bartender plays his part well. He slides the vodka-tonic toward her and takes away her empty. He pushes the whiskey-soda to me. Picking it up, I say, "Cheers."

Her wedding ring flashes as she holds the new cocktail. She clinks her glass against mine. She swivels in her chair, sipping, then says, "Have a seat."

I look at the leather stool. It's a coveted trophy, but with a little discipline, I'll have much more than a leather stool underneath me. Before I taste my new whiskey-soda, I say, "Tell me about yourself."

She says, "Are you going to sit down?"

"Depends on how interesting of a story you're going to tell me."

"What do you want to know?"

I say, "How'd you end up in this bar all alone?"

"Do you really care?" she says.

I stir my drink, waiting for her to answer.

"The University Hospital's Summer Gala was at the Monona Terrace."

"Oooh la-la, fancy schmancy, open bar?"

"All doctors do is drink. I swear they are the unhealthiest people. The God complexes. I had to get out of there."

"You're a doctor?"

"Hell no, I do prescription sales for this new drug. I'm visiting the University Hospital all week. You ever get hepatitis. I'm your girl."

She keeps talking about her work. The way to sell to a doctor is not directly, but indirectly—to be thorough, but never wasting time. How their gaze often roams her up and down. They know the stats; there's ten other drugs like it. For them to sign the deal, they need to be seduced by her charm. She's lucky her mother taught her how to be an actress.

I watch her words tumble out, her cheeks redden, and her pupils dilate. Words, words, and more words. She needs to talk. She has such warm and inviting lips, the perfect shade of red. She is lonely. Does her husband know where she is? She's by herself a long way from home.

Rachel plays with her hair, she sucks down her vodka-tonic fast, she is doing everything at once and almost doing nothing at all. I am patient.

A familiar vibration strikes my pocket. Sophie. Another text. I ignore it.

I continue to ask questions about Rachel's work until I know too much about it. I move on to the city she is staying in: Madison. She likes it, she supposes, but it is nothing like New York. I agree. The people here eat too much, drink too much, and know too much with too little to do. It's scary in a way, too many people knowing your business. So, she says. I don't disagree. It's getting harder and harder to go out without seeing someone I slept with. I don't say that. I let her talk. She is seducing herself now.

Rachel speaks about the Upper East Side, about her friends, and the rent. It's all the stuff I've heard before from other people, about other places, but it is important, nonetheless. She thinks she could live here. She thinks she could live anywhere. She's lived in New York City her whole life.

I ask about her family. Her mother was born on Long Island and moved to the city at 26 to pursue acting. She met Rachel's father at a theater playhouse—he was there with another woman, but the moment he saw her mother, he fell madly in love.

Her father grew up in Queens. He died in a car wreck when she was 10 and her mom never remarried. I peek at her hands. Her right covers her left. She starts asking me questions.

I'm from a small town in Northern Wisconsin that no one's ever heard of. My parents got divorced when I was a kid. My dad drinks himself stupid every night in my childhood home. My mom moved to Minneapolis and enjoys the suburban lifestyle with some finance guy named John. I only ever see her at Christmas. She wonders when I'm going to propose. I don't say that last part to Rachel. Instead, I mention that I'm a graduate of the fine university here and a full-time poet.

She asks about my publishing history. I make up some magazines. She doesn't cross-reference them with her phone, but she does say she's going to look me up later. I say that I'll give her one of my books, if I ever see her again. She says her husband is in publishing, so she already has too many books to read.

She admits she comes to the city too often to count, but it's her first time staying downtown. It's so much more alive.

I'm surprised I've never seen her before.

She isn't. She usually keeps to the hotel room.

My ears perk up as I wonder which one.

Tonight, this isn't like her, but based on what's happened lately, she needs to relax.

I don't want to know any more than that. Digging too deep turns a hook-up into a therapy session. My eyes catch the diamond crowning her left hand. Setting down my whiskey, I say, "What are you thinking about?"

"Nothing," she says, playing with the furthest tip of her hair. Her eyes big and glossy.

"Are you saying I have you speechless?" I quip.

Silence slinks between us. A midnight wind washes through Rachel. She's a long way from home. She trembles. It's subtle this trembling. A subdued resistance to the temptation she yearns to let in. The air prickles her arms.

Rachel pinches her eyelids shut and opens them wide just as fast. She's forgotten the time, no doubt. She looks at her phone. On the screen, the flash of her husband's ghoulish smile. She pulls out her purse and drops her grinning husband inside. She says, "It's late and I have work in the morning."

"Let me walk you back to your hotel." It's a reasonable request.

"I'm perfectly fine. What—my hotel's just across the Capitol Square?" she says.

I shrug. "There's at least one that way."

"That's not that far." She slings her purse over her shoulder and asks for the check.

I've got to pull her back somehow. "But there are criminals out there who prey on tourists."

"I'm not a tourist."

"Oh yeah, are you from around here?" I ask.

Rachel is taken aback as I hide my smile. It's the game I want to play with her. Little fights with our words—a jousting match, swordplay.

"Trust me," I say. "You need an experienced tour guide like myself."

"Usually when someone says 'trust me,' it means 'don't.'"

"Fine. Fine." I cast off her words with a soft, encouraging voice. "I respect that. I respect you. Hope you enjoy the rest of your time in Madison." I get the bartender's attention and signal for the check.

"You're leaving too? What? You struck out, so now you've got to get home to your girlfriend?"

Honestly, I'm getting out of here because I don't want to miss my chance to walk out with her. I don't say that. Instead, I say, "As much as I want to soak this seat in whiskey, I've got to write in the morning, so—"

I set cash on the bar. "It was a pleasure meeting you, Rachel. Remember to look me up. Maybe buy a book or two."

In one swift turn of my heel, I walk away—a clean break.

I can't look back. If she sees how desperate I am for her, she'll disappear.

Once more, our conversation hangs on that metal wire.

TWO:

"WAIT UP—" Rachel's voice calls from inside the bar as I exit.

Out on the street, the night swoons. Royal-blue darkness shades the stark white dome of the Wisconsin Capitol building. I wait outside in the August heat, beaming at my luck. Rachel's dress rustles toward me. Her heels click on the pavement—each step bringing us closer to what we want: to make love for no reason other than we can.

We walk the Capitol deck, a white-tiled promenade tucked along the Capitol walls and columns. Much dreamier than any city street.

"You ever gotten the tour of Madison?" Inspired by the cool air, a rush of romance sweeps through me. The fingers of whiskey puppeteer my hand, and I dare her to take it.

Raising her brow, she uncrosses her arms, drops her shoulders and lets out a short laugh. She says, "You think you're slick, don't you?"

I beckon her to grab my palm. "I don't want you getting lost. It's a boring tour and people generally wander off if I don't hold their hand."

Rachel surrenders with a groan.

When she clasps my hand, I announce, "Rachel. This is the center of the city: the Wisconsin State Capitol. It was built…a long time ago. Modeled after the United States Capitol. In fact, Lady Liberty on top points east, toward DC, in honor of our country."

She stares skyward. "It's really tall."

"Tall indeed, it's the tallest building in Madison. City ordinance states that nothing can be taller."

"How tall is it?"

I look up at the great spire and give it my best guess—I mean I'm spewing knowledge leftover from a third-grade field trip. "A thousand feet."

"That's not a thousand feet. Maybe four hundred. What kind of tour guide are you?"

"Moving on!" When we're by the great columns before the Capitol entrance, I ask her, "Do you want to go inside?"

"We can do that?" She says. "It's after midnight."

"Yeah, it's always open," I say. With confidence, I pull the door handle. Immediately, I'm met with a thud. It's locked. "When did they start—?" I try another one, just to be sure.

Rachel's laughter mocks me. But it's the most 'her,' I've felt all night. She's loosening up. If it takes a few pratfalls to get back to her hotel room, I'll play the victim. I don't mind.

"Come on." Her feet scuff the ground.

My phone vibrates. I silence the low hum by jamming my fist into my pocket. It's Sophie, of course.

Rachel's a few paces ahead. I answer it.

"What's up?" I whisper.

Sophie murmurs through the line, "Where are you?"

"Kovski's," I say. "Probably going to stay here. It's late." Rachel checks over her shoulder to see if I'm following

her. I quickly whisper, "I love you, bye." And hang up.

Rachel hugs herself, a forlorn silhouette in the streetlight. Her red dress colors the full moon night. I go to her. My hands find their way around her shoulders, and I bring her into me. She collapses against my shoulder, and I stroke her lower back.

There's a weight to love. For her, it is about 1.5 carats and adorning her finger. It used to be heavier. A weight she gladly carried. She put everything she owned into too. But when it came to talking about the future with her husband, it turns out the future has no weight—they still have no kids, no mortgage, no plan, at least not one being followed. And yet that nothingness weighs more than everything she owns. A burden heavy enough to make her stumble.

For tonight, I'm going to carry that weight for her. Our secret pact. We don't need to say a thing. We don't need to know about the past. Or plan the future. We live in this moment, nothing more and nothing less, seduced by desire.

In the shadow of a large rose bush, I interlace my fingers with hers. The cold metal chills my skin. Her warm hands clutch mine. I pull her toward me again and she trips over the tip of my toe.

Rachel catches herself with a brush against my chest. The urge surges through her. She shouldn't surrender. She shouldn't be out with this man, this child. But there's something about me. She shouldn't press her lips against mine. And yet, she does.

When we kiss, it's what we've been waiting for. We sway like new dancers. Without grace, without music, we bounce off the Capitol wall, fighting each other back. Our monsters inside rage.

"We can't." Rachel resists. "We shouldn't do this."

I'm too busy kissing her neck. I explore the line of her

ear. Its discovery leads back to her jaw, then to her lips. This is the love I crave. Passionate fire, clumsy, and perilous. Sophie and I burned this way.

"Come on." Rachel grabs my hand.

"Where are we going?" I say, stepping with her.

"The Continental."

I can't help, but smile.

We wobble down the Capitol steps, arm in arm. At the corner, a second monument to Lady Liberty, cast in black steel, overlooks State Street, her arm guiding our way to her hotel.

A homeless man lies at Lady Liberty's feet, staring at us. "Can you spare some change?"

I toss him a couple ones from my vest pocket. Some of my tip money. Whatever. Poor soul.

Rachel squeezes my palm harder knowing I'm a good man.

After the next block, the Continental glows.

Behind two-story floor-to-ceiling windows, you find a gold and marble lobby with a long chandelier, descending from the vaulted ceilings, that dangles over the grand center staircase. It's the kind of place wedding magazine editors send someone to write about every few years.

Before we enter, I glance at the bell stand. No one there. Behind the front desk, the night agent sits at the far end of the counter, staring at his phone. It's the slow time of night.

I lead Rachel to the elevators. She asks, "Been here before?"

As those bronzed steel doors glide to a close, I say, "Once or twice."

"You're such a player, aren't you?" The elevator hums.

"A gentleman never kisses and tells," I say, playing

it cool. She knows the type of man I am. Right now, I've got Cupid's arrow sticking straight out of my ass and plan to yank it out before work in the morning. I pull her to me before she can think twice about what we're about to do.

We kiss, heavy and reckless. A breath escapes her lips every time we break away. She presses hard into me, giving me her weight. I take her in. I take her all in.

The doors slide open. She straightens up like a housewife and tugs the wrinkles from her dress. We step out—one behind the other, distant. In the hallway, we're two prudes hobbling to bed. I guess she can only love me in private, away from the prying eyes of judgment. I realize there are cameras on that elevator.

Rachel removes the keycard from her purse. Swipes it against the lock. And pushes down the handle. A red beep blocks our path. She swipes again. And red. Again and red. She's doing it too fast. I can't stop myself any longer. I take the card from her. Hold it against the pad like I've done a thousand times. The green light turns on. Her hand presses down and we stagger inside.

Frenzied hands. Frenzied lips. The thud of my button-up hitting the floor. I reach around her waist and unzip the teeth of her dress. I slide it off her shoulders—I've been dreaming about this moment all night.

Rachel wears these old lady undies, the spandex thick and soft. "Sorry. I wasn't—" She yanks them down and flings them at the door. "Planning on having sex tonight."

What's before me, vulnerable and naked, is the real Rachel. A haunting befalls me. Her eyes, green like Sophie's, dark and serene, send a chill through my body. I shiver.

Rachel crawls onto the bed. Adrift in the king-sized

mattress, she lies open before me, her hips glowing in the streetlight that cuts through the blinds. I glimpse the valley between. She asks, "Are you going to kiss me or what?"

I lurch forward. There is no past. There is no future. There is only now. I drop to my knees. She pulls me closer, her fingers digging into my hair. I bury my face between her thighs. A surge of craving electrifies my tongue. Her back arches. She moans and moans as I devour her.

THREE:
bellboy

 Y PHONE ALARM CHIRPS. Rachel doesn't stir. The plush hotel blanket, half on me, winds tightly around her. I shut it off. She's a heavy sleeper, or she's not used to such late nights. Judging by the pounding between my ears, it's a combination of a few things.

The clock reads 7 AM. I'm going to be late for work if I don't run. I yawn and stretch.

Being in a hurry and being quiet is a skill I've mastered. In well-practiced choreography, I scramble into my clothes in the faint light. It takes two attempts for my undershirt before it's the right way around my neck. I nearly snap my ankle stumbling over Rachel's heels in the hallway.

Before I leave, I turn back to look at her one last time. She slumbers. I think to myself, Rachel, I'll always remember you. You taught me something: married women know how to fuck.

As I glide down the elevator to the basement, her taste lingers on my breath. I take the nametag out of my pocket and pin it back into the breast of my vest.

The doors open to the vestibule of the hotel's underground parking garage. Through the glass exit doors, the guests park their cars and bring their luggage into the hotel. Beside that door, there's another door. A discreet beige door with a key reader.

I pull out my wallet. Tucked inside its folds is the skeleton key to the hotel. I tap it against the keypad. A green light blinks, and the lock unlatches. I enter like last night never happened. A perfect escape.

In the windowless, high-ceilinged laundry room, I walk past the line of the washing machines and dryers. They spiral with white linens.

Two housekeepers, Carmen and Josephina, fold white bed sheets. I say, "Hola," as I pass.

Carmen, the older one, says, "Buenos días," in a soft, friendly voice. Josephina, braces covering her smile, nods. As I pass, they giggle together.

Josephina calls out, "Your fly is open."

I stop and look. Down there, my turquoise underwear glares at me through the hole in my crotch. I zip up. I say, "Thanks," and carry on. They keep on laughing. At least they're looking.

At the time clock, I punch my code in and press the key against the pad. Anything before 7:08 and you're on time. The clock of the digital screen says 7:07. From naked to work in under seven minutes, this has got to be the fastest commute in history. I might have to do this more often.

Hungry and mildly nauseous, I swipe a muffin from the cart for the morning buffet to heal my tender stomach. I head back through the laundry room and walk up the parking garage ramp. I've done this enough to know that I can finish my breakfast by the time I arrive at the hotel lobby's side entrance.

Weaving between the two large hotel vans, I stuff the rest of the muffin in my mouth and chew. I walk through

the side door and head to the bell stand in a slight hurry, acting like I valeted a car.

The bell captain stands behind our oversized chestnut podium. A six-five suit with straight razor cheeks, round eyes, and a short frown plastered on his big, square head. His hands cradle the vehicle log. He senses my footsteps and checks his watch. "Where have you been?"

I give him an easy smile. "Parked a car."

"Bullshit. We haven't had a guest all morning."

I take out the fiver I keep in my pocket for occasions like this one. Making tips is what he's about, and if I'm pulling in cash, he doesn't bother me. It pays to be prepared. "What can I say? He was outside waiting for me."

The bell captain scans me up and down. "Wipe the crumbs off your vest. This is the Continental, not a Best Western."

"Aye, aye, captain."

The captain leans in and whispers, "And zip your fly."

Brushing away the muffin crumbs, I realize he's right, my fly is open again. I zip myself up.

Between the hangover buzzing in my ear and last night's work shift, I could use a cup of coffee. I sidestep the bell stand and make for the luggage closet, the bellman's entrance into the front office.

I pull out my keycard and swipe it. I walk through the closet filled with polished brass luggage carts and stacks of suitcases. It's a good place to hide out when I need a break from being nice to guests; anyone can 'organize the luggage.'

The dopey, fat-bellied bellman named Givens occupies the mirror, fixing his tie. I don't acknowledge him. I step into the next room, where the concierge answers phones.

And there she is in all her glory: the coffee maker.

The pitcher contains the sheerest film of coffee burned to the bottom.

"Sorry, I took the last cup," I hear over my shoulder. If it were anyone else, I'd be upset, but it's Eva. She leans back in her chair and sips her coffee mug with her pinky out, adding a slurp for sport. Her headset microphone pushed up above her head.

"You're a monster," I say to her.

"Shouldn't have been late to work. Aren't you supposed to start at seven?"

"Keeping tabs on me?" I say.

"No." Eva swivels, full circle in her chair. Obviously bored. No one calls before 8 AM, so she's always extra snarky until then.

Wrinkles gather beneath her eyes and along her cheeks—Eva's a couple of years older than me. An immigrant's daughter with a face sun-kissed from a childhood of early mornings. She left the farming community she was born into for college and never looked back. She fits in here. Her hands and feet are far too dainty for a life of tending crops or raising babies.

Sitting on the edge of her desk, this is our morning dance. It's how we both stay sane. Everyone's got their co-worker they get along with best, and for me, it's Eva. Sure, I want to fuck her, but she's made it abundantly clear that she respects herself too much to go on a date with a guy in a relationship. I should've never told her about Sophie, but I don't know, I sort of opened up to her about my girlfriend and why I worry about us so much. The funny thing is, I appreciate Eva all the more for the rule. Doesn't mean I still won't try. Come on, Eva fills a skirt too well for me not to dabble.

"What'd you get into last night?" I ask her.

Eva leans her elbows on the desk. She puts her knuckles below her chin, and says, "It was the full moon last night. I went to the Monona Terrace and watched it rise."

"Sounds like something a witch would do," I say. I pick up a Panda stress ball on her desk.

"I forgot to bring my eye of newt, so I couldn't cast any spells."

"You should've told me. I was at Foolproof," I say, tossing the ball up to myself.

"I just wanted to kind of be alone." Eva swipes a loose strand of her black hair behind her ear.

"You're kidding."

"You're a writer. I'm sure you know the feeling."

That's why I love talking to Eva. She gets it. "Of course. And a good writer knows that a story needs more than one character. Promise to call me next time. I'll be there."

"How's Sophie?" Ah, yes, there's the rub. Her little phrase lets me know I've strayed too far. Eva's one of the good ones.

"We're looking for a bigger place," I say. "She thinks—"

Eva drops her headset to her mouth. "Hello, Continental Hotel. Yessir, you can drink the water out of the tap. Yes, it's the same water we use for our laundry. Not the exact same water." She rolls her eyes, puts a finger gun to her head, and shoots herself.

I snort, loud. Eyes wide, she mouths, "Oh my God." Her voice cracks as she speaks into the mic: "Yes, sir. Yes. Just call back if you have any more stupid questions. I mean—questions. Just questions."

"Did you really say that?" I fling the stress ball at her.

Eva catches it and buries her head into her chest, black curls spilling over her face. She wipes the tears from her eyes as we cackle together. She exhales and tosses her hair back. When she smiles, the corners of her lips draw tight and her two front teeth slip out—a grin with puppyish charm.

The front office manager, Haseem, in a clean-cut suit, his hair coiffed, stomps out of his windowless office and goes to the printer. "What's so funny?" Haseem grabs the printed pages. As he taps the paper straight, he says, "Is it cause your fly's down?"

I look down—a wide-open canyon stares back at me. "I'm sorry, boss. I don't know why no one told me sooner." My voice trails toward Eva.

"Well, fix it. Eva, I want you to start training with Dave on the front desk today." Haseem walks back into his office. He slams the door behind him.

"Front desk, huh? Let me get some of that dirt off your shoulder." I pat her shoulder.

Eva preens, "Thank you."

"Why didn't you say anything about my fly?" I feel betrayed, even the housekeepers noticed it. She didn't, of all people, stare at my crotch once? That's absurd. The boss sees, but Eva doesn't? Come on.

Eva says, "I didn't want to tell you."

"Why? Because you didn't want to admit you were staring at my crotch?"

"No, because I think it's hilarious!" Eva keels over the desk hooting.

I don't find it funny. "Can you help me?" I say, innocent, I swear.

"I think you can zip it yourself. And you really shouldn't say that sort of stuff to me, especially at work."

"No!" I plead my case to avoid an HR nightmare. "It keeps opening. This is the third time in like 15 minutes."

"That sucks. Maybe, we have a safety pin somewhere." Eva digs through the top drawer of her desk—a mess of pens, business cards, and chocolate bars.

"Exposing your stash, huh?" I swipe a mini-Snickers bar. I unwrap it and pop it in my mouth. I reach for another one.

"Hey! Hands off." Eva slaps my wrist. She keeps searching.

"I've got a safety pin," Givens says from the doorway. I bristle at the sound of his reedy voice. Glasses teetering on the bridge of his nose, beads of sweat gathering at his temples, his chubby fingers still spindling around the tie, the bastard's been watching us.

Eva gives up and closes the drawer. "No luck here."

"Alright." I step into the bell closet. "Where is it?"

Givens plucks a safety pin holding up the bellman schedule on a corkboard. He puts a thumb tack in its place. He hands it to me.

I take the safety pin and turn to the brass bell cart. My back to Givens because I'm sure he's a perv. As I try not to give myself a dick piercing, I ask, "Were you spying on us?"

"No, not at all. I heard you were looking for a safety pin." Back at the mirror, Givens redoes his tie. He thrusts the tip of the tie through the loop and pulls with the other hand. He raises his head, pushes his glasses up with his finger, and says, "How's it look?" The tie ends at the hill of his bulbous stomach.

I snicker at his faux pas. "Fits you."

Givens yanks the tie apart again. "Don't lie to me." He grunts, runs his fingers through the knot and undoes it. "I hate these things." And he's back to trying to tie it. When he's nervous, he sweats. When he's frustrated, he sweats more. Yet, he remains smiling through his cadre of emotions never revealing a thing he's thinking.

I say, "I'm sick and tired of always seeing you out of the corner of my eye. You're like a goblin or something. If you've got a problem with me, say it." I push the pin through the fold of my pants and press together the safety pin.

Givens takes the two ends of his tie and looks at them with his brow creased. He puts one end over the other, shakes his head, and restarts. He puts the other end over the other. He nods. "Here we go." He checks the length. He straightens the tie over his midsection, doesn't like it, loosens the knot, and plays with the length until the long end hangs over his waistline. He looks up at me. "What were you saying?"

"Come on, Givens, answer my question."

"My name is *Ryan*." He undoes his tie again. "Not Givens."

"Yeah, yeah," I've known him for a couple of years. I can call him whatever I want. He's in my life, not out of desire, but out of the fact that we work together and must communicate sometimes. Also, he's a friend of Sophie's. They went to grade school together and maintained their friendship throughout college. I'm pretty sure they talk about me behind my back. Even worse, he calls himself a writer too. I know his type—a stalker in need of an excuse to spy on people. "Givens, what did you hear?"

"Look at this." He points with his index finger to the brass nametag on his right breast. "What does this say?"

It says *Ryan* in big black letters. I don't want to give him the satisfaction. I turn my back on him and head out the lobby door.

"You're awfully paranoid," he calls after me.

"I'm not paranoid." I watch him from the doorway, still struggling with his tie. "Let me do that." I grab the ends of his tie and tie it for him. For a moment, I want to strangle him. "I know what you're thinking, and whatever you perceive in that egghead of yours is made-up, alright? You have nothing to worry about. Eva and I are work friends." I fumble with the tie. "God, your neck is enormous." I manage to get the tie around him in some reasonable fashion. When I tighten it, I tighten it too tightly around his neck.

He squeals, "Hey!"

I say over my shoulder, "Mind your own business." Before he can respond, I push open the door to the lobby.

As soon as I step onto the marble tile floor, a woman, pulling a pack of cigarettes out of her purse, walks into me. I outstretch my hands and catch her before she falls. In my arms, Rachel flips her brown hair back to look at me. "Madison's finest poet, huh?"

I smirk. "Are you alright, miss?"

Rachel straightens her pinstripe blazer. "I looked you up this morning." She sticks a cigarette between her ruby lips.

"You missed me that much?"

Her frown doesn't quite say she was happy with what she found. She mumbles because of the cig, "Everything makes sense now." She isn't three-deep in liquor anymore.

"If you're following me," I recoil. "It's cool, but word of advice: don't be so obvious about it."

"Don't you have work to do, bellboy?" She walks through the side exit door.

I run ahead and get it for her. I say, "You need a lift to the University Hospital?" I jingle the van keys hanging from my belt loop.

Stepping outside, Rachel says, "I already booked with the other guy." She lights up and a silver cloud leaves her lips. She glances at my vest. "You know the one in the suit and tie?"

"Nice," I say, aware she's testing my aptitude for jealousy. "He's a good driver." I remain confident. "Not the best driver, but he'll get you there."

Rachel says, "That's all I need." Her gaze roams the curb looking for her chariot.

"Sure," I say, "it's all you need, but it's not all you want. I can tell you that much. He doesn't know the city like I do. He has no idea how many back roads you can take to get where you need to go."

"The usual way is fine by me," she breathes deeply into her cigarette.

The growl of the van engine comes up from the parking garage. I look hard into her, "Have a good day at work, Rachel."

"See you around," Rachel says, checking my nametag. "Daniel." Rachel pats out her cig in the hotel ashtray as the white hotel van pulls up to the curb.

Glare-proof sunglasses on, the bell captain looks out the driver's side window. "Ready?"

I guide Rachel into the busy street, stopping traffic.

She asks before stepping into the hotel van. "Why do you have a safety pin on your pants?"

"Someone broke my zipper last night," I say.

"Lucky guy."

I blush as she disappears into the van's far backseat.

The bell captain looks back at Rachel. "Would you like an ice-cold bottle of water? We keep them handy for our guests."

"I'm fine," Rachel says as I slam the van door.

I signal to the next lane of traffic to stop. A black BMW sedan brakes and waits.

The van speeds forward and merges into traffic. I walk back to the curb. In the reflection of the hotel front glass, I check out my crotch. Thrusting left, then right, the safety pin does its job. Realizing people can see me through the window, I gulp when I see the front desk. Eva and Givens wave, laughing.

Damnit.

I quickly turn my back on them and hang by the valet stand at the curb. I'm going to be here for a while. Stupid zipper.

But I don't get it—how often do people look at my dick?

FOUR:
old-fashioned

OPHIE'S SITTING WITH SOMEONE. A man. She's smiling. Through the window of the Old-Fashioned, I see her profile with him. Casual. Flirtatious, no doubt.

Sure, I'm 20 or 30 minutes late. It doesn't mean she can find a new man.

I stopped at a bookstore on State Street and looked at all the new books I'll never find time to read. Sophie doesn't understand the fascination. She's more of a reality TV fan. No plot, all drama.

The Old-Fashioned is a large, speakeasy-style restaurant with a long, gleaming wood bar, famous for its Old-Fashioneds and a greasy burger served with fried cheese curds.

"Sophie!" I say, ignoring the maître d, she can't be bothered anyway—this place is barren except for an old couple in a booth obviously here for the early bird specials.

I walk to Sophie's table and exhale when I see the man she's with—the waiter in a white shirt and brown apron. He's got an ear piercing, a big Roman nose, and curly brown hair that glistens with oil. He spots me and

stands. "Looks like your knight in shining armor has finally arrived."

Sophie smiles. "Thanks for keeping me company, Tyler."

"I'll bring you back a refill."

"You're the best," Sophie says.

"Could I get a classic old-fashioned with rye?" I ask before he steps away.

"Sure." The waiter tarries off to the bar. Sophie watches him go, then she turns her exquisite green eyes to me. Her stubby chin, angled cheeks and button nose are perfectly framed by the soft fall of her long, wavy mahogany hair.

"New friend?" I say. I take my rightful place across from her. On a sticky day like today, the waiter's heat clings to the grooves of the wooden chair. I lean forward to let it air out. "Sorry, I'm late."

Sophie frowns. "Where were you last night?"

"I was at Kovski's."

"What do you do when you're over there?"

"After the bars, we play video games. And sometimes, we're really drunk and the games go really late."

"Didn't you work this morning?"

"We skipped the bars part."

"So, you got wasted at your friend's house on a Tuesday?"

"And played video games." Sophie doesn't need to know about the married woman. Or any of the other women. She'd leave me in a heartbeat. What she doesn't know doesn't hurt her. It doesn't hurt us. I love her, you see.

What's love to me, you ask? Love is simple. That patter in the chest followed by an urge between the legs. It's yes in a world filled with no. When you know love, you go with the flow. I made love to Rachel last night. Tonight, I'm making love to Sophie. At least, hopefully. After being together for so long, it's harder to seduce her than it is to seduce a stranger at the bar.

Her excuses for saying no multiply anytime I'm horny. She's got a headache. It's too late. Or she's too gassy. If she understood how much I need her body, she wouldn't be so prudish, and then we could give each other orgasm after orgasm until we die of happiness.

"Why shouldn't we break up right now?" Sophie snaps.

When she goes loud, I go low. "Whoa, hey. Something's bothering you. What's going on?"

"You think you can show up whenever you want and I'll always be there. When we first started dating, you would never ever be late or not answer my texts."

"I answered your phone call."

"But you were super short and weird about it. It sounded like you were outside."

"We were playing this big trophy hunt game. Kinda got really into it and lost track of time. That's all. It got super late and I crashed on his couch. I'm going to do better. I promise. You are the most important thing in the world to me, and all I want is to see you happy. I love you." I give her my most watery eyes.

Sophie was the first girl to tell me she loved me. I didn't say it back right away. Too dumbfounded by the statement. Me? I thought. How could I be so lucky? We started dating our senior year in college. She studied art. I studied writing. We met at the library at the shared computer kiosk. I sneezed. She said, "Bless you."

Those were her first words to me: "Bless you." And mine back: "Thank you." We used the world's most polite pick-up lines. I didn't think much of it until I looked at her—did a double-take. She was a wild beauty with emerald eyes, rimmed red, hungover from the

Thursday night bar specials, racing to print out her art history homework.

Sophie peeked at me, her gaze lingering on this mysterious man writing a poem before his morning class. Our hearts pattered. I told her my name and that's how Sophie and I began.

Call me a nerd or a romantic, but the poem I wrote that day included the line I'll never forget—*soft, sweet sneezes fill my heart with glee.* (Hey, I wasn't always an incredible writer.)

I break the silence. "I was thinking about you today."

She says, "I hope you think about me every day."

"Can I talk?" I say. "I was thinking about you today because they installed this painting in the hotel lobby. This monstrous thing. Splashes of gold on white canvas. It looks pretty cool, actually, but I thought about the stuff you used to make in college—those psychedelic ink-blot paintings. Ever think about selling your work to corporate offices?"

She sighs. "I know I should be getting my work out there. But it's like, those are too heady for an office."

"Might be worth a try." I suggest.

"What's the point? I already have a job."

"Because you love it?"

"Sometimes I think I was an art major because I craved people's attention and the classes were super easy."

"But I love seeing you paint," I say. "We should go home right now, stretch out a canvas, lube up with cadmium yellow and make art."

Sophie blushes.

Our hearts still patter, but the beats aren't always in sync. Dating someone for so long evolves. In the jade of her eyes still shines the look I fell in love with—a way of seeing me that no one sees. I can hide a lot of things from Sophie, but not what I feel for her. She knows me too well. She'll know the moment I stop loving her. Like I'd know if she stopped loving me. That's what love truly is: a connection that transcends time and space, beyond any physical reality. We sense each other, even when we're apart.

If I cheat on this woman, can you really call it love? At these late-night lounges, sipping cocktails of loneliness and longing, I meet women doing the same. Inebriated by sorrow, we fall into bed together and let ourselves feel again—the existential urge to fuck just to remind ourselves we're still alive.

Sophie used to be beside me, but lately, she's too tired or busy. Somewhere along the way, she got on the straight and narrow without telling me. She beckons me to follow her, but I prefer late nights and love sessions that go on till the sunrise. We haven't done that since her brother's wedding. I don't know why.

The waiter comes back with our drinks. "Your old-fashioned and an iced tea for the lady. You guys ready to order?"

Sophie says, "We might need more time."

I already know what I want: "I'll take the cheeseburger, medium, with cheese curds."

"Oh, alright." Sophie asks Tyler, "What's your favorite?"

"What are you talking about, Sophie?" I interrupt their charade because this is ridiculous. She's just trying to find an excuse to talk to him. "We come here all the time. You've tried everything."

"I'm just wondering—"

Awkward, Tyler leans back on his heel. "I mean, you can't go wrong with the burger and curds." He flashes me a smile. "Or...there's a secret sandwich. An Iberian smoked ham sandwich. Doesn't sound like much, but trust me. The chef imports the ham from Spain. A big slab of this meat,

soft French bread, and some butter. Divine."

"C'est magnifique," Sophie says. "I'll take that."

Of course, she does. These games we play. I laugh to myself and let it go. She has every right to be mad. If I were in her shoes, I'd probably try to fuck the waitress to feel better. That's the difference between us. She'd rather bleed me with needle after needle rather than kill me. If I really wanted to break up with her, I'd just tell her and get it over with.

Sophie won't tell me what's bothering her with words. Instead, this whole dinner will be pieces of a puzzle I have to put together. It's annoying, but I do it. She's the only woman I will ever do this for.

Sophie asks, "Do you love me?"

"I do," I say. "Hey, aren't you supposed to be the one to say that?"

"Don't be cute."

"I can't help it," I say. "Because I'm sharing dinner with the most amazing woman on the planet."

"Please stop. I'm serious. What's the matter with you?"

"I'll be on time from now on. I get it." This line of questioning is getting old.

"It's so much more than that." Sophie goes on. "Where do you see us going?"

"Do I have to remind you?" I sigh and recite the list we've created over the years. "A house on the shore of Lake Monona with a pier and view of the Capitol, where we can swim in May and ice skate in January. Two kids. A golden retriever that never stops barking at the neighbor's weed whacker. And a minivan." I know this is exactly what she wants to hear, so I can't go wrong.

"A minivan?" she says. "You'd drive a minivan?"

"I'll be a soccer dad. I don't care. You might hate the beer gut."

For the first time all night, Sophie relaxes. I pressed all the right pieces together and set her at ease. She's been going off at me lately. I thought it was her period at first, but it keeps happening. She wants to know where I am, what I'm doing, and why I'm not home. But when I am home, she wants to lay around with me all night. Not even fuck, just lay there, side by side, and watch TV and go to bed.

"How's the poetry book coming along?" She asks. When she says it, though, she believes in me. Most people scoff when I mention poetry. She cares. That's the thing. Sophie cares, and she's been there for the struggle.

"It's…" I say, choosing the best words. Funny, I usually have words for everything. "It's taking longer than expected." She doesn't say anything. She listens, unmoving, unblinking, unnerving. "It's hard. The stuff I'm coming up with. It's just—it's just lame. I don't know any other way to describe it."

She says, "You're a great writer. You've got to believe that."

"Imagine going to school for four years studying English. A language everyone knows. And now you're out in the real world, you have to ask people to pay you for 14 lines of words that rhyme. For some reason, as soon as I try, it's impossible." Sometimes when you tell the full truth, it makes everything quiet.

"It's going to be alright. Okay?" she says. "Don't judge yourself too much."

"What if I'm not good enough? And I never will be." I say, laying it on thick with sadness.

She reaches her hands across the table and holds mine. All the glassware makes this awkward, but I appreciate the gesture. We gaze at each other, and for a moment, we forget everything and smile.

"I love you," I say again.

"I love you, too," Sophie says, like music.

Sophie understands the creative struggle. That's why she gave up. She used to paint all the time. Especially in college, I'd show up at her studio apartment. She'd be on a paint-splattered sheet, with a paintbrush in her mouth, a cutting board dolloped with oil paints, and a canvas on the floor. We never made it to the bed in those days. Instead, we'd barely say 'hello' before our mouths found new places to kiss on each other's bodies. Afterwards, we showered off the wet paint smeared against our bare skin.

With her job at a cosmetic company, she analyzes sales and strategy. What used to be a spontaneous spatter of cadmium yellow on loose white canvas has turned into hope for veridian green to appear at the bottom of balance sheets.

"Can you stop being such an idiot?" she says, serious again.

"I promise I'll do better," I reiterate. I don't know how many times she needs to hear it before she believes me.

I keep alive this image of Sophie on the floor in her studio, rolling carelessly in the wet colors. Her smile was as bright as the sunlight pouring through the two-panel windows. I remember her that way in case she forgets, which we're all apt to do as time passes. I'm sure she remembers a version of me when we were young and naïve. Before we graduated. Before we moved in together. Before we became like this.

Then again, it didn't last long before I first cheated on her. It wasn't out of spite. It's because we weren't official. She found out about it because she saw me texting some girl I met at a bar with Kovski. I won't tell you her name because, honestly, I don't remember it. Sophie didn't hit me. She didn't raise her voice, and she didn't cry. She looked at me with those jade eyes. And I felt it. All of her love was burning for me. That's when I told her, '*I love you,*' for the first time. In a way, my cheating pushed our relationship to a new level.

A level of trust we took with us when we signed a lease together. In downtown Madison, between our two jobs, we could afford a nice one-bedroom in an apartment building at the top of Frat Row. The heart of the college town pulsates outside our windows when we make love.

The food arrives. The waiter begs us to enjoy our meals. I don't miss the extra glance he shares with Sophie. She's got my chest rattling tonight. I've got to change my ways or I'm going to lose her, but it's hard to walk a straight line all the time.

As I pick up my burger, I ask Sophie, "Want to head to Whiskey Jack after this?" I take a big bite. The grease runs down my chin. They know how to fry an onion. Perfect haystack crunch.

"*Ew.* No." Sophie says. She sizes up her sandwich. The French bread glistens with melted butter around a slick slab of ham.

"But it's Ride-the-Bull night! Chelsea's going."

"How do you know?"

"She texted me about it."

"Really?" Sophie says. "She texts you?"

"From time to time, yeah?" I say. "She knew you wouldn't be into it so we're teaming up to convince you to come."

Sophie shoots me a look. "It's a work night."

"Live a little," I say. "Sometimes you make me feel like we're old."

Sophie says, "We have to be responsible."

"We won't be out late. We grab a drink with Chelsea and Kov, go for a ride, then go home."

Sophie chews. "Fine," she says, mouthful. She swallows. "I haven't seen Chelsea in forever."

FIVE:
ride-the-bull

OPHIE AND I PLOP DOWN on two leather stools at the bar called Whiskey Jack. I drumroll my hands on the counter, looking around for Will Kovski.

In the far corner, a big-horned, brown and white mechanical bull grazes at the center of a knee-high, blue cushioned pad. Strobe lights flick their beams across the large, wood-raftered hall. This saloon-inspired pleasure palace calls to the party animal crowd.

Right now, it's still too early. A few regulars play Pop-a-Shot at the back, next to the pinball machines. After ten, though, this place will be crawling even on a Wednesday.

Coming from the bar's basement, Kovski carries a tall tower of plastic cups that bend backwards over his head like the tail of a strange bird. "Hey, Danny! And Sophie? What an honor." Kovski sets the cups on the bar. Automatically, he loads up the space beneath the bar top.

Yes, this place serves drinks only in shatter-proof pint plastic cups. Three drinks will get you stumbling out the door. Four and your next memory will be either waking up somewhere or hugging a toilet. And you'll probably have pissed yourself. That's a lot of liquid. There really should be a warning sign.

When Kovski's done sorting cups, he takes the last one, flips it up to himself in the air, catches it, and scoops ice into it. "What do you want, Soph?"

"I'll do a tequila soda."

"You skinny bitch." Kovski smiles. "Haven't changed a bit."

"What can I say? I like what I like." Leaning on her elbow, Sophie asks, "So, you guys were up late last night?"

Before Kovski douses the ice with rail tequila, he glances at me. I nod. Kovski knows what to do. "Oh. Yea." He pours two big glugs from the tequila bottle. "What time did we finally hit the bed? One? Two?"

"Four," I answer.

"That's why I'm so exhausted today," Kovski says. "I got up two hours ago. We were so drunk last night. I don't know how you're functioning." He presses the soda fountain over the drink for a second and sticks a lime wedge on the rim.

"You know hangovers are all in your mind," I say.

"My mind, body, and spirit definitely feel it. Full three-dimensional hangover." Kovski sets the tequila-soda in front of Sophie. He does the same routine for my whiskey-soda.

"Hair of the dog?" I say, offering a toast.

"You're an animal, but what the hell?" Kovski grunts and pours himself a shot.

The three of us cheers. I catch that glint in Sophie's eyes that I love so much. That tell that she's being naughty. She sips her cocktail and comes away coughing.

I take a sip of mine. The whiskey burn pinches my face when it hits the back of my throat.

Kovski takes his shot like water and spritzes an extra shot of soda into the top of each of our cups. "You got to stir it." Kovski wipes down the counter.

Kovski's the type of friend I talk to every day. We always know what's going on, where we're at, and if we'll see each other that day. Blonde hair high and tight, he's a tall guy, muscular, tattoos on both arms, and a half-day's shadow on his cheeks. Good looking, sure, but it's his playful, silver-blue eyes that stand out. As a bartender, his drinks are strong and he's bad at counting. Women adore him. Sometimes, I envy him. He's grounded and walks with purpose, even if that purpose is debauchery.

Sophie swirls her straw. She takes another sip. "That's better." When she smiles at me, I lose myself. It's her hidden power. Sophie's got the strings of my heart and moves me around like a marionette.

I flitter the straw around the edge of the cup and take a hearty swallow. That cool burn, rye and oak, soothes my aching mind. Some days I love this woman till death do us part. Other days, she's a distant memory. Why is that?

Sophie gets up from her stool. "I've got to run to the bathroom." She walks off. I watch her go until she's out of earshot.

Kovski asks, "Why are you so smiley?"

I can't believe I'd ever say this, unless I, myself, got married. "I banged a married woman at the hotel."

"What?"

I say louder, "I banged a married woman at the ho—"

"Shh...I know what you said. Sophie could come back any second. What the fuck?" He puts his hands on the bar top and swings himself over the bar. He sits on the stool next to me. "Tell me everything."

So, I tell him the highlights and end with what happened at the hotel this morning.

"A married woman." Kovski shakes his head, impressed. "What were you on last night? What if her husband finds out and comes looking for you?"

"He's going to fly all the way from New York to kick my ass?"

"Hey, you never know. But like, why? Why her? Of everyone in the bar, in the city, why her?"

"I would've backed off if she told me to, but she never did. If you saw her, you'd understand." Kovski still looks at me in shock, I go on. "And then, she fuckin' gave it to me. She passed out in my arms. Used me for my body. That's it. That's all it was. Un-fucking believable."

"My man." We slap hands. Kovski respects the game. "Are you going to text her?"

"I don't have her number, and that's the best part, no strings. Well, except she's staying at the hotel."

"She's a guest at the hotel?"

"It's fine. She works all day. Worst thing to happen? I have to drop her off or pick her up. Maybe fuck in the van along the way."

"Dude. I've got to give it to you. This is either a new high or a new low. I'm not going to judge, but wow. Just wow."

"Thanks for covering for me."

"As often as you stay at my place, Sophie might start wondering if we're fucking—heads up."

Suddenly, two hands cover my eyes. A sprightly woman's voice announces, "Guess who?"

Judging by the ocean breeze perfume and soft palms, I smile. "Hmmm…Dwayne 'The Rock' Johnson?"

"No!" the mystery woman squeals, pulling apart her handmade blindfold.

I can see again. And what I see is Sophie coming back and taking her seat. I swivel around, almost wiping

my nose across Chelsea's cleavage. "Chelsea? I never would've guessed."

"You think I have man hands?" Chelsea says. "Sophie?" Chelsea displays her hand for Sophie. French-tipped fingers, glowing tan, and a sleeve tattoo of the mythical Hydra—the nine-headed monster Hercules slayed.

Sophie retakes her seat and pushes up a well-meaning brow. "Sorry, honey."

Chelsea examines her hands in horror. "Wait. What?"

Sophie meets my gaze. I let out a burst of air. We both laugh together. We got her. Sophie says, "We're kidding! You have great hands."

"Not sandpapery at all," I say, playfully.

"Hey, I moisturize," Chelsea says, slapping me in the shoulder. I wish she would stop touching me. Sophie watches every small gesture. I tie my hands to my sides. Chelsea should know better. She sits next to Sophie, setting her purse on the counter. "What are you drinking?"

"Tequila-soda," Sophie says.

"Meh," Chelsea says.

Sophie and Chelsea are best friends from college. They met sitting next to each other in French class—Chelsea used to cheat off S   ophie's tests. One day, Sophie caught her. Ever since, they're inseparable like Kovski and me.

To say Chelsea is attractive is to say rain is wet. There's nothing I can say about her body that won't make me sound sleazy. Because I'm a gentleman, I'll be delicate. Icy-blonde hair cut sharply at her shoulders with bangs. Her daddy bought her a nose job in high school. She's slim, without being too skinny. She shows off her belly button piercing in summertime. Even now, it peeks out beneath her Smiths band shirt that she split open in the front and fringed along the bottom with a pair of scissors. She's a little bit all over the place.

Kovski, fiddling with the bull remote control, sees Chelsea and comes over. "What can I get you?"

"Hey Kov," she says. "Margarita, por favor."

"Rock'n'roll." Kovski gets to it.

Chelsea turns to Sophie. "So, did you get the promotion?"

"Promotion?" I ask, "What promotion?"

Sophie says, "I didn't want to tell you in case it wasn't real. But yeah, I should find out by next week if they want to make me a sales manager. My boss keeps winking at me."

"That's a good sign." Chelsea winks.

"Maybe he's into you?" I add because men don't just wink at women.

"Ken? Yeah, right." Sophie laughs it off. "He's got a wife and kids. He's goofing around. I hope it means I got it and they're sorting out the paperwork."

"What would you be doing?" I say, "I'm surprised you haven't told me."

"Someone has to be home to tell," Sophie says. "Anyway, I'll have my own sales team, and I'd earn commission off their performance. Six figures."

"Holy fuckin' shit." Kovski squeezes lime into Chelsea's margarita.

"Now, you know why I only told Chelsea." Sophie says, "I don't want to jinx it."

"Guess drinks are on you tonight," I say. "A round of green tea shots, my good man."

Kovski slides Chelsea her drink. "Coming up stat."

"Oh no," Sophie says, "I have to work tomorrow."

"But we have to celebrate!" I say.

"You see?" Sophie says, "This is exactly why I didn't want to tell you. It hasn't happened yet. And you're already acting like it has."

"But you're obviously going to get it. Your boss is winking at you for crying out loud," I say. "Why not believe you got it?"

"I don't want to feel bad when I wake up."

"It's just a shot, Sophie. Geez." I say.

Sophie holds up her cup. "Plus, however much was in this, it adds up."

"Put this one on the list too," I say. "Kovski. Four shots please."

"Easy, peasy." Kovski pulls out an unmarked bottle from the rail. Looks at the blue liquid. It's not the right mix because it's not the right color. The next one he pulls out is electric green. That's the one.

Kovski doles out the shots. We each grab one, except Sophie. "I told you I didn't want a shot."

"It's on the house as a good luck charm," Kovski says.

Sophie eyes the glass. She picks it up. "To…me?"

"To Sophie!" I say, clinking my glass against hers. I throw my head back.

The green liquid leaves behind a soothing trail down my throat. A slight buzz vibrates in my ears. These are the kind of nights we remember forever. Best friends all together, hanging out and celebrating for no other reason than we can.

I nod at Sophie. "Not so bad, huh?"

"Yep." She smiles.

Chelsea says, "How did you know I love green tea shots?"

"Everyone loves green tea shots." I put my arms over Sophie and Chelsea's shoulders. "Who's ready to ride the bull?"

Sophie reacts first, stifling any excitement Chelsea was about to announce. "No way, Danny, we should be getting home."

"We'll go home after we ride the bull," I say, everything is a compromise with her. I wish for once that she would get on my side from the start.

"You can if you want." Sophie crosses her arms.

"I'll do it," Chelsea says.

Kovski pulls a gigantic novelty orange cowboy hat off a hook on the wall behind the bar. "Giddy up."

Chelsea dons the oversized hat. "How do I look?" She strikes a pose in her frayed denim shorts before strutting over to the bull. Sophie and I get up and follow her. We stand at the edge of the pad as Chelsea mounts the machine, her bare legs splayed behind the bull's large hump.

"Ready?" Kovski says.

Kovski presses the button and the bull gyrates beneath her. At first, she laughs, her fingers gripping the rope. The bull bobbing up and down. She throws a hand in the air and yells, "Yeehaw!"

Kovski kicks it up a notch. The bull spins and bounces up and down harder. Chelsea grips the rope with both hands. Back and forth. Back and forth. On a hard bump, she slips and clutches the bull's neck.

One wicked spin sends her flying off. She hits the blue mat, facedown.

"Are you alright?" Sophie shouts.

She turns over, laughing hysterically. "How'd I do?"

He says, "12 seconds."

"Woo!" she says. "New PR."

"You're lucky I took it easy on you." Kovski grips her forearm and pulls her to her feet.

"My turn," I announce. I scoop the hat off Chelsea and hop on the bull.

I grab the rope with one hand and as I put the other in the air, Kovski cranks the knob on the remote. A mischievous smile pricks the corner of his lip. I fall forward and hug the bull's neck.

Up and down, side to side, I cling on. My thigh muscles tighten hard around the slippery back of the bull. As the bull spins, it rocks forward. Then back. When the front drops hard, I flip off the top of the bull.

I land square on my back and stare up at the rafters of the old saloon, wondering how the hell I got here. Chelsea, laughing, comes over and pulls me up.

Sophie stands on the sidelines, arms crossed. Seeing Sophie so far away, I clamber over to her, the adrenaline coursing through my veins, and I pull her toward the bull. "Your turn."

"Danny, please." She stumbles, almost falling onto the blue pad. "I'm too tired. I just want to go home."

"You're leaving already?" Chelsea says, joining us at the edge of the mat.

"It's been a long day," Sophie says.

"I'll probably take off too," Chelsea says. "Tonight was fun." The two women hug.

"Glad you could make it out." I try to hug Chelsea, but she's sucking down her drink.

"Sorry," Chelsea says with the straw in her mouth. She finishes the margarita. Setting it on the nearest table, she throws open her arms and we embrace.

Chelsea blows on my ear as she hugs me. When we let go, she smiles with a twinkle in her eye. "Good seeing you," she says.

As Kovski and I go to the bar together, I ask him, "How much do I owe you?"

"Let's see. Three drinks. Four shots." Kovski clicks on an imaginary calculator in the air. "Carry the one. Drop the zero. Add fourteen. Total's ten bucks."

"I love you, man." I say, digging out my wallet.

"Hey, you didn't finish your drinks," Kovski says.

Kovski pushes a full green tea shot toward me. He clears away the other three empty shots. I say, "Sophie didn't take her shot?"

"Don't think so."

I look back at the mechanical bull, but no one's there. Sophie's by the door, tapping at her phone. Chelsea waves at me from the exit before she disappears outside.

"Fuck it." I knock the shot back real fast. I leave Kovski a twenty. I doubt he even added any of our drinks to the register.

Sophie and I walk home together. Our backs to the Capitol, the breeze off Lake Mendota hits us with a warm mist. These nights in August feel as lazy as a hangover. We sway our way up the little hill that Sophie and I call 'our little hill.' At the top of Frat Row, we go to the tan brick apartment building. Special only for its age. It's been around as long as the students have been coming to campus. It got a few facelifts over the years, but the bones are the same. We're just another pair of roommates listed in the log of its history. It'll outlive us all. In the upper left-hand window, we always keep the lamplight on. If we're mice, it's our hole in the world.

When we crawl back inside, it's late. We don't turn the kitchen light on. The fatigue of the long day sits on my shoulders more than ever, especially with our bed in sight. My body aches for rest, but my soul yearns for the night to never end.

Sophie slings her purse on one of the hooks by the front door. She takes off each of her heels in front of me,

leaning on the wall for balance. I watch her shorts cling to the curve of her hips.

When she straightens up, I put my arms around her waist and press myself against her. Her hand finds the back of my neck. She pulls me in for a kiss.

The soft wetness of her mouth sticks to mine as we release. She runs her tongue over her bottom lip, tasting me. I dive my lips to her bare shoulder and plant short, heavy kisses up her neck to that one spot behind her ear.

Her perfume *Unmistakable*, I breathe her in. My love for her hardens. As I grind myself into her, she steps away.

"I'm not in the mood tonight."

"Not in the mood?" I say, closing the gap between us with a short step. "Are you sure?" I run my hands down Sophie's sides. Unlike Rachel, Sophie remains a statue. I unhook her bra.

"Please. I have a headache." Sophie says, taking another step back.

My hands fall limp, I say, "Fine."

She says, "Are you coming to bed?"

"Yeah, I'll be in in a minute," I say. "I've got to drink some water."

Sophie disappears into our bedroom. I linger on my boner, waving at me through my pants. She never noticed the safety pin.

SIX:
scenic route

T'S FUNNY. THE CAPTAIN IS the same name I call my cock. Except one prick gives me pleasure, and the other is just a prick.

The bell captain and I post up at the bell stand at 9:15 AM. It's after the commute rush that takes over the first two hours of the bellman shift. After rolling one of the bronze carts back, I temper my heat with a nice, long lean on the counter. It's a posture that says, 'Don't bother asking me to do something, I'm not going anywhere.' It's my favorite stance when the lobby dies down and time moves to a crawl. Sure, time is money, but at a service job where you make below minimum wage, that time spent had better be worth the money. Until then, I lean.

Between the last two late nights, I'm a little winded, honestly. The wad of fives and ones bulging in my vest pocket says otherwise. I might be tired, but I'm still bringing that five-star service with a smile. The guests can sense the pheromones. They may not know it, but they're talking to a once-in-a-generation talent. No one can charm a person better than I can.

The bell captain leans too. Except he can't lean down to his elbows like I can, he's got to, at least, look like he's in

charge. He used to wear a vest, but he was promoted after Francisco retired. Hence, the suit and tie. Which means in the clothing authority hierarchy, people will naturally talk to him first before me. That thought makes me really lean back. I've got time to kill.

Since I've been working here since college, I was up for the promotion too, but I didn't want the job. It's a paltry pay bump in exchange for the responsibility to schedule the bellmen. The bell captain sold all his free time for an extra $2 an hour. I can make that in a ten-minute guest ride around the Capitol. It's about power. He wants to tell people what to do. Too bad power requires respect. If he tells me to do something and I don't do it, he has to do it or he has to fire me, and he still will have to do it. Tell me, who really has the power?

My gaze moves from the lobby to the front desk. Dave and Haseem stand behind the tall, curved counter, its veneer shining in the artificial light. To Haseem, the front office manager is the next step in a long career as a hotelier. He fits the part too. His suit is pristine down to the cuff links. His receding hairline, tousled and styled with product, and his attitude toward guests toes the line between snide and generous. Without fail, he stands at the part of the desk in the shadow of the grand staircase. Like me, he's found the spot where he's least likely to be engaged by a random guest.

Dave is my age—handsome enough with a mustache and a dry sense of humor. Despite his wit, he's a lame duck when it comes to the opposite sex. Some people don't care how they come across. He wears a rumpled suit, fit enough for his skinny frame, but he looks more like a clothes hanger than a mannequin in it. When he's bored, he goes to the doorway into the front office and peers in. Everybody knows he's got a thing for Eva, except maybe Eva.

His entry is my excuse to peer in alongside him. Through the half-opened doorway, I spy Eva pushing up her headset microphone. Dave says something to her. She says something. Dave says something while he smiles. Eva laughs, big and toothy. Her eye catches mine, admiring her. She picks up the phone and hits a button. The bell stand phone rings.

I reach over and grab it before the bell captain can. Her voice cuts across the line. "Creeper."

"What's so funny?" I say.

Dave looks over his shoulder and his smile fades. He lets the door close behind him and turns to the center computer at the desk. His hand on the mouse, his index finger clicks and clicks and clicks.

No longer in view, Eva says, "Dave asked, 'What's a number's favorite dessert?'"

"Can I book a shuttle?" A female voice talks to the bell captain. Rachel.

"Are you going to guess?" Eva asks.

"Let me see." The bell captain checks the shuttle schedule.

"Sorry, there's a guest." I hang up. Rachel averts her eyes and adjusts her purse on her shoulder. I tell the bell captain, "I'll take her."

"No, no, I've got it." The bell captain says, writing his name on the log.

"But you've got that manager's meeting at 10. I don't think you'll be back in time."

The bell captain crosses his name off and writes mine instead. "You're right. Go ahead."

"I'll pull the van out front." Finally, some action.

As I push through the revolving door, I hear over my shoulder, the bell captain asks, "Have you ever been to Paradise?"

I march to one of the two 15-person passenger vans. Had to get a special Class C license to drive this hunk of metal. The blind spots abound, especially backing up in morning traffic.

Where the Continental is located on the Capitol Square, there's no avoiding congestion. So, backing up a shuttle van blind requires timing and finesse. As the back-up beep sounds, I check my mirrors and let the vehicle edge backward. At a certain point, I must let go and trust no one's going to ram my bumper. There are enough dings to prove otherwise.

Slow and steady, ready to stop at any moment, but still rolling. There's enough time for me to check Rachel talking to the bell captain through the revolving doors.

I watch the bell captain flirt with Rachel. His style is called cocky-funny. I read about it in a book on women. Deride her to ride her. It's brutal if it's done wrong. You end up insulting a poor woman for no other reason than the fact that you're not funny. Humor requires clever banter more than attitude. For the bell captain, he's better off relying on his height rather than his jokes.

Through the glass, he's smiling in his dumb way, and she laughs with him. Maybe I'm wrong, but she could want him. She is married, remember?

I almost hit a runner in these tiny white shorts. The van rocks to a stop. I sigh. Turns out the runner is definitely a dude. I shake my head. Men shouldn't shave their legs. It can be confusing.

Giving the van some gas, I check my rearview. An endless line of cars zoom past behind me. I wait for a hole. Just enough space to assert myself. A Honda passes. Then a truck. Between a Camry and a motorcycle, I see my opening. My fingers tighten on the wheel. The Camry passes, and I swing out. The van butts into the lane. I swing the wheel back, then hit the accelerator. It jostles forward, pulling parallel to the curb in front of the hotel.

I roll down the driver's window and watch Rachel and the bell captain through the lobby glass. Every time it looks like the bell captain is going to open the valet door, he turns back and says something else. She wants to go, but she can't shake him.

In watching their interaction, I learn how to wrap Rachel around my finger. I can tell from her heels striking on the marble tiles to the sway of her skirt that nothing intimidates her. She's from New York. She probably regularly sees things on her daily commute that would rattle half this town.

Her divorce papers will clear the courts by the end of the week, I imagine. She'll be free again to love, to lust, and to live. She learned marriage is just another excuse to bind people together, to spend thousands on celebrating 'love,' and to combine bank accounts. Only to find out in five years, in ten years, as the children grow up, that the love they felt was a fleeting feeling that passed long ago. What they've been doing is acting, and in acting, they played their part for as long as they could, but now, the show's over and the audience has moved on. It happened to my parents. One slip-up leads to another and another.

Even if she says she is 'happily married,' she cheated on him. That's not happy. Her husband doesn't fulfill her wild desires anymore. Not like I do, Rachel needs a man who can let the tiger out.

The bell captain could fit the bill. He's handsome enough. Yet, his personality is about as inspiring as a plastic bag stuck in a tree. She needs debonair. She needs physicality. She needs to be laid down and made to feel

no remorse. That's why when she looks at me out of the window, she knows she discovered her match—the man who sets her free.

I take matters into my own hands. Exiting the van, I open the valet door for Rachel and say in a bad cockney accent, "Your chariot hath arrived, m'lady."

Rachel, relieved, heads out to the van.

The bell captain yammers onward, following her, "I swear, The Dice has the best cheap drinks in town." Failure with women is often described through the word 'cheap.' "I can take you there after you're done working today?"

Rachel turns to face him. "You'll still be working?"

"No." He smiles and takes an aggressively small step forward. "I don't mind showing you around." The captain towers over her and takes a quick peek at her breasts. She notices, shifts her arms slightly to cover them, and takes a small step back. He doesn't understand this tiny dance of failing romance.

"Maybe another time?" Rachel heads around the van as I signal to the oncoming traffic to halt.

She ducks her head as she enters the van. As I close the door behind her, she whispers the words, 'Thank you.'

Unmistakable perfume clouds the van's worn-out grey leather interior.

A thin layer of dark pantyhose flows down Rachel's legs into her stilettos. White gold jewelry dangles from her wrists, neck, and ears. I hadn't noticed the small, round scar in her left nostril. A sign of a nose ring. She must've been wild. I adjust the rearview mirror. Her wedding ring shoots into view. I find her eyes.

"Was your boss flirting with me?" Rachel leans forward between the seats. "Do I have a 'fuck me' sign on my head or something? Don't men see this ring? It means back off."

"Do you fault him for trying?"

She puts on a pair of big, all-black sunglasses. "You know where you're going?"

"University Hospital."

"You remembered?"

"It's my job." I maneuver into traffic. Silence permeates the air as I switch lanes and brake at a red light.

When the light turns green, she says, "How's your girlfriend?"

The van jolts forward. Rachel flies back into her seat. Not a good look, but I steady myself. New Yorkers know how to get down to business. She's direct. I like that. I contemplate telling her the truth.

Rachel's a guest at the hotel. Avoidance as a tactic is impossible until she's back in New York City. Should we create a shared tryst? Anything like that requires commitment to the truth, but it's taking me too long to think of a proper response. I go with my usual, "What girlfriend?"

"Don't lie to me. I can tell you're taken." She fixes the sunglasses on the bridge of her nose.

A bead of sweat forms on the back of my neck. I wipe it away and decide to try my hand at humoring her. "Why's that?"

"You fuck too slowly."

"That's a problem?"

"Single guys fuck like jackrabbits. Pounding and pounding and pounding. They can't contain themselves. But men with girlfriends fuck like they can get it all the time."

"You know this from experience?"

"Maybe I do." She leans forward between the front seats again. There's a smack to her lips when she says, "You seem like a guy who can't contain himself at the buffet table, Daniel." The way she says Daniel, I feel undressed somehow. She must know I hate the way my full name sounds—that's why I never go by it. "What's her name?"

I admit, "Sophie."

"I knew it!"

"You're happy?" I say.

"Now," she says, "I don't feel so shitty about what happened. As long as I wrecked someone else's life, I know I'm not the only terrible person."

"You feel guilty?" I ask.

"You don't? Are you a sociopath?" She says. She digs through her purse for something. She says to herself, "I know I put them in here somewhere."

I say, gripping the wheel tighter, "I guess I haven't thought much of it. It was fun while it lasted and it's over. Sophie doesn't need to know. We have one life to live, you know?"

"Don't I know—Aha!" Rachel pulls out a pack of cigarettes. "I started smoking again. Do you mind?"

"In here? No way." I say.

"Please? I've got a full day of meetings and I need it."

"You're an addict."

"Can you make an exception?"

"Sorry," I say. "Last time I smoked in here, I had to detail the whole thing myself."

"Well damn." Rachel clutches the pack in her fist.

Her wedding ring catches the light. Why did she do it? Why would she break her trust with her husband? Because she can get away with it. With traveling, it's almost too easy and she has needs. What hubby doesn't know doesn't hurt anyone? She gets her fill. He's still satisfied. Life goes on. Happily married.

Then again, there's a reason for everything. As a writer, I must ask. I take a shot in the dark. "How long has it been?"

"I don't know. It's my second pack this trip."

I swerve around a car taking a left-hand turn. "No, since you and your husband started having troubles."

"Hah!" There it is again, that jeering laugh. "You don't know what you're talking about."

"It's okay, you can tell me," I hit the pedal to burn through a yellow light before slowing to a crawl in morning traffic.

"I don't need a therapist," she says.

"You'd be surprised at how many people spill their guts to me."

"What if I open up the window and smoke?"

I smirk. "You're fiending." I flick the turn signal and veer off the well-beaten path. I head into the heart of the UW campus, desolate in early August.

"Where are we going?" she says. "This isn't the way."

"You want to smoke, right?" I pull off at an outcrop in the road in front of the first dormitory ever built on campus. It's on Madison's tallest hill overlooking Lake Mendota.

I flick on the hazard lights, and my shoes hit the pavement. As I open the passenger side door, I say, "Pull one out for me."

Pack in hand, Rachel exits the van, using the safety bar for stability. When she sees the view, she says, "Oh yeah, this is great."

"Remember, I accept tips." A windless summer's day in Wisconsin greets us. The sunshine bounces off the vibrant leaves. It'd make any girl weak in the knees.

Rachel puts both cigs in her mouth and lights them.

She takes one out and offers it to me. "How's this for a tip?"

"I'll take it," I say, sticking the pink lipstick-stained filter in my mouth. I breathe in the smoke. A faint buzz shivers down my spine.

Rachel leans back on the front of the van. Cool and casual. So confident in what she sees. She blows out a hail of smoke.

Together, our smoke lingers above us before evaporating into the endless sky as we stare at the wide blue expanse that is Madison's largest lake. From our view, we have the campus classrooms at our back and the empty dormitories below us, a winding path of trees gilds the shoreline that leads into a nature preserve a mile away. We are floating above it all.

"Good call, Daniel."

"Please call me Danny."

"So, is this what you do, Danny? You take every guest here?"

"Yep, this is all part of the tour," I say. "Aren't I a great guide? I'm the reason why the Continental has so many five-star reviews."

She narrows her eyes at me. "You're terrible."

"It's lonely coming to a city and not knowing anyone. I make it a little easier, don't I?"

"I don't know what to say to you." She blows out. "You're a bellboy." I raise my brow at her use of 'boy.' I'm a bellman. "What's between us is nothing. It's less than nothing. You know what I'm saying? We can't do what we did last night ever again."

"Is that what you want? Even if your husband will never find out?"

"And what about your girlfriend?"

I suck in, gather my thoughts, and blow out. "For

some reason, I feel I know you. Is that a strange thing to say? I feel I've met you before. I feel we've met each other even before we met at the bar the other night."

"Don't try your stupid lines on me." Her forest green eyes squint in the sunlight. Her breath creates a veil between the lake and us, she declares, "I don't want you to get the wrong idea. What we did was wrong. I won't let it happen again."

"I get it. We'll just be friends from now on," I say as innocently as I can.

"We fucked," she laughs with a snort at the end. "We can't be friends."

"Who says?"

"Everyone," she breathes out smoke. "How old are you?"

"Does it matter?" I say, flicking ash.

"I want to know if I'm dealing with a child."

"I'm 27." Goosebumps prickle my arm because I know I'm close to losing her, I say, "What are you? 32?"

"Don't you know you're never supposed to guess a lady's age?"

"Am I talking to a lady?"

"I'm 39." Her cheeks blush. "Happy?"

"What's your favorite color?" I ask.

"Blue, why?"

"Better be careful Rachel—we get to know any more about each other and we'll end up friends. Mine's red, by the way."

"You're so full of shit. I can smell it." Her smile tells me I salvaged a victory. She tosses her burnt-out cig into the grass.

"Well, Rachel," I toss mine beside hers, a puff of smoke escaping. "It's time to take you to the hospital."

"You don't have to sound so morbid."

I open the door for her. She slides in. We drive along

the tennis courts, the baseball fields, the three-story brick gymnasium, and the whole cluster of agriculture buildings en route to the University Hospital. All so empty this time of year.

When I pull up curbside to the hospital entrance, I hop out. She barely has her seat belt off when I open the side door. She turns, surprised, to see me greeting her already. I ask, "Let's get together tonight."

She sinks back into her seat. "You don't quit, do you?

I don't care if I'm too forward. There's something about her I can't shake. Instead of a one-night stand, we can be a fling. A fling until she goes back to her normal life in New York City. There's nothing wrong with that. She's lonely, and I'm addicted. I say, "I'll take you to Fresh. It's on the Capitol Square. They don't have the same panty-dropping specials as Paradise, but I think you'll love the food. The wine isn't bad either."

I hand her a hotel business card facedown from my vest pocket. On the back, I scribbled my number. It pays to be prepared. "Give me a call if you want to get together as friends."

Rachel takes the card between her fingers. "You know I'm not going to call you?"

I shrug my shoulders, saying cockily, "I understand old ladies need their rest."

"You're a funny one," Rachel says, before slipping the card into her purse. She slides out of the van. I offer my hand to help her—she takes it. In this electric moment, our bodies ripple with anticipation, a silent tryst sealed in the current passing between our palms.

When Rachel gains her balance on the cement, the business of our daily lives returns. I'm a bellman and she's a guest. She digs into her purse and pulls out a five. I gladly take it. This innocent tip masks our guilt. I smile. "Have a good day."

Rachel heads to the hospital entrance and doesn't look back.

As I pull the van forward, I laugh at myself. *Pi*! That's a number's favorite dessert. Not bad, Dave. Now I've got to come up with a joke for Eva.

SEVEN:

After work, I ring apartment number 911. Seeing Rachel again today got me all hot and bothered, but she never texted me. That's why it's important to have other options. I get sad if I'm by myself for too long.

The expected static buzz doesn't come. I press the plastic button on the wall again. I ring it a third and fourth time.

The high-pitched hum vibrates the security door. I'm inside. The Empire was the talk of the town in the '90s. Now, it's in the shadow of newer high-rises. On the way to the elevators, the puke-pink lobby always smells of stale beer. I shake my head. This place is basically another dormitory, except it's private and marketed to the wealthy upperclassmen or grads.

The elevator glides to the ninth floor, and I strut down the next hallway.

Passing the slurry green carpet of the laundry room reminds me of the time I vomited in the third-floor dryer. It's what happens when you chug a pint of whiskey over ice. I was trying to outdrink some business school clowns. Those asshats said I'd never get a job as a writer after I graduate. I spent half the party arguing into my phone with this girl to come out, but she wasn't even in the city at the time. That was the last time we ever spoke. They tricked me into taking the call outside and they locked the door behind me. I wandered the hallways of The Empire, drunk and lost. I'm sorry to whoever found the remnants of my mistake on laundry day. Promise I hold my whiskey better than that now.

I knock on the apartment door. It creaks open and I'm met with the aroma of vanilla.

"Hello?" I announce. Stepping inside, I see a plate of fresh-baked cookies. The apartment is an open-concept kitchen and living room, with a piece of Sophie's art on the wall. A charcoal nude she sketched of a sunbather on a large crème canvas hangs over the couch. Pans and cookie sheets soak in the sink in the middle of the breakfast bar. I'm not finding what I'm looking for. I walk into the living room. "Where are you?"

This place is one of my favorites. The fourth wall is a window with a view of the towers and valleys of downtown Madison. In the far corner of the frame, I can make out the spouting fountain of the University of Wisconsin library mall—the line between city and campus. At the other end rises the Capitol dome. Between them, stretches a mile of bars, eclectic shops, and restaurants all along State Street.

There's always so much going on. I watch the people, ants crawling along the sidewalks. My gaze lands on the cleavage of a woman walking into the building—huge tits considering these heights.

"In here." I hear and head to the closest bedroom.

Propped up on her elbows, Chelsea lies on her stomach across her bed in a white t-shirt and black yoga

shorts, an antique book open in front of her. She has two posters on her walls: one of Audrey Hepburn and the other of Lady Gaga. She's one of those women trying to change the world. She's one of those girls who thinks she's damaged and pretends she's had it rough. I try not to judge, but when she talks, I know the roughest thing she's ever done is get fucked in a bathroom stall at Sloe Gin. You're welcome.

"Hello there, *Daniel.*" Chelsea kicks her feet in the empty air as she smiles at me.

Daniel. It's more phonetically pleasing to her upbringing. She grew up in Maple Bluff on the posh side of the city, where the Wisconsin governor resides. In that neighborhood, the residents throw balls, instead of parties; they play lacrosse in their backyard, instead of football; and when it comes to speaking of their charming neighbors, they whisper.

Chelsea is destined to be a lawyer defending the guilty. She says we don't give criminals proper rehabilitation. Her literature degree makes her think Dostoyevsky is scripture, and her critique of modern society is *abominable.*

I slap her ass as I sit down on the bed. "I see you got dressed up to see me." I peek at the cover of the book, but she snatches it away. "What're you reading?"

"You're going to laugh." She presses it into her chest.

"What is it—the Kama Sutra?"

"That'd be fun. No. It's War and Peace." She stands up and places it on her desk.

"Just doing some light summer reading?"

"I knew you wouldn't understand."

"Are you that bored?" I stare at her smooth tan legs. My cheeks flush with warmth.

Her summer classes ended in July. Since then, she's

been on summer vacation until the new semester starts in a few weeks, after Labor Day.

"Tolstoy has a way with words that transcends time." Chelsea sits on the bed and puts her arm around my neck. She lays her head on my shoulder. Her short, blonde hair tickles my cheeks. "It feels like I'm there—connected with Andrew and Pierre."

I can't help looking at her shirt, where two staunch nipples salute. "Do you feel like that when you read my stuff?"

"Of course, I do," she says, looking up at me. Her plush lips gleam in the evening-lit room. "I just wish there was more of it."

"Someone's got to stop distracting me."

My choice of words makes her sit up, she says, "When are you going to break up with Sophie?"

I look off. I don't really want to talk about this. "I was thinking next week or the week after."

"What are you waiting for?"

"She's got this promotion thing. I don't want to ruin her chances at that, especially if she's going to be sad. Like it's a big deal."

"But you keep saying you'll do it, yet you don't do it." Chelsea grinds on my lap. "Don't you want me?"

"You're my muse. I need you." I throw my arms around her, squeeze her tight, and kiss her neck.

"Hey…" She puts her hand on the back of my head. I can feel her quiver. "*Daniel*". She mumbles. I kiss her lower and lower until her t-shirt is in the way.

I tug at the ends of her shirt. The fabric caught between our bodies. Chelsea leans back and pulls it off, spilling her breasts into my face. Tossing her shirt aside, she pushes me back into the mattress.

The thing is, I always thought Chelsea was pretty.

We'd get drinks all together. I got to know her. Her life. Where she's from. What she wants. Likewise, she learned about me, like friends do. Maybe I had love's sunglasses for Sophie because, for four years, I never saw the real Chelsea.

Chelsea straddles me, grinding against my fly, unable to let her lips escape mine.

When I got home from Whiskey Jack one night when Sophie and her were doing a wine and whine night, believe me, I saw the real Chelsea. Drinking straight from the bottle, she paraded around in skimpy purple and pink booty shorts, the edge of the cloth escaping into her butt crack. Sophie was too drunk to catch me staring.

Chelsea works at getting my pants off. First, she struggles with the hook on my belt, then she struggles with the metal button. I think of Sophie. Her nimble fingers would work along my waist, her fingertips brushing against my skin. I soften at the sudden gnashing of my zipper. Chelsea's hands are too eager, indelicate. My love loves time.

Things were so good between Sophie and me, despite a few hidden dalliances on my end, that Sophie didn't think twice when she excused herself to bed, leaving me alone with Chelsea. And Chelsea was in trouble. She needed help finishing the bottle. Being the gentleman I am, I obliged.

Chelsea hooks her fingers into my belt loops and pulls. Caught under me, I lift my butt so she can get my pants down to the floor. Stuck on my heels, she kneels and yanks them off. She lets out a well-earned sigh.

I grabbed the bottle from Chelsea and took a swig, the lip of the glass sticky with her saliva. When I handed the bottle back, she took a pull. She handed it back to me. Back and forth it went, no words, just a knowing smile.

Closer and closer. Our hands grazing each other's as we passed the bottle.

Chelsea's hands, heavy and rubbing, start at my calves and work up my thighs. Feeling returns to me. I open my eyes and stare into the whirling ceiling fan. It's the same brand as the one in Sophie and I's bedroom at home. Her fingers move up my legs until they're back at my boxers.

Soon enough, the bottle was empty. We were out of breath, our lips stained red with pinot noir. I called a cab for her. When it arrived, we were on my building's front stoop. Her eyes lingered on mine. Mine lingered on hers. I told her to text me when she got home. She said she would.

And she did.

Chelsea gropes me through my boxers. She squeezes and pulls, squeezes and pulls. I work up the feeling, but I need more. I pull down my underwear, hoping the fresh air helps.

"What's the matter?" she says to me. Her hand clasps around the captain, shaking life back into him.

This isn't right. She's on her knees and I respond with this? I say, "It's been a busy week."

Chelsea opens her mouth wide and clamps down. Chelsea's head goes down and back up. She gasps for air, still rubbing the captain. "You're tired, that's okay. We can stop." She lets go, and I ache for her touch again.

"No—no, keep doing that."

"Are you sure?" When she gives me that innocent smile, in an instant, she resurrects the dead. The captain greets her. "Oh, hello." She gives him a good rubdown.

I'm anxious that he'll fall again, so I grab her under the shoulders and pull her toward me. I need to be inside her now.

In a rush, she's on top, bouncing up and down. A constant squeak fills the room at each push of her hips. Sophie comes to my mind. Her body. Her breasts. Her love. Never like this. Never immediate like this. I close my eyes and feel Chelsea, her rhythm as she slides. We don't need words. Our love flows out of us like rivers, a flood of dreams and deep desires.

Kovski tells me to leave Sophie for her, but I always refrain. There's so much grounded in our history together. I lose my steam. Chelsea senses it too.

I redouble my effort. I sit up, squeeze Chelsea's ass as she grinds into me. Hot and wet, she rubs herself into a fervor. Her breasts slapping against my chest. But it's no use.

I think of Rachel. The cold grip of her ring pressed against the captain.

The blood surges through me at the memory. I exhale. Chelsea groans, swiveling her hips until she can't take it anymore. A rush overtakes her. She wraps her hands around my shoulders, moaning until she's breathless.

It's my turn.

I flip her over, her legs spread, and I lay the captain into her. Each stroke brings me closer to Chelsea and away from my thoughts. Chelsea clears it all away. Everything. The past. The future. Until there's nothing left, except her and I. Eyelids half shut, we grunt, toiling away our mortal lives. The pressure building inside my body overtakes me. I let loose inside her.

Shit, I forgot a condom. I pull out fast. "You're on birth control, right?"

"Are you kidding?" She sits up and stares into the wet trail leading from the base of her. Her mood changes. "I thought you were going to pull out?"

Reaching for my boxers, my pants, my shoes, I'm short of breath. "It'll be alright." I don't need a child in my life. I don't understand how I can be so reckless. I deserve this. I'm hyperventilating. I try to take deep breaths. "It's just one time," I say, in between breaths. Usually, I pull out, even with a condom. "It can't lead to anything. You can get that pill. You can buy the morning-after pill." I reach for my wallet. "How much is it? $80?" I draw out two twenties and hand them to her. "My half."

"Your half?" She stares at it.

I prompt her with the cash. "Go on, take it."

"What are you doing?"

"I'm giving you money."

"Seriously?"

"What?" We're both staring at the cash, and then, we look at each other.

She says, "How could you forget?"

I draw a blank and say, "So, are you on the pill or not?"

"You're an idiot, you know that? Do you pay attention to anything I say?" Chelsea imitates me as if I'm a bumbling fool. "My half. You should pay for all of it."

"Fine." I draw out my wallet and offer her two more twenties. "Do you want me to walk with you to the pharmacy?"

She scoops up the bills and counts them. "Men."

"Hey, I don't want a kid."

Chelsea says, "You should probably listen to the people you fuck. Or is your ego too big for that?"

"It's not my ego that's too big." I smirk.

"You're so gross sometimes," she laments. "I told you I've had an IUD since I was 18." Fresh air reenters my lungs. I reach for the cash in her hands. She pulls it away. "No way! This is asshole tax."

"Come on, that's not funny, give it back." I stick out my hand like I'm waiting for a tip at the hotel.

"You should've remembered." She wads up the money and throws it into my face. It hits me in the nose. In shock, I do the only thing I ever come here to do. I grip her waist and push her back into bed and climb on top of her.

"Hey!" she says. "We're having a serious conversation."

"Wouldn't you rather have round two?"

"You're already ready to go? I thought you were tired?"

"What can I say? The muse revived me."

"You don't have to leave?"

I check my watch. Sure, I should be getting home, but the captain can't get enough. I say, "No way. I'm paying good money for this."

"You are such an as—" I kiss her hard on the mouth before she can finish. Our tongues gnash wildly together, her fingers digging into my hair.

We bury this conversation, like all our conversations, the best way we know how. She pulls her mouth away from mine to catch her breath, and she says the most perfect thing any woman has ever said to me. She whispers in my ear, "Fuck me."

Being the gentleman that I am, I oblige.

As I lay the captain into her again, a notification beeps from my phone on the floor. I know I shouldn't look, but it could be Sophie after all. Unable to pull away from Chelsea's wanting lips, I sneak a glance at the screen. I stop. It's not Sophie. It's an unknown number. Rachel.

Chelsea pulls at me to keep going.

I tell her, "I have to get home."

Without saying it, she knows I mean Sophie.

"Okay." Chelsea sighs. She gets out of bed and goes to her dresser.

Putting on my shirt, I say, "You know you're going to have to be there for Sophie after I break up with her."

"I will be." Lifting plaid pajamas up her bare legs, Chelsea says, "Like a good friend should. Then, after the initial shock is over for her, you and I can be together guilt-free."

"Of course," I say, kissing her. She teases me with her tongue. "Anything for you."

In the elevator, heading down, I reply to Rachel.

EIGHT: *fresh*

TECHNICALLY, I'M NOT LYING WHEN I text Sophie: *I'm meeting an old friend visiting from out of town for dinner. Don't wait up.* Rachel is from New York, and she is, at 39, probably my oldest friend. Now that I think about it, Rachel's a woman, which means she's probably lying about her age. She must be in her forties!

I can't imagine being that age. I figure it's filled with baby pictures and playing house. And you live your life like the lives of people they talk about in magazines. Nothing's special anymore. And the belief that this is how it is from now on hangs on you unquestioned. Fuck that, this is the time to be alive. Rachel knows it too. We both hate getting old. So, we do things to stay young forever. Like fuck the bellboy at a three-star hotel. Or get dinner with a woman who wears a wedding ring.

If anything, this meeting is an extension of my job. I take my concierge duties seriously. That's all. Rachel and I were strangers, we fucked, and now, we're going to be friends. We shouldn't do this, but at the same time, it's exhilarating, isn't it? On the other end of this walk, waiting for me at Fresh, is a woman who couldn't stand another night without me.

I realize midway around the Capitol Square. There's a lump in my inner sport coat pocket. Feeling the box, immediately, I remember. It's the engagement ring I bought for Sophie. Knowing her tendency to organize my stuff, I hide it in the one place she'll never look: my sport coat. I ran home to grab it because I thought it'd be funny. But there's nothing funny about hiding an engagement ring in my pocket all night.

My whole body shakes at the thought. I love Sophie, but I don't. I can envision my life without her, yet I can't. We are good for each other, though we aren't. How do you break up with someone you love because you don't love them the same way anymore and you don't remember why or when it changed? It's not something to do quickly, and the longer I wait, the more inseparable we become. We end up hating each other, but we need each other. Is that still called love? Or are we hopeless?

A rush of crispness hits me when I sit down. Rachel wears a leather jacket and a slate skirt that shows off her legs—much more in her element than all those stingy business outfits. I suppose I feel overdressed. I don't care. An overdressed gentleman fares better in the company of women than an underdressed slob.

Her black-lined expectant eyes sparkle. Rachel leans forward against her hand in anticipation. I lean forward, too, in hope. We are embarking on a journey to newness. There can be no wrong answers, no ill-talk, no hated topics to avoid. We don't know each other. We are strangers together, two unknown dancers finding rhythm in each other's company.

Rachel orders a glass of red wine—*merlot*. I order whiskey *on the rocks*.

When the waiter, a middle-aged man with a stubby chin in a white tuxedo, brings us our drinks, he knows there is a small show going on between us and dares not interrupt. He keeps his conversation short and his demeanor professional, albeit always with a knowing smile. She orders the salmon and I get the duck. He leaves us to each other.

We clink our glasses together, I think, in celebration. From here on out, Rachel and I discover the lost treasures we never knew we were looking for. Under our secret tryst, we can revitalize each other's passions for life.

I smile at her. Is it too much? She smiles at me, not enough? I ought to treat her as a friend. She ought to do the same. As I stare into her eyes, I think, now, this is what I want: mystery—not knowing what will happen next. In her gaze, I can see she feels the same. There is still distance between us, but we're drawing closer.

"Tell me, Rachel," I begin in my sly way, "how do you do it?"

"Do what?" She swirls her wine glass.

"How do you attract such good company? I mean, I look around and quite frankly, you seem to have found the most exquisite man in this room, dare I say, even the entire city."

"Shut up! You are so full of yourself," she says. "Why are you wearing that sport coat anyway?"

I say, with a coy frown, "I know how much you respect a man in a suit."

"Because of your boss?" She chortles. The wine laps up the sides of her glass. "You're funny, you know that? You wouldn't believe what he was telling me on the cab ride back. I thought you were picking me up, by the way. That's why I didn't text you earlier."

Nice to know.

"I don't care if you make 60K a year, hunt turkey, and went to the University of Whitewash for Hotel Science or whatever the hell he said. He's a total hick."

"It's Wisconsin," I say. "Not New York."

"You're normal, I think," she says. "You know the difference between polite conversation and boring the shit out of someone. I mean, even this morning, did he ask me out?"

I think about how she ended up here with me in a similar fashion, but I don't mention it aloud. "Everyone goes to Paradise. Best bar burger in the city."

"Maybe I should've taken him up on his offer."

"What? Is this place not good enough for you?" The white-clothed tables speak much louder than I do.

"There's no panty-dropping deals." She smiles.

"Oh, is that the vibe we're going for tonight?"

"No. No. It's a joke." Rachel sips her wine. She's going through it pretty fast.

"How long have you been married?" I ask, kind of out of the blue, but it's been burning me up.

She looks off, exhales, and turns back to me. "Seven years. Been with him for ten."

"How'd he do it?" I can see she doesn't understand my wording. "How'd he propose?"

"You want to talk about this?" she says.

"If you're up for it," I say. "It's good research for me."

"So, it's serious between you and—?"

"Sophie," I say.

"It wasn't unromantic if that's what you're thinking. It wasn't quite romantic either. It was July, one of the hottest on record, and our AC broke in our apartment. We went to Central Park to get some fresh air. Near the carousel, his shoe was untied. He bent down to tie it. I let my mind wander around as I waited for him.'

"I'll always remember looking at a little girl in a yellow raincoat with a purple balloon shaped like a dog. You know the kind that clowns make? And I thought it was so odd because it wasn't even raining that day." Rachel leans back, looking off in memory, twirling her hair. "That little girl smiled and pointed behind me. There, Tate was on his knee with this ring stretched out in front of me.'

"I cried. I couldn't help it. I, of course, said yes. How could I not? I was in love with him."

Rachel said she *was* in love. It makes me wonder. "Are you still in love?"

"Of course," she quickly says, "why wouldn't I be?"

"I'm nervous," I say. "I want to believe that the love I feel for Sophie will last longer than a few years. I want to believe that, but I don't know. I can't see that far ahead. Is that wrong to say?"

"Isn't it kind of too late for that?" Rachel says. "You don't cheat on a woman you love."

"What about you?"

"Tate is my entire life. Sometimes I hate him, but it doesn't mean I still don't need him." She shifts in her seat. "I don't know if it's right. We've changed—him and me. For so long, it was wonderful, but I'm afraid..." She scratches at a rumple on the white tablecloth, "I'm afraid we forgot what made us get married. He works all day. I have to travel. Our weekends are booked with weddings and birthdays. Everything is so planned. There is no time for anything new. It'd disrupt the whole system. We're the social versions of ourselves all the time, and when we're home, we turn off and go to our separate spots to recharge."

So, this is the weight she carries. The same weight she held against me the other night.

Her hands shake to her wrists. She wipes the tear away from her cheek and sniffles. "I'm sorry. I didn't mean to say any of that." When she looks at me, her gaze becomes wide and glossy. Afraid her weight is too much, too soon.

She rests her left hand near the middle of the table. I reach out and lay mine atop hers. Warm, soft, and shivering, her wedding ring presses back.

Rachel pulls away, cognizant of what she let happen. "Why am I doing this?" She finds her purse and sighs. "I have to go."

"Please." I tell her. "Sip your wine and enjoy some company for once. So, you did something wrong? And you've been together for what, ten years? I think you earned a consolation fuck after all that time."

"That's not how marriage works." Rachel pushes her chair back. She's out the door if I don't say something clever.

"Teach me," I say. This gets her attention. She leans back in her seat. "I mean, I love Sophie like you love Tate. How do I do it? Become a married man."

"You don't actually care. You already got your prize and now you'll say anything to get seconds."

"So what?"

"I'm a woman—with thoughts and feelings."

"I have those too…?"

"What I'm trying to say is that you—you don't actually want to be with me. You want what you can get and when I leave, you'll move on to the next poor woman and you'll forget this thing between us ever happened. And I'll be at home, wondering why the fuck I fucked a guy like you."

"Least you have good taste," I say.

"It's wrong!"

"To be honest, when I wake up in the morning, I'm no different from the man who goes to bed." The whiskey

scorches down the back of my throat. "The characters and scenes are the same every day. Then you come along, and instantly, my whole world has changed. I see something in you and when I'm with you, I feel it click. We would be better off staying away, but there's no excitement in that. Is there?" I wait for her to respond, but she doesn't. "You can't tell me you don't feel the same way."

"Listen, Danny," I'm happy she recalled my proper name. "I think you're a bit eager. Don't you think?"

"Eager?"

"Yes."

"How?"

She says, "Where to begin?" She lifts her wine glass and creates a list in her mind. "First, you come up to me at the bar."

"Easy, I saw you looking at me. I thought maybe you were lost."

"I looked at you?"

"Your look said it all."

"And what did it say?"

"Find me," I say. I wanted to say 'fuck me,' but that's a bit direct, don't you think?

"Hah." She keeps going. "Second, you tell me you're a poet and it turns out you're my bellboy."

"Technically, writing is my day job. I moonlight as a bellman, but I don't mind being called your bellboy."

"Would you be quiet for once? Then, this morning, you took me for a ride and asked me out to dinner. Now you're telling me you have these insane feelings for me? What am I supposed to think?"

"I think you skipped the part where we had sex."

"Exactly!" Scared of her voice, she lowers it. "That's all this is—a one-night stand."

"Why are we having dinner together?" I say, swigging the rest of my drink.

"Because—" Rachel says as the salmon and the duck arrive on large white plates. The duck still smokes. I order another whiskey. She another wine.

She goes on. "I guess I need a friend in this city."

"So, here we are." I set down my empty glass.

"Here we are." She picks off the rosemary from her salmon.

"And that's all this is," I say, taking up my fork and knife. "Two friends having dinner together."

"Let's eat," she says and we dig in.

This place knows how to cook a duck to just the right medium rare. Sizzling, the crispy skin crunches as I cut off a nice strip. The juices flow. I blow on it to cool it down.

Rachel stabs, silently, at her salmon, its flaky meat coming apart at the plunges of her fork. "Are you going to tell your girlfriend?"

"No. Are you going to tell your husband?" I say, chewing the salty meat.

"I don't know."

"You would?" I say. "Aren't you afraid that it'll end things?"

"We betrayed their trust. It's the only way to get it back."

"If Sophie told me that she cheated on me, I would never forgive her."

"That's a double standard."

"What Sophie doesn't know doesn't hurt her." I cut myself off another slab.

"How many times have you cheated on her?" Rachel asks.

"Enough."

"More than twice?" My look tells her to up the amount. She squeals, "More than ten?"

"Maybe," I say. Never tell any woman the true number. It never does you any favors.

"You're awful."

"Am I? How many times have you cheated on your husband?"

"Once."

My whiskey arrives. I take it from the waiter. This is not what I want to talk about. I thought we'd laugh about the other night, not dredge up repercussions. She's a long way from home. It shouldn't matter.

I raise my glass. "I feel honored."

"As you should." She points at the bulge in my sport coat. "What is that?"

"What?"

"I've been staring at it all night. In your jacket."

"You mean you've been staring at my bulge?" I smirk.

"What is it?"

"It's funny, really," I say, considering drawing out the ring box. "But I don't think you'd find the humor in it."

"Try me."

"I'd rather not."

"Fine," she says. "If you're not going to tell me. I don't want to know." She sips her red. Purple hues decorate the corners of her mouth.

"Do you really want to know?"

"No," she says, "not anymore."

"It's a box of condoms."

"You're disgusting."

I didn't think my joke would land that flat. Not knowing what else to say, a silence sits on the table between us. My mind rages. Damn my mouth. She'll think it's a box of condoms if I don't show her. In fact, I want to show her. I want someone to know how serious I am about my girlfriend. I haven't even told Kovski yet. Someone should know I have this ring. Why not Rachel? She's someone who doesn't matter in the grand scheme of things, and she's been at the altar before. She can give me pointers.

I draw the box from beneath my coat and out in front of me.

"Oh my God," Rachel stares at the box. "You have got to be kidding me."

I open the lid and let the brilliance of the ring shine across our conversation. "What do you think?"

"Are you serious?" she says.

"What?" I can tell by her tone that this is not what she was expecting.

My gesture gathers the look of the restaurant. Even the waiters come to a standstill. It's as if the whole world waits for her answer. I can see how this gives off the wrong impression.

"Unbelievable." Rachel throws her napkin onto the table and stands up. "What is wrong with you?" She slings her purse over her shoulder.

"You don't like it?" I say, snapping the box shut.

She curses herself. "I should've known better. You're a fucking child." She presses her hands on the edge of the table. "You don't have a clue."

I slide the box back into my pocket. "What's wrong?"

"What's wrong? This whole night is wrong." She picks up her wine glass and drains it into her mouth. "Think with your head for once and you'll know." She drops the glass to the floor. It shatters. She sneers, "Un-believe-able." Her heels smack the hardwood as she walks out.

The silent room studies me. The waiter carries over a dustpan, broom, and the bill. Sliding the check over to me,

he says, "Pay at the bar." Whispers fly among the tables as he sweeps up the broken glass.

By the time I've paid the tab and head for the door, the place has already roared back to life. I leave as another anecdote for someone's water cooler tomorrow.

Outside, I scan the square for Rachel. She couldn't have gone very far. Not seeing her, I bet she's going to The Continental.

I round the first corner of the Capitol Square when I spot her. She wanders off the curb. A taxicab jolts to a stop and blasts its horn. She doesn't flinch. The cab screeches its wheels after she clears the bumper.

I catch up with her outside an ice cream shop. Painted in the window, a smiling cartoon cow licks an ice cream.

"What's the matter with you?" I bark, harsher than I meant to. Rachel frowns, mascara trails down her cheeks. I stop in front of her and say, gently, "What's going on?"

She tries to sidestep me, but I block her path. She pauses, not looking at me.

"Get out of my way." She sniffles.

"It was harmless," I say. "It doesn't mean anything. It's not like I was asking you to marry me. I wanted your opinion." I put my arms out wide for a hug. She ducks under them. "Rachel, please, listen."

She stops, but she doesn't turn to face me.

I sidle up to her side. "What's done is done. There's no point dwelling on it. And you might as well have fun while it lasts." There's no better argument for us to keep fucking than simply because we already got away with it. Chelsea and I had the same kind of conversation.

"I don't know what came over me. We shouldn't have done that." A tear trickles down her cheek.

Ever so softly, I say, "Let me walk you back to the hotel. When we get there, you'll walk inside and I'll walk home."

"You will?"

"Yes."

She drops her chin and nods. I put my hand at the small of her back and move us along.

We walk for two blocks and don't say another word. She clings to me, her sobs muffled by my shoulder—the only thing holding her up.

Outside the hotel façade, I pull her back from entering. I say, "Are you going to be alright?"

Her lower lip trembles. "It's a beautiful ring. It is. She would be such a lucky girl."

We stare at each other, lost in the night's events. She wobbles on her heels. Another tear steals away from her mascara. I want to say something more to make her feel better, but I don't know what. My little finger wipes away the tear.

Rachel says, "I leave tomorrow." She puts her arms around me. As she hugs me, she whispers, "Let's promise to never do that again."

"I promise," I say, "if you do."

She lifts her head from my shoulder, eyes glistening. We don't hesitate—our lips catch each other. Desperate for connection, our tongues collide. The night darkens around us as we kiss beneath the streetlights.

"Oh God," she gasps, pulling away. "No, no, no." She buries her face in her palms and slips into the hotel's revolving door.

Through the lobby window, she waits beneath the grand staircase. She glances at me, and I smile. She turns away, disappearing into the elevator. The weight of her lips still lingers on mine.

The ring box thuds against my pounding chest.

NINE:

T'S MUCH LATER THAN I THOUGHT. My stomach growls. Rachel left so fast, there wasn't any time to pack up the duck.

I close the door to my apartment quietly. It scrapes the wood trim before the lock clicks back into place. I turn the deadbolt, my neck muscles tense, awaiting the sharp click—*thunk*—the door latches. Sneaking into my own home is a shameful thing, but I don't want to disturb my slumbering girlfriend. Sophie deserves better, I know.

Sophie and I have been living together for two years. Twenty-four months exactly since we committed to this test of our relationship. We were proud the day we signed the lease. Happy, too, not to need to trek to each other's respective apartments anymore. We saw each other every day anyway. We figured we should live in closer proximity, immediate proximity, instant access, 24 hours a day. It's not that I wasn't thrilled with the idea. I was. I am. I still am, but it's these moments when I feel that the whole idea was something born out of fear.

What that fear is, I don't know—like a trembling in my chest, that no other woman will ever compare to her and letting her go would be the biggest mistake of my life.

When I'm with her, it all fades, replaced by a warm certainty that she is there—a rock on a shore I'm anchored to. With her, I can face the worst hurricanes, real or imagined.

Cracking open the door to our bedroom, the living room light casts my shadow over the bed. I take a deep breath. This is it.

Shutting the door behind me, my eyes adjust to the darkness. I go to the side of the bed and kneel. I open the ring box. Our whole life changes tonight. With a toothy, optimistic smile, I turn on the lamp on my nightstand.

Then quickly frown.

Sophie isn't here. I press my hand onto the down blanket. It deflates beneath the weight. I check my phone. There's a message from Chelsea: *Next time, stay for dinner.* It's a picture of her topless beneath a white apron. I don't care. There is no word from Sophie.

While I'm here, I pull open the drawer to my nightstand. Solid wood, but nothing fancy. I find the nail file that's been in there since freshman year of high school. I drag the nightstand away from the wall. I run my fingers down the pocked corner of the wood. From top down, each notch a marker for another woman won.

With the nail file, I saw into the wood and blow away the dust. If nothing else happens between Rachel and me, at least this counts for something. I push the nightstand back where it was.

Satisfied with my work, I turn on the TV. Some reality show cast-off sobs over losing the love of his life. Pathetic, but I need the background noise.

My mind rattles. *Where is she?*

Looking around for a note, I step into the kitchen. Usually, she leaves me something to tell me where she's gone and when she'll be back. I don't find anything.

The condiments quake in the door as I swing it open. I reach into the meat drawer, draw out two slices of ham, and dangle them into my mouth. I chew the salty, pink meat. The slices go down fast. I grab another handful and shut the door. I ball them up and shovel them into my mouth. It cures my hungry gut. I wash out a cup sitting on the counter and fill it with water. I gulp that down too.

Sophie must have forgotten to text. That's all. I do it all the time. Not a problem. I'm not going to be like her. I don't need to worry about where she is because I trust her.

I'll wait for her to get home with an old friend of mine. Pulling out a snifter and a bottle of Gentleman whiskey, I pour a full glass and go to the couch with the bottle.

Lying under the coffee table, I pick up a pen and a white envelope from the University of Wisconsin asking me for donations. I look out of my window into the street, bright headlights flash by and disappear, and the streetlamps cast grey shadows throughout the darkness. *Where is she?* echoes in my mind.

I put my pen to the blank space on the back of the envelope—

I'm in for
a long night. My love
doesn't love me anymore. She doesn't
say it. We are slipping
apart. Every day,
a grain of sand falls.
Soon we'll be empty,
of each other, craving
a new side
for our fill.

Pen down, I take up my whiskey. The first taste always wets my tongue and scorches my throat. All the germs die back there. All the bad stuff burns away, followed by that sudden buzz of alertness.

I reread the poem. I should really do an open mic one of these days. Just to show off a bit. It's hard in summer, though. Without college students around, venues don't host many events for the arts.

I think Sophie said she was seeing a friend of hers tonight, obviously not Chelsea. She's a good girl. It's not even midnight. I'll give her some time. I'm just lonely, that's all. She'll come back. She has to. She lives here. Still, my mind drifts to the possibilities of her being with someone else.

It's impossible. Sophie would never do such a thing to me. She couldn't. She's told me more times than I can count how much she loves me. Today, we didn't kiss goodbye before work. Hell, I barely saw her. She was getting ready, waging her daily battle with the mirror. I can't interrupt.

Why do I worry? I had my fill today already. If she wanted another go, I'd be too tired to do it. I'd lie to her about why I'm not feeling it tonight. I have to wake up early, that's a favorite. I had too many drinks—that's a common one. She'd understand. As long as I keep my eye contact direct and my answers short, she believes me. That's the secret to a believable lie.

I sink into the couch, switch the channel to baseball, and take another drink. It's the bottom of the fourth and there's a runner on first. One out. The batter steps to the plate. He looks at a strike. He swings the second time. On the third, he cracks the bat into the ball. He drives it to the pitcher. The pitcher tosses it to first. Double play. I take another drink.

It's the idea of her with another man that gets me. I mean her, Sophie, getting ready for someone else. Dressing up in heels, putting on perfume, trying to impress another man who isn't me. I cringe at the thought.

I can see Sophie smiling, her fingers wrapped around a wine glass, her face made to look better than perfect. Her eyes look deeply into his. His eyes look deeply into hers. They are getting closer to each other. He says something. She laughs. Her cheeks crease with a smile. What did he say that was so funny? I can almost make out the words. Why doesn't she laugh like that around me? I drink the rest of the snifter.

I pour another one.

Cheeks blushed by the zinfandel. Sophie's wine glass is empty. His is too. He asks if she's ready to go. She is. He stands and waits for her to get to her feet. As they walk out of the restaurant, he puts his arm around her waist. She leans into him like she's cold. She's not. She enjoys his company. She feels safe, almost comfortable, in his embrace.

I gulp.

They split a cab together. He opens the door for her. She feels impossibly grateful. He says his address first. She doesn't mind being dropped off second. They talk on the cab ride. Tomorrow, she won't remember the conversation. It is those kinds of words they are speaking—waiting words, words before saying goodbye, small talk. It means nothing, but she enjoys them, him, anyway.

The whiskey sends flames into my gut.

The cab reaches his house. He owns his own home. He could take care of her with none of the worry. She imagines what it must be like on the inside. He invites her to take a look.

A VACUUM ERUPTS SOMEWHERE BEYOND my closed eyes. I refuse daylight's calling and deepen my shoulder into the couch cushion. The empty whiskey bottle clinks as Sophie smacks it with the vacuum.

Sophie whispers to herself, "What the fuck." She picks up the bottle and sets it on the coffee table.

I blink awake. The shroud of Sophie's long mahogany hair rustles in and out of frame. Body heavy with last night's slow, unwinding nightcap, I push all my strength into my rib cage, and I slide my legs onto the floor. I rub the sleep out of my eyes.

Sophie finishes vacuuming and shoves the machine into the hallway closet. She comes back with her white Converse shoes and sits in the armchair.

"Off somewhere?" I ask her.

"I met a realtor last night. He's got an apartment on Monona Bay that's not on the market yet. He says we can see it today."

"I bet he'd loved to show you it too." Men do that. They make promises that are too good to be true to women they like.

"Don't be like that," she says. "It's not like that. This could be it, Danny. This could be the place we always dreamed about."

"Probably because he's just trying to get into your pants. How'd you meet this bozo anyway?"

"I was out with Chelsea, and she wanted to talk to these guys." Sophie tightens her shoelaces and stands. She goes to the mirror and checks herself out, fixing the way her azure dress falls across her chest. "So we were talking and it turns out one of the guys is a realtor and he has this apartment."

"You were out with Chelsea last night?" I ask.

"Yeah." Sophie grabs a pair of earrings off the breakfast bar. She puts them in her ears.

I don't know what to say except that she's lying. There's something going on, but I can't call her out on it. She'll wonder how and why. I can't just say Chelsea and I were hanging out without her. She'll suspect much worse. I sigh and get up from the couch.

I cross the room, skimming my fingers along Sophie's back as I pass her. Rachel's bare skin, bathed in lamplight, flashes in my memory. I grab my shoes and slip them on.

"You're not too hungover?" Sophie says.

"For our dream home, never." I stand.

"Do you need to change?"

"I figured there was no time."

"You should change."

"No, it's alright. No one will notice." Sure, I'm in a rumpled shirt, but when I reset the collar and button it up, it looks better than most mouth breathers.

"You stink," Sophie says.

"Oh." I smell my pits. They're rather woodsy. "I'll be right back."

In our bedroom, I scramble out of my clothes. I don't know why I am so nervous. These hangovers always leave me feeling clammy. I peel off my sweat-stained clothes from the night before. If Sophie went out last night, it's fine, I trust her. She wouldn't be with me if something happened. She's not that kind of woman.

I jump into a pair of blue jeans, roll on some deodorant, and button myself into a clean khaki Oxford.

Headed to the bathroom to brush my teeth, Sophie calls to me. "At least it looks like you were productive last night."

Through the mirror, my mouth full of toothpaste, I see pinched between her manicured fingers the poem I wrote last night. "No!" My heart drops to my gut. I quickly spit and rinse my mouth. "Don't read that."

It's too late. She sets the poem on the coffee table. "Is this about us?"

"See? I knew you wouldn't understand. It's art. That's all."

"What do I have to do to show you that I love you?" Sophie says.

"I know you love me."

"Then what's this?" She points to the poem. "Because this stuff comes from a deeper place than what we talk about. So, what's going on?"

My pulse shakes. Sweat beads at my temples. Sophie watches me, eyes wide, ready to take in whatever I'm about to say. I hate her for it. Hate that she can do this. She does everything right.

This is what couples are supposed to do. They're supposed to talk these things out, listen, and discuss how to move forward from here. The poem does come from a deeper place. The echo chamber in my chest that knows that Sophie's not the one. She can't be. Not after all the things I've done behind her back.

Here's the moment though, if I want to break up with Sophie and be with Chelsea for real, this is it. One sentence and I can end it.

And yet, when I look into Sophie's pleading emerald eyes, love sparkles back at me. I'm transfixed. She loves me. There's no one I think about more. That's why I can't tell her the truth—it would turn her beautiful love into molten hate.

"I'm going to stop drinking so much." I tell Sophie. "Whiskey gives me crazy thoughts. I've got to cut back."

Sophie pats my shoulder. "I think that's a good idea."

"I love you," I say.

"I love you too," she says, pecking me on the lips.

Sophie parks her Civic on the curb in front of a cream brick townhouse with a grass front yard lined with lush pink and fuchsia petunias. A hummingbird feeds from a sugar lantern hung over the corner bushes.

At our backs, across the street, a beat-up metal pier extends into the waters of Monona Bay. Every night, we could sit on the end of it dangling our feet in the water as we look out at the Madison skyline. The waves softly lapping against the rocky shore.

"Hello there!" The realtor, a tall, chummy guy in a polo and khakis, sits on the swinging bench on the front porch.

"Sorry for being late," Sophie says. "Someone overslept."

"Someone didn't know we were touring an apartment today."

The man greets us at the top of the porch steps with a laugh. "I've been there. Don't worry. I understand. Sander

Monroe." He clamps my hand so hard I have to wrestle it away from him.

"Right this way." Sander opens the door and gestures us inside. "At the top of the steps. You'll see."

Sophie gives Sander a little, nervous smile before she charges up the steps. Even after five years together, I check her out. Her slender brown shoulders glow beneath the spaghetti straps of her dress that flows to her ankles. Her white sneakers quack on the hardwood stairs.

At the top landing, Sophie stops and turns to me. Her excited smile spreads to mine. "Are you ready?"

Already, I can see through the glass door the sun-filled home. Sophie pushes the door open, and we enter.

Windows line every wall. In the frames, the Capitol dome peeks above the shoulders of the downtown high-rises, one of them being The Continental. Beneath it all, the great blue Lake Monona shimmers. This would be the view from our living room every day of our lives.

"Check this out." Sophie rushes through the empty living room and into a sunroom. Following her, she dives into one of the two plush wicker chairs. "Imagine this. Imagine it, alright? It's October. It's the first frost and the leaves are all changing. And boom! Hot coffee. Think of all the inspiration! I could put my easel here and maybe paint again," Sophie says. "You could write and just look at that. All the time."

"You don't think it'd get old after a while?"

"Old?"

"I mean, yeah, after awhile we'd take it for granted like there it is again, the big boob in the middle of Madison."

Sander butts in. "Have you ever gotten tired of looking at boobs?"

Fair point.

"Why'd the last tenants move out?" I say. There's something fishy about this place. I know it.

"Murdered." Sander slashes his throat.

Sophie and I check each other.

The realtor laughs. "Nah, I'm joking. They bought a house," he says so matter of fact that I grind my teeth.

"I bet you got a nice commission off them," Sophie says.

"It didn't hurt." He smiles, not too big, but you can tell he's proud of himself. Judging by his looks, he's still fresh to real estate.

"Was it your first deal?" I say.

"God, no," he says, laughing. "No, no. I've sold 25 houses last year alone. I barely make any money off rentals. Usually, I pawn them off on younger salespeople, but this place is made to fly. Why not earn a few hundred bucks for a night's work?"

I retort, "You're really that confident that this place will get rented today?"

"There's another couple coming through tonight and the listings' not even live."

"Come on, let's see the rest," Sophie gets up and leads us to the kitchen. Small, but still bigger than the one we have. The cabinets, the sink, the oven and fridge covering three of the walls. The fourth is big enough for maybe a shelf and the trash bins, but not much else.

"We'll need to eat in the living room," I say. I check the cabinets, look under the sink, peer into the fridge. They cleaned the place well.

"We do that now anyway," Sophie says.

"How's the bedroom?" I ask.

Sophie leads us from the kitchen, through the corner of the living room, down the hallway that ends with a bathroom, and into a large bedroom. The realtor lurks in the doorway. I avoid his friendly gaze.

The master bedroom eats up most of the apartment's square footage. The master bath is huge—big enough to lie spread eagle without touching anything. The walk-in closet is nice, though Sophie insists that it will be 'hers.'

"Why?" I say.

"Just wait," she says. "You'll understand."

The bedroom itself can only fit a queen-sized bed, but I'm not complaining. Sophie leads me into the other bedroom on the opposite side of the hallway.

Sophie enters first, spinning to face me in the center of the room. "What about this as your office?" she asks. Out the window, the same view as the sunroom stretches before us. "Well?"

My chest thumps as I stare at the Capitol dome. I think of Chelsea and how mad she's going to be, but I must believe that Sophie is the woman of my dreams. I mean, look at us—we're standing in our dream home.

Turning to Sophie, I smile. "It's perfect."

"Should we do it?" Her grin mirrors mine.

"I don't know. Should we?" I make a dumb face.

"Yeah?"

"Yes," I nod.

Sophie jumps into my arms and kisses me on the lips. I nearly fall over. She hits me so hard.

ELEVEN:

TWO FINGERS PROD BENEATH MY RIBCAGE. It jolts me. Eva sets her tray next to mine on the lunch buffet line, laughing at my reaction. "Someone's jumpy today."

"You want me to do that to you when you're not looking?" I say. I run a knife, dripping, with jelly, across a piece of white bread.

The hotel provides us lunch in a windowless break room in the basement. There's always a sandwich and salad bar with a variety of meats and veggies. Sometimes we get fed the leftovers from over-catered weddings and conferences at the hotel. I suppose it's a good perk.

"You'd love that." Eva grabs a plate and two pieces of bread. She slathers both sides with mayo. Unlike me, she takes her time to make her sandwich. "Who was that woman you were with last night?"

"What woman?"

"Come on. Ryan and I saw you."

"Givens was there?"

Eva nods.

"I was giving her the tour of the town. You know how I take my concierge duties very seriously." I smush together my peanut butter and jelly.

"I know you do. But there's one problem. I'm the hotel's actual concierge. Like that's my job title." Eva adds bacon, tomato, and lettuce to her bread.

"I'm trying to take off some of your workload," I say, picking up my tray.

"You have a girlfriend. What the fuck are you doing?"

"Don't worry about it." I snipe at her. "You're talking kind of loud." I pick up a plastic cup out of the stack next to the soda machine. I fill it up with ice and root beer.

"Don't worry about it?" she says. "You're being an asshole. And as your friend, I should have the right to call you out on it." She cuts her sandwich in two triangles.

"It was nothing, okay? She threw herself at me even though I told her about Sophie. I pushed her away."

Eva grabs a plastic cup. "Didn't look like it."

"Did you see me go into the hotel?" I say, stepping back as she fills up a cup with water. It's close enough for me to smell her cinnamon perfume, warm and refreshing.

"I guess not." Eva picks up her tray. "Why were you even out with her in the first place? Did you tell Sophie what happened?"

Together, we head to the only open booth on the other side of the room. "No, she doesn't know." We pass a table filled with the gray-shirted maintenance guys. "Sophie doesn't need to." A smattering of housekeepers and kitchen workers sit at the next one. "I'm doing it for work. The woman's husband is a publisher."

We set down our trays and sit across from each other.

"You're going to give her your work?"

I nod.

"What work?" Eva asks.

I smile. "You want to know?"

"I think the whole world wants to know what Danny Clark has in store for them."

"Don't tell anyone." I lean in close. "I'm writing a book of poetry."

Eva chokes on her sandwich as she snorts with laughter.

"What?" I say. "What's so funny?"

Clearing her throat, she asks, "A book of poetry?"

"Yeah?"

"You're serious?" she says.

"Do you know my major in college?"

"Ummm…women's studies?"

"Ha. Ha. That was my minor. It was poetry!" I bite into my smushed together PB & J.

"Poetry!" She mocks my hyperbole. "Fine, fine, that's a good major, bright future in that." She cackles. "Go on, tell me about it."

"It's about love and all the stupid shit we do to feel it."

"You have the experience." She bites her sandwich and chews.

"Anyway," I say, "I'm going to give it to her to give to him when it's ready."

"Wow," she says, "look at you—wining and dining the publisher's wife to get closer to him. Sounds like a foolproof plan."

"Believe what you want Eva, but I'm a good dude and my intentions are pure. You would know if you ever went on a date with me."

"I would never go out on a date with you."

"Why's that? Am I so bad?"

"Do you want me to answer that?

"Why do you hang out with me? I mean, you could get lunch with Dave or Givens or anyone else really."

"I find your life entertaining."

"So do I. Let me know when you want to join it for real." I wink at her. "We could hit up Whiskey Jack after work tonight."

Eva says, "No thanks."

The radio on my belt crackles to life. It's Dave. "Danny, we need you to take Mr. Flores to the airport."

I say into my radio, "I'm on my lunch break. Tell the bell captain to do it."

The radio buzzes with Dave's voice. "He's on a run."

"Mr. Flores is going to have to wait," I say into the radio.

Eva pipes up, "Danny! He owns the hotel."

I shrug. "Then he should have a car and he can drive himself to the airport." Unlike most people, I have boundaries and won't get bossed around.

Haseem comes on the radio, "Danny, do this now. Thank you."

"Ooh, you got Haseem on the radio." Eva dips a carrot stick into some ranch dressing and crunches.

My head sinks to my chest. I shovel half of my sandwich into my mouth and chew. "Could I get Ryan's number?"

"I'm surprised you don't have it."

"Keep forgetting to save it." I swallow.

"Trying to cover your tracks?" Eva says, pulling out her phone.

"No, I want to switch shifts later this week."

"Sure," she says, sending his info.

"I'll see you up there," I say.

"See you up there." Eva bites into her sandwich.

I add my tray to the pile on a grey kitchen cart, wondering what if I could leave all these late nights behind and really be with someone like Eva. No one talks to me the way she does. Even if we only had a few minutes together and she called me out on some bullshit, it'll still be the highlight of my day.

I glance back at her. She's busy scrolling on her phone. Maybe she's right, we have no connection.

Back in the lobby after the airport run, I check the clipboard and find Givens' name. I skim my finger over the schedule…we don't work together until tomorrow. That's long enough for him to blab to Sophie—I can't risk it.

I wish they weren't friends. No doubt, they talk about me.

Now that Givens has seen firsthand proof of my indiscretions, his moral compass is a threat. He's going to take it upon himself to make sure I'm punished rightfully for it, unless I can convince him otherwise.

I'll call him, invite him for drinks tonight, and pretend I'm interested in what he's writing. Once he's comfortable, or comfortably drunk, I'll bring up the whole misunderstanding with Rachel and spin it my way. It should work. Givens seems lonely. He'll be seduced by my mere company.

TWELVE:
memorial union

GIVENS PICKED THE TIME AND PLACE. Surprised by his authority, I agreed.

The Memorial Union Terrace is the melting pot of Madison. Covered in a variety of yellow, orange and sky-blue metal chairs and tables, the triple-deck terrace faces the blue helm of Lake Mendota. Lovers and children sit with their legs dangling off the docks, splashed by the ever-living water.

On an easy breezy summer day like today, everyone meets at the Terrace. No one can resist beers beneath the sunset.

When Givens sees me, he pushes up his glasses and waves. It's a squeeze to get to him on the middle deck. He must've gotten here early because he scored the center table in front of the stage. An ice-water sweats in front of him. Making my way to him, a pitcher of beer and cups in hand, I sidestep a mom and dad exchanging their baby between them.

Sliding between two chairs, I catch myself looking at this rocker girl, probably a junior stuck here for her last summer before graduation. I trip over the nose of a guitar

case and I douse her red Doc Martens with beer. Catching myself, I say, "Sorry."

Despite her punk vibe, plaid skirt, tank top, and cotton candy pink hair, a smile inflates between her dark lips. She pulls the guitar case upright between her legs. "No, no, my bad. This thing is always in the way." She reaches down and mops her boots with a brown napkin.

As much as I want to ask her if she's in a band playing tonight and, eventually, if she needs help carrying that guitar home after the show. It's not a good look in front of you-know-who. Instead, I carry on.

"Givens!" I say, and his eyes narrow immediately. "I mean, Ryan, Ryan, Ryan, how are you this fine evening?" My enthusiasm sickens me. I've got to pretend to be his best friend or my mission will fail.

"Where have you been?"

"Come on, it's only fifteen minutes." I check my watch, maybe forty-five. "Yikes. Lost track of time. Writing, you know how it is." I took a few shots of whiskey with Kovski before I got here. We talked about my plan. He thought it might work.

"I hope it was something good." Givens whines, "I don't understand why you'd call me up to get together and you come late."

"That's how it is with me." I take a seat. "I figured you, of all people, would get it."

"Well," Givens says, swirling his water cup as he stares at me. "You're not wrong about that—except if you really cared, you'd be on time." He takes a satisfied sip.

"We've been working together for what?" I say, changing the subject. "Two years and we've never gotten drinks together. That's a long time—too long."

"Don't think I don't know what this is about." He sits back and crosses his arms. I wonder how he could possibly know my intentions. While I try to devise a counter, he continues, "If you're trying to get me drunk so you can make fun of me. Let me tell you, it's not going to happen."

"You think I invited you out to mock you?" I'm flabbergasted, honest, I am. If that's my reputation, no wonder nobody joins me for my after-work benders anymore.

"I've heard about what you do."

"Oh, come on, Giv—" He shoots me a look. "Ryan," I start again, "give me more credit than that. I'm not that kind of person."

"I saw the photos of Dave."

"That was an accident, I was drunk and I didn't think anyone would share it." Dave wanted to go out and pick up girls, except he got too drunk and ended up hugging the toilet around midnight. I snapped an ugly video of Dave and shared it with a couple of maintenance guys. Turns out those guys are the biggest gossips. I never meant for the whole hotel to see it, but Dave was lights out. With eyes like scarecrows, his voice sick with too many margaritas, he pleaded to God for mercy between his bouts of dry heaving. It was hilarious. Haseem gave me a few days' suspension without pay for that one. I didn't mind it. Sophie and I booked a cabin in the woods with my time off. We broke a dry spell that weekend.

Dave and anybody at work never looked at me the same way after that. It is what it is. People need to learn how to accept that no one's perfect and it's okay to look dumb every once in a while. It's not a big deal.

Givens fiddles with his cup.

I continue in a reassuring tone, "But I'm not going to do it to you. You and I are friends. I respect you, and I

hope you can respect me." I pause. "Why'd you even want to meet up if you thought I was going to fuck with you?"

His puffy and lightly bearded cheeks huff. "I thought it'd be nice to get to know another writer." I can hear the slight wheeze of air entering and escaping him. Givens sips his water and smacks his lower lip. "You promise not to mess with me?"

"Yes, of course. Seal it with a cheers?" I say, pouring him a cup of beer.

"Don't mind if I do. Might help calm the nerves," he says, taking the beer. "Because I've got a surprise for you."

"Oh yeah?" I pour myself one.

"It's open mic night!" He throws his hands out for the big reveal. "We've got to sign up!"

I fill up my cup with beer. "Oh God, really? I don't know."

"Come on," he says. "Sophie tells me you're such an amazing poet. I've got to hear something. You even said you were writing before you got here. That's commitment."

"Sophie's not wrong, but I don't have my notebook with me."

"Anything on your phone?"

"Not that kind of poet. It's more in the moment, pen and paper."

"Here's a challenge." He takes a pen from his backpack and pulls out a G2 Pilot. My brand of pen. Huh. He tears out a page from his notebook. "Write something down and read it tonight."

"Right now? No way," I say, slapping down the pen on the loose paper. It flutters in the light breeze.

"Why not?"

"I need...I need inspiration," I say.

"I knew I liked you." Givens raises his cup. "Cheers to that."

A loud hiss comes from the stage.

My retired poetry professor, Miss Arabella Holmes, a tall, ancient woman with long braids, dyed red, sets up the microphone center stage. The stage lights illuminate her. She ran this open mic when I attended school. Square glasses, no chin, and a frumpy frame, she half-limps as she walks, holding a black fedora. She speaks into the mic, "Alright, everyone, open mic sign-ups are open. If you want to get on stage, come up here and put your name on one of these slips of paper and drop it in the hat. It's random, so you might go first or you might go last. When I'm out of slips of paper, sign-ups are closed."

On the front of the stage, Miss Arabella sets the fedora, a stack of square white paper and pen. She hobbles off.

Givens stands.

I say, "What are you doing?"

"I'm signing up. Want me to sign you up too?"

The blank page glares at me. "There's no way. No way. I wasn't prepared for this. If I were, I would've brought my notebook. I'm not reading something I wrote for the first time. It takes time to craft a good poem. Days, weeks, years. I can't."

"Danny," A smug smile plasters across Givens' big cheeks.

"Stop looking at me like that."

"It's okay to admit that you're shy," he says. "It's surprising to me, but, you know, it makes sense. You have all this bravado, but like a true writer, you hide your feelings in your work."

"I just don't have anything ready!" I snap.

"Suit yourself." He weaves through the maze of crowded chairs and tables on the way to the stage.

The rocker girl hands a pen to the chortling Givens. Of course, the guitar. She's playing tonight. Can't wait to look at her for five minutes. The guitar is a bonus. He signs up and drops his name into the hat. They come back together. Rocker girl catches me staring. She winks. I snap out of my gaze, and she turns back to her friends as soon as she sits down.

The rocker girl reminds me of Sophie, a version of her I knew ages ago. Sophie used to wear leather cuffs and spikes. She'd rip a hole in a tank top to give it an edge. She wore thigh-high boots at the dance club on our second date. I never realized it was just a phase.

I left Sophie home alone again. She wanted to stay in because she had a long work week. The usual blah blah blahs. She wanted to watch this remake to some movie people forgot about. We'd already saw the old one. I couldn't bother doing that. Give me something real. Sophie thinks it might help my creative process to compare two ways of telling the same story. Friday night is not a night to do homework. It's a time to go out and shake hands with the devil.

Sophie believed me when I told her I'd be going out with Kovski, which wasn't technically a lie.

Givens returns. That's when I realize, it's so obvious. To seal the deal on Givens' word, I invite Sophie to come here. When she does, he hears we signed a lease together. He knows what I did must not have been my fault. And we all continue our happy bliss never needing to know the truth.

"Let's get a picture," I say to Givens, pulling out my phone. "I want to send it to Sophie."

"Really? Okay," he says. We smile together with the stage and the lake as our background. "Just don't send it to the work chat. I don't want people to think I'm an alcoholic with all this beer on the table."

"Paranoid much?" I text the photo to Sophie.

I message her: *Guess who's at the terrace? You should come out now. It's open mic night!* I hit send.

Within minutes, she responds. *I'm kinda of tired, but have fun tho.*

Of course, I always have to prod her. *Come on, Soph, it's not everyday we sign a lease to our dream home.*

She types, then stops. That means she's trying to find the perfect excuse for not coming. I wish she would be spontaneous for once. Feels like years since she got caught up in the whirlwind. Hell, we haven't had sex in public since senior year, amongst the books in the basement library stacks. Why does everything get worse when you get older? People lose that sense of danger, of getting caught, of doing something wrong even though it feels right at the time. Sophie used to have that, but she lost it. She relies on me to complete her because I haven't lost it—that urge to feel alive.

My phone buzzes. Sophie typed back *On my way.* The impossible happens sometimes.

A stark reality hits me: why wouldn't I do the open mic? Sophie would find that so strange that I'd randomly be hanging out with Givens. We never did that before, why now? Because I'm hiding something. That's why. She'll figure it out. No, I must perform.

On the stage, Miss Arabella picks up the hat. There's one slip left. An old guy in a visor and carrying a banjo aims for it. I can't hesitate.

I scramble to the stage, bumping the rocker girl's elbow. "Hey…" she says.

I yell back, "My bad." A kid on a scooter cuts me off. I hit the brakes. Banjo guy reaches for the last slip. I have to do what I have to do. I sprint and swipe the paper before he does. I write my name down.

The banjo player says, "You son of a bitch. That was mine. Now I don't get to play."

On the stage, Miss Arabella towers above us. I offer her the slip and she drops it in the hat.

"Too slow, Marv. I'll plug you in at the end."

"Least, I know I'll be last. If you can't find me, I'll be at the bar." Marv walks off.

"Thanks, Danny. Makes my ears bleed listening to him practice the banjo."

"Funny. That's my act too, except I play the mouth harp."

"That's too bad." Her hand mixes up the slips of paper. "I figured you read a poem."

"That was a joke. I am," I say. "I'm actually coming up with it on the spot."

"Your work always did have a sense of urgent irresponsibility." Miss Arabella walks off stage to a small table, where she sits during the show.

I head back to my seat. When I pass the rocker girl, she subtly nudges me with her elbow in the thigh. Not hard, but noticeable.

I shoot her a look. She says, "My bad."

That minx. I say, "If we bump into each other anymore tonight, you're going to have to buy me dinner."

"Keep dreaming," she says, turning back to her friends.

When I sit down, I tell Givens that Sophie plans to join us.

Givens says, "What was that?"

"What was what?" I say.

"Between you and her," he says, but it's not patronizing. Is he curious?

"Nothing. Banter. That's it."

"How is it so easy for you? If I said what you said, I'm pretty sure she'd break my nose."

"Give yourself more credit than that," I say. "But it's true, you say that line wrong, you're a creeper."

"I think if I say any line, she'll laugh at me."

"The problem with most guys is that they think they can get the whole pie in one line. It's a thousand lines. Like writing. You share a moment here. A story there. You're building something with every touch and every word. It takes time."

Givens thinks about it. He nods. "But what if you've let it take a lot of time and nothing's happening?"

"You must not be building toward something." He doesn't get it. "Think of it as a story's climax. For instance, that girl, right? If your goal is to take her home tonight. That's the story's climax. How you get there is from point A to point B to Point C and so on."

"But what if I'm not that kind of man?"

"Shut up, yes, you are, every man has to be that man if he wants to ever have sex. It's the same thing whether you just met her or you've been married for decades."

"Are you trying to take her home?" Givens asks.

"Hell no. Why would you even ask me that? You could. Which," I nudge him here. I know he's already painted a bad portrait of me, but I'm going to prove to him that I'm a misunderstood masterpiece. "if you wanted to, here's what you do. Keep making little advances, not big moments. You did it right with the pen thing at sign-ups. We're going to be here all evening. Start too strong, it gets awkward. Give it time, some eye contact, a compliment after her set, maybe some banter, and then, make the ask."

"How do you think of all this?"

"College was a very good time for me." Realizing I have his full attention, I pivot to a more pressing topic. I tell him. "I'm writing a book about it, actually."

"You're writing a book on dating?"

"Better." I lean in and whisper. "I haven't told anyone yet, not even Sophie." A smile perks the corner of my lip as he leans forward. "I'm writing a romance novel."

"A romance? No way. Makes sense for a poet." Givens basks in the glow of my secret novel.

"I probably shouldn't be telling you since you and Sophie are such good friends." I back off. "I wouldn't want you to read too much into it."

"Come on, Danny, it's me. Of all people, I know fiction is fiction," he says. "But fiction usually comes from a place you know. Is yours based on a true story?"

"No, no, of course not, if I had the main character's life, I'd kill myself," I say.

He claps his meaty hands together and sits forward. "Let's hear it."

"There's a college graduate named err—Andy. He's going through some tough times. He's got a dead-end job serving tables 14-hours a day at this restaurant, but he's got a degree. The problem is his degree is in writing, and unless he gets published, it's basically useless, you know?"

"I don't agree," Givens says, "but keep going."

"Now, Andy has a problem. He's got this beautiful girlfriend named umm—Britney, whom he has been dating for years, and he plans to marry her. I mean, he's got the ring and everything. He's waiting for the perfect time to pop the question. But then, a drop-dead blonde walks into the restaurant one day while he's serving. He can't keep his eyes off her. Once more, this blonde gives him her number. Tells him to call her."

"He's got to call, right?"

"Bingo," I say. "They go out, and he tells her that they can only be friends. Andy's an honest man. Like the gentleman he is, he walks the blonde woman home. All this time, Andy's not making any moves because, you know, he loves his girlfriend. This woman, though, is making moves. Andy holds strong, but for how long? This woman is a total bombshell ready to explode." Givens leans in, on the edge of his seat. "When they get to her door, she forces herself on him. Andy pushes her off and tells her he is still in love with his girlfriend. It just so happens that Britney's friend is walking by and sees what happened."

"What does Andy do?"

"The only thing Andy can do. He tells Britney's friend the truth."

"What happens next?"

"I don't know yet. I haven't finished that part." I pause, seeing if Givens has grown cognizant of any of the story. "Maybe you can help me. What do you think Britney's friend will do?"

Givens places his palms together and looks up at the sky in thought. "I think the friend would understand the truth. From what you're saying, it doesn't sound like Andy is very truthful at all, even if he calls himself an 'honest man.' Why would he even agree to get dinner with this bombshell? Does he tell the friend that he's having second thoughts about Britney?"

"No." I say. "He doesn't because Andy isn't having second thoughts. She threw herself at him and kissed him. He let that happen. In truth, he kind of enjoyed it. That thrill of something different, new."

"Definitely sounds like a romance," Givens says.

"I know it's juicy," I say. "But what I'm stuck on is the next part with the friend. I'm leaning toward writing that the friend doesn't tell Britney anything about the kiss because the friend shouldn't get in the way of such things."

"Then again," Givens says, stroking his chin. "If the friend doesn't tell Britney, there's not much of a story anymore. Where's the suspense?"

I'm starting to think Givens didn't see a thing last night. I reach for my drink and take a satisfying gulp. "What if it ends there?"

"What are you writing? Some moral porn romance? We need the nitty-gritty." Givens pounds his fist on the table. "You've got to dig deep on this character. Bigger issues are going on with Andy than this one girl. Maybe there are a few girls, and the friend knows about all of them. Maybe Britney is naïve to it, but Andy doesn't hide it that well."

"That's an interesting subplot," I say, buying time. Now I wonder how Givens knows about the other women. I bet he's bluffing. "What do you think I should do?"

"It's your story, and you should write it how you want it. But what I'd say is, Andy needs to keep up the charade for a while, really build that suspense, so he does certain favors for the friend. When you build up the plot enough and it gets to the point where only the truth can be set free, boom, the truth comes out. The friend betrays Andy and lets Britney know." Givens pats his finger against his lip. "Ooh, what if Britney is getting something on the side too? That'd change everything." Givens takes a drink. He smacks his lips. "I love brainstorming. Don't you?"

Red-hot rage buzzes through my veins, flushes my cheeks, and pricks goosebumps along my skin. Givens knows something that I don't. "Is Sophie cheating on me?"

"What?" he says. "Why would you ask me that?"

"Tell me." I grip my beer, ready to pitch it into the ground.

"Where did you get that idea from?"

"It's obvious, isn't it? It's obvious you know something that I don't. Tell me, Givens. Is she cheating on me?"

"It's Ryan."

"What's the big deal?" I say. "Givens, Ryan. Ryan Givens. They're all your fuckin' names. Tell me, Ryan, is she cheating on me?"

"Why don't you ask her yourself? Better yet, maybe you should tell her about all the girls in Andy's life that aren't her."

"You don't know what it's like to be in love." I say, swallowing down the rest of my drink.

"I know how to treat someone with respect. Maybe you should tell Britney the truth and see what happens." Givens pulls off his glasses and cleans them with the hem of his shirt. "Or like sharing your stuff on stage, are you just too scared to?"

Miss Arabella stands center stage and digs through the hat. She pulls out a name and announces it. It's not Givens or me. I can breathe again.

For the first act, a violinist plays a somber tune filled with screeches and haws, but it gives our conversation a rest. I've said what I needed to say. Laid the seed. If he respects me, he understands and won't say a word. If he doesn't, he'll tell her the truth and watch me squirm.

My back stiffens with nerves. I try to relax against the stiff metal chair. These terrace chairs are famous in Madison. Anyone who goes to the University of Wisconsin has a memory of trying to steal one. What's so special about them? There's an allure of bygone days when we didn't know any better. Throats dry from talking

with friends and refreshed by pitcher after pitcher of Wisconsin ale. This is one of the few student unions in the U.S. where you can drink on campus. The chairs are not particularly comfortable, but you forget because you're getting blitzed in public in such a beautiful place.

One late drunken night, after the Union closed, chasing a girl, of course, she and I nabbed a chair and ran. We almost got caught. The security guard chased us, but the donut holes haunting his waistline held him back. We were too far ahead. We hid out in her apartment and made love on her living room floor. In the morning, I snuck out and took the chair as my prize. Don't remember her name and lost her number. It was the perfect getaway. The chair remains on my balcony, gathering rust and rain.

The mic'ers go up and down from the stage. Each time Miss Arabella pulls a piece of paper from the hat, my chest tightens and my throat dries. When I hear I'm not next, I bury my nerves in my beer, trying to stay calm. All the while, the blank page stares at me.

We're on the eighth slot, some sleight-of-hand magic act, when Sophie shows up, and walking close behind her, there's Chelsea.

They weave through the throngs of tables and chairs, but I have no idea where they can sit. We couldn't save seats.

Rocker girl comes to our rescue. She says her friends have to get to a show at the Majestic and offers up two chairs from her table. Bummed they couldn't see her play, the friends get up and go. We snag the empties. Sophie sits next to me. Chelsea sits in front, partially blocking my view of the stage. Can't say I mind.

Sophie hugs Givens before she sits down. "Are you reading tonight?"

"Another scene from the novel."

"The novel?" I ask.

Sophie says, "When can I finally read the whole thing?"

"Still fine-tuning. I'm a mad scientist twisting all these knobs. A word here. A plot point there. That's why it's so great reading at these. Not only do I get to hear it out loud, but I can tell where I lose people."

Chelsea blurts out, "You should let Danny read it. He's a writer."

"I'll take a look, if you want," I say. I dream of one day writing a novel. The fact that Givens has written a book and I haven't even started one drives me bonkers.

"That's what I need!" Givens squeals. "Someone to tell me how to give the words more depth and meaning."

"Yeah. Yeah. Send it my way whenever."

Givens taps his beer cup against mine. "Cheers to that!"

As I sip, Sophie and I lock eyes. I blow her a kiss. She looks away, blushing.

Chelsea asks, "So, you're reading tonight?"

"I am." I proudly announce, "Givens, I mean, Ryan practically begged me to do it."

"Otherwise, he would've chickened out," Givens sneers.

"I wasn't scared," I say.

"I think it's exciting," Sophie says. "What are you going to read?"

Chelsea says, "You should read the one about the two caterpillars." I wish she hadn't said anything. I stopped sharing my work with Sophie around the same time Chelsea and I hooked up the first time. Sophie judges it too much. You heard her before? She thinks everything is about her. Chelsea knows better than that.

Sophie says, "Two caterpillars? I don't think I know that one."

"Yeah, I showed you it a while back," I lie. "It doesn't matter. I'm cooking up something else, something completely new." I hold up the blank page for them to see.

They look at each other. Sophie says, "I don't get it."

"I'm writing something off the cuff," I announce.

"You're making it up on the spot?" Chelsea asks.

"It's so epic," Givens says. "I'm going to record it."

They're impressed, but they can't feel how hard my heart pounds. It's exhilarating and hell at the same time. As soon as Miss Arabella calls my name, I'll be naked in front of all these people, in a metaphorical sense, of course. I haven't done one of these since college. The nerves make my mouth dry. I swallow more beer.

Of course, as soon as her friends leave, the rocker girl gets her name called. *Nina*. Not that it's important that I remember. It's a good name for a rock'n'roll singer. Almost like Nirvana, with the feminine luster of Madonna. She pulls out her shimmering red-and-black guitar from its case and takes the stage.

Chelsea says, "Can I get a drink?"

"Of course," I say. I grab the pitcher and pour her one. That was a bit over-eager. I follow up with Sophie. "You want one?"

"I'm good," she says. "Sticking with water tonight." Sophie barely drinks. She used to. She tore up the streets. When we'd grab dinner, we'd drink ourselves under the table. Meet up with our friends at Chaser's and fuck off the rest of the night. Talk shit and gossip about each other, the school, and the people around us. Nothing mattered.

When our crew split up and moved away, the city got hollower. We didn't have the same need to be seen out together. She didn't like drinking all that much. Blame it on her rosy cheeks or how dumb it makes me act. She says the first, but believes the second. She deals with me at bar call. I get it.

Chelsea says, "You've got to celebrate. Congratulations on the new apartment."

"I'm alright," Sophie waves away the pitcher.

"New apartment?" Givens asks. "Where?"

I smile at him. "Sophie found this sweet spot on Monona Bay."

"No way," Givens says. "That's so far from the hotel."

"And from me." Chelsea pouts. "I'll never see you, Sophie."

"We'll be around," Sophie says. "Just because we don't live downtown doesn't mean we'll stop going out to dinner."

"Or grabbing drinks," I say. "I'm going to bike to work. Probably lose a few pounds."

"It's totally worth it for the space and the lake," Sophie says. "I think we could raise our first kid there."

I choke on my beer. "Yeah, that too."

Nina plugs her guitar into the amp and strokes her pick hard down the strings. She quickly tunes her guitar by ear.

To think that this is where Sophie and I are going. If we have a kid, I'd be a dad like my dad, but different. I get to decide how my kid is raised. Sophie will be the mom and we will all live together and call ourselves a family for the rest of our lives. It sounds so simple, but why does it sound so hard?

"It's a bold move." Givens cackles, but no else does. "Get it?" We all look at each other. Givens continues. "Because you have to move and you probably have to break your lea—"

Nina launches into a rock'n'roll riff that drowns out Givens' voice. She strums through a power chord-driven

break-up song about being young and wild and free. Her chorus whines—

> *"Breakin' hearts, like drinking booze,*
> *it burns at first, then goes down smooth,*
> *maybe I've got issues, but so do youuuu"*

—the rhythm intoxicating enough to get a few people out of their seats. The floor in front of Nina fills up.

Sophie doesn't want to leave our seats. Chelsea and I go up anyway. I'm hoping it will get me away from these thoughts about having a kid with her. Givens joins us, too.

Chelsea and I dance together, head thrashing, moshing into each other, forgetting all our cares in the world. I lean on Givens as I do an air guitar solo. Givens laughs, pretending to play the bass.

From the stage, Nina glances at me. A smile lights the corner of her lips before she screams the next verse. I don't know what she says. I'm so lost in her everything. The black nail polish and eyeliner, the fake tattoos on her cheek, and her voice that overpowers that beating guitar. She rages at the night.

That's what I crave.

If Sophie doesn't want to dance, Chelsea fills her place. Her hips bounce side by side. Her neck is a loose crane, and her hair flops over her face. She's into it. We rub shoulders again, and she gets me to groove with her at a safe distance, of course.

I'm surprised Chelsea is so cool about the whole lease thing. I'm sure she knows we can still maintain our secret affair. It'll be even easier. Her apartment building is along my commute. I can pop in and the captain can say hello to her real quick.

Sophie comes up, stiff as a board. Out of jealousy, I'm sure. I grab her hand and try to twirl her around, but she doesn't want to and lets go midway through. She settles into a spot and sways, bobbing her head to the beat. I bump against her playfully. Sophie puts her arm around my waist, making me sway with her. She centers me, keeps me in line; her demeanor is a reminder of how important regimen is to a life on track.

Chelsea stops dancing too and joins our sway. Her little finger slips into my palm. It completes the circuit between the three of us and it electrifies me. Struck by inspiration, I tear loose from them and go back to our table and write down a few words.

When the rocker girl hops off stage, everyone on the terrace roars. Beneath the hail of cheers, Nina slices a path between Sophie and Chelsea on her way back to her seat.

I write on as Nina returns. She looks over my shoulder as I finish the final line. For some reason, and I know it's stupid, I sign my name at the bottom. Makes it feel complete.

"Look at Shakespeare," Nina says.

"More Bukowski," I say.

"I love Bukowski," Nina says. She opens her guitar case and stuffs her guitar inside.

I reread the poem. Switch around a few words here and there, but for the most part, it'll work.

Miss Arabella returns to the stage. She pulls out a name. For the first time, I hope it's mine. "Ryan Givens," she says. "Welcome back, Ryan. I hope you're doing more of your sci-fi book."

"Of course," Givens announces and makes his way to the stage.

Refilling my beer cup, I shake my head. I lean over and tell Nina. "Great song by the way."

"Thanks." She smirks. She knows.

I want to ask her more about her writing process, but Sophie and Chelsea return to their seats. I'll have a chance later. I should listen to Givens' story anyway. Knowing him, it's probably terrible.

On stage, Givens hugs Miss Arabella and approaches the mic. He clears his throat and reads from his phone. "This is an excerpt from *2677*. My sci-fi epic set in 2677, where space mining is big business.'

'If you remember last week, I ended the reading with Sola getting captured after her and Apex's failed mission to steal Lord Denmark's war plans for the invasion of Nuknoku. Sola got sent to the maximum-security space prison—El Serondo. And that's where we begin, Apex, our hero, lands a Vulture, which is a spacecraft that kinda looks like a motorcycle, near the ventilation shaft of the prison ship."

Givens clears his throat. His voice, deep and resonant, transforms him into this warrior-like figure as he reads—

"Crawling through the air vents, Apex recalls the last words Sola said to him: 'Don't save me.'

Apex promised Sola that he wouldn't come back for her. Their mission to save their home planet is much more important than any reconnected friendship between a pilot-smuggler and a rich importer. But Apex lied.

On the commlink as she was captured, he couldn't muster the words to say to her. They clung to his throat. Somehow, the same man, who once survived twenty Orcane fighters, alone in the jungles of Cass, armed with only a laser dagger, was afraid of three little words."

I whisper to Sophie, "What do you think so far?"

Sophie puts her finger over her lips.

Chelsea refills her cup. "It's pretty good, right?" Beneath the table, she must've slipped off her heels because her barefoot finds my calf.

I finish my beer and offer her my cup. "Fill me up."

"I think you can do it yourself," she says.

"Oh, okay." I grab the pitcher from her. Our fingertips graze each other as Chelsea passes me the half-empty pitcher. As I pour myself a beer, her foot finds my crotch. I overfill my cup and spill beer on the table.

Sophie jerks her elbow away and snipes, "Seriously?"

I mop up the spilled beer with a napkin. Chelsea's toe skims down my thigh and disappears. She turns back to watch Givens read—

"Apex removes the grate from the air duct above Sola's cell. He lays on his stomach and looks over the edge. He can't believe it. Her cell is empty. It can't be. He must be wrong. He goes to the next cell and peers in.

Not finding her in any of the cells. Apex winds through the ventilation shafts."

How is Givens able to keep coming back to the well?

It's hard for me to string together enough sentences to make sense of anything. I'll start with this idea. Get all hot and bothered about it. I'll write a page or two in my notebook, get tired, and give up. Never finding that magic again for that one story or poem.

Givens probably doesn't drink when he writes. I have to. It shakes things up a bit. Tears down the cobwebs. I get stale if I'm sober too long. That's what I'm getting from Givens' story. It's good, sure, but there's nothing fresh about it. Guy saves girl. We've all seen that.

Sometimes I wonder if every story has ever been written—what's the point of making more? I'm supposed to be writing for money, but I can't even start a story without thinking about how I'm adding more trash to the garbage heap of humanity.

The thought sends me to Sophie for warmth. I slide down and rest my cheek against her shoulder, her skin sticky with humidity. Chelsea glances back at us. I smell *Unmistakable*. That fragrance fills me with chills. I straighten up and try to pay attention, ignoring my sudden desire for Rachel.

"You can stay here and rot to death," Lord Denmark comforts Sola. "Or you can join the Legion and I'll give you a life filled with more wealth than you've ever dreamed."

Between the rusted grates, Apex sees Sola, her back to Lord Denmark. Lord Denmark, the power-hungry oligarch and leader of the Legion, the totalitarian regime sweeping the Andromeda Galaxy Order.

"Why me?" Sola asks.

"Someone with so much talent shouldn't rot in a jail cell," Lord Denmark says. "What is your answer?"

"It sounds like I don't have a choice," Sola says. "I'm going with you."

"My beautiful girl." Lord Denmark puts his fingers beneath Sola's chin.

Sola swats his hand away.

"Ouch," Lord Denmark cackles. "The guards will take you to the decontamination showers. You'll be joining me for dinner at suntide."

As the armored guards take Sola away, Apex thrusts through the vent. He crashes into the floor. Woozy from the fall, Apex clambers to a fighting stance, drawing out his laser dagger.

"I won't let you take her," Apex says. Apex swings his knife at Lord Denmark, but a guard's paralyzer hits Apex in the throat. He seizes. Dropping the dagger as he drops to his knees, quaking.

Sola yells, "Apex, no!"

"No more games." Lord Denmark orders, "Guards, take him to the boiler room."

Sola mouths the words, 'I will save you.'

The butt of a guard's rifle smacks Apex across the forehead, knocking him out cold."

Givens lingers in the silence. The terrace erupts in applause. There were good points, sure, but I need to hear it again because I got too distracted by Sophie and Chelsea.

"Go, Ryan!" A man screams from the top deck.

"Thanks, Marv," Givens says into the mic before stepping off the stage.

Miss Arabella says, "Incredible as always." She pulls out a slip from the hat and calls out. "Danny Clark."

I shoot to a stand, nervous as hell. I chug my beer and pull the paper out of my pocket. I lean over and kiss Sophie on the lips. Chelsea, not to be undone, secretly squeezes my ass.

As I head to the stage, Givens calls out, "Good luck."

When I step up to the mic stand, it's too tall for me. I clasp the thing to lower it, but it doesn't give. Miss Arabella shuffles out. With one twist of her wrist, the mic lands in front of my mouth. A metallic screech reminds everyone that it's on.

About one hundred expectant eyes follow my every move. I find Chelsea and Sophie sitting, side by side. And there's Givens, the whole reason why I'm even up here in the first place. The ham. He's got his phone out. He's recording. He's trying to embarrass me!

I'm not going to let him.

I breathe in and I summon something from deep in my chest. For some reason, the thought I had while standing between Sophie and Chelsea and staring out into the black horizon was of the color of darkness. How late at night, when I get home and enter Sophie and I's bedroom. There's just enough light from the window to see, but not enough for anything to have color. Instead, it's this grey-black like the night is holding back the day.

I say into the microphone, "My name's Danny Clark and I'm a poet—'

"In the grey-black, the endless
battle between light and dark,
I search for you
to bask in your glow.
As the new day awakens,
it's still midnight in my soul
and I'm stuck in yesterday—
when you filled the hollows
of my mind and how it felt
to know with such certainty
true love. Now, I dream
of knowing anything
with as much certainty as I once knew love.
The courage it takes to go forward,
blind, into the darkness
and expect to be enlightened."

With a dramatic pause, I stay a moment, taking in the space letting time stand still. The place is silent before Sophie, Chelsea, and Givens clap, loud and hooting. It's good to have friends. Their passion floods the terrace with a burst of applause. Soon enough, it's replaced by the tide of conversation. Miss Arabella approaches the mic stand.

"Good job, hon." Miss Arabella says, as she passes me enroute to the mic. "I can tell you've been writing."

"Thank you," I say before stepping off stage. Sophie, Chelsea, and Givens await at the table. Nina, carrying her guitar case, heads for the parking lot.

Seeing her walking away, I catch up with her. "Hey! Are you leaving?" I say, part of me was hoping to chat with her some more.

Nina stops and looks back at me. "Going to my friend's show at the Majestic after I drop my guitar off. You and your friends want to come?"

"We can't." There's no way Sophie would be up for going to a concert tonight. Chelsea would be, but I've got to be a good boyfriend. Sophie and I made a big decision. We should spend the night together.

"I dig your music. What's your social?" I ask, innocent enough. "I'd love to check out your band." I hand her my phone to type in her name.

"For sure." She finds herself and hands my phone back to me. "Do you have any of your work online?"

I admit, "No. The publisher is making me keep it under wraps for now. Soon, though."

"I'll follow you back. Good meeting you, Danny."

"See you around, Nina." Her eyes beam when I say her name.

Guitar in hand, Nina walks down the sidewalk. I watch her go. I realize I'm watching her go and quickly turn back to the table.

Sophie glares at me. Chelsea too. Reality sets in.

When I'm back at the table, Sophie asks, "What was that about?"

"I've got a new fan," I say.

"It looked like you got her number," Chelsea says.

"What? No," I say. "I want to check out her band, so I asked for her social. She was good. Or am I crazy?"

Givens says, "She was great. I'd check her out."

"Thank you. See?"

Sophie says, "I saw what I saw."

"Maybe you should get your eyes checked," I say, a bit too harshly.

"I know you, Danny. And I know that look you get when you want something. You gave her that same look."

"I thought you'd be happy for me going up on stage. But this. This is what you want to talk about?"

"We shouldn't have to talk about it, but we do because you do stupid shit like this right in front of me. It makes me wonder. Do you even love me? Or are you still that uncertain that you have to write poetry about it?"

"We just signed a lease together," I say. "How much more proof do you need?

Chelsea and Givens, uncomfortable, share a look.

"Tell me you love me," Sophie says.

"You want me to say it here? In front of everyone?" I say.

"Your answer shouldn't be a question." Sophie picks up her purses.

"Where are you running off to?"

"Home."

"Fine. If that's how you feel, go. But it was nothing. I'll even unfollow her. Here—" I pick up my phone and unfollow her. I mean, I'll follow her back later when Sophie isn't around. "Happy?"

"All you had to do was say it. Why is that so hard?" Sophie turns on her heel.

"I love you." Sophie keeps walking. I call out, "I love you!" She carries on into the night.

I get up to go after her, but below the table, Chelsea squeezes my hand hard, holding me back. Instead, I see the empty pitcher and say, "Another round?"

"You're not going to go after her?" Givens asks.

"What's the point? This is what she does. It's not my problem she's jealous."

"You should talk to her," Chelsea says. "Smooth this over."

"You believe me, right?" I ask. "Nina was good."

Her left eye twitches. Chelsea considers saying no, but she says, "Yeah, of course. She was really good. I dug her voice. Sounded like the Yeah-Yeah-Yeah's."

I say, "Totally."

"If you guys aren't going to go, I'm going to go talk to her." Givens jumps to his feet and springs after Sophie.

I shake my head, hoping he won't mention Rachel. I trust him. He understands that it was a big misunderstanding. I have been and always will be loyal to my one true love. Why else would Sophie and I be together for so long? The lease really is the perfect cover-up. And who knows? Maybe I'll like living further away from downtown. It'll help me live with more intention because it'll be a long walk to stumble home from the bar.

Alone at last, Chelsea's icy eyes narrow at me. She digs her fingernails into my flesh. It hurts. I yank my hand away from her.

"What the hell?" I say, rubbing my clawed knuckles.

"You signed a lease! You told me you were going to break up with her," Chelsea says, her teeth clip each word.

"I'm sorry," I say. "I really am, but I've been with Sophie a long time and I'm staying with her. Maybe, what you and I have. Maybe, we have to end it."

"But you don't love her," Chelsea says. Her fingers skim down my chest, stopping short of my waistband. It's enough to make me reconsider.

"Of course, I do," I say.

"Really?" Chelsea leans in. Her lips close enough to make me feel the rush of her breath against my cheek.

"You can't change my mind," I say, in a whisper.

"Is that so?" Chelsea bites her bottom lip.

I peer over her shoulder and scan the space for any signs of Givens or Sophie. In the middle of the crowded terrace, my hand finds the small of her back. I kiss her hard. Caught in her riptide, the waves of her tongue crash and swell against mine. She suddenly leaves me gasping for air.

Chelsea says, in a smoky rasp, "I'm going to show you why you're making the biggest mistake of your life." She pulls me in again. I fall headfirst into her seas.

THIRTEEN: *love*

THE MOMENT I LET GO inside her, I feel everything at once: her body, my body, our skin, the cotton sheets, the hum of her dryer spinning, the heat of the apartment, the lights of the city, the breadth of the earth, the weight of the universe in a heartbeat. Then, I'm lost in the black hole of her bedroom. Her dark shadow creeps up the walls.

Chelsea's atop me, her hands pressed into my chest, slowly raises her waist, and lifts herself off. The sticky warmth dribbles out of her onto the sheets. She gets on all fours and crawls up to kiss my lips. I close my eyes, turn my chin, and let her kiss my cheek. The warm press burns like the other women's burn. She could be any of them, and the longer the kiss lasts, the more of them I feel and the less I feel for her. All of them leave me drowsy.

Lightly panting, Chelsea relaxes against my shoulder. She says, "I love you."

My eyes burst open. "What did you say?"

"Oh God!" she says. "Sorry, I meant to say I love this. I mean, I like this." Her hand frantically squeezes mine as she shimmies closer to me. "I'm crazy about you." Her mouth is an inch from my ear.

I push her aside, swing my legs onto the floor, and search for my clothes in the dark.

The longer I don't look at her, the more she whimpers. She breaks down. "No, it's true. I love you, *Daniel*."

"Why?" I yank out my boxers, bunched up in her goose down duvet. After I wriggle them up my legs, I search for my jeans.

"Because you give me something no other guy has before," she says.

"An orgasm?"

"Shush. I'm serious," Chelsea punches me in the shoulder. "No, you make me feel less alone."

"That's why you love me?"

"It's poetic, isn't it?" Chelsea says. "I thought you'd appreciate it."

"You feel alone?"

"Yeah, with law school and summer, friends are on vacation and I'm living here watching the sunrise and fall every day. Besides my roommate, if you're not around, I could go days at a time without seeing anyone. At least you give me some variety. And I feel that same loneliness on you. Like is this all there is?"

"I'm not lonely at all."

"I think you are, but you're too afraid to admit it. That's why you go out all the time. Tell me the truth." She says. "Do you love me?"

Frustrated, I finally find my pants and belt in a heap near the door. "You knew the deal when this began." I pull them on one leg at a time. "When we wanted someone to fuck, we'd fuck. Nothing more. You remember that?"

"But that was a year ago," Chelsea says. "I didn't think we'd last this long."

"There is no we. It's just you and me." I put on my pants and grab my shoes next to them. I never took off my socks.

"Why do you keep coming back?" Chelsea says.

"I'm addicted to your sexy ass."

"And Sophie doesn't have a sexy ass?"

"I mean, you've seen it. Why do you think I signed a lease with her?" I feel around for my shirt under the bed. Giving up, I flip on the light. Tears leak down Chelsea's cheeks.

"How can you cheat on her and act like everything is normal?"

"It's—" I say, trying to explain as I continue to look for my t-shirt. "It's—"

"What is it?"

"Jesus, let me finish."

"Go on then!" Chelsea crosses her arms.

"It's because it's easy and doesn't cause us any pain if we never tell her. And there's no point in telling Sophie because between you and me there is no love. We're just f—" Suddenly, the room fills with white and red lights, and an angry buzz permeates the air: the fire alarm. "Ah, for fuck's sake."

Chelsea jumps out of bed and puts on her closest pair of pajamas and a robe. She pulls my shirt out from under the pillow and tosses it at me. "We have to get out of here." She drags me out the front door.

For some reason, I feel like I'm forgetting something.

College-aged people pour out of the rooms and into the hallway. The alarm howls across the air. Some of the people sleepwalk, some stagger drunk, but the consensus is that some idiot pulled the fire alarm. The elevators are not running, of course. We funnel into the congested stairway.

On the way down the nine floors to the lobby, there's no smoke or any smell of burning. We jostle our way through the exit doors.

In the courtyard, the summer air, cool and deep, greets us. We gather around the flagpole, staring up at

the massive, red-brick apartment building. No smoke, no smoldering, nothing. There look to be about two hundred people outside by now, all of us staring upwards, wondering what the fuck?

The fire trucks arrive screaming, and the men in yellow suits file out. They walk inside. Judging by their dawdling pace, this should all be over in a matter of a few minutes.

Chelsea's glossy, pink eyes make me want to say something. I say, "Just because we see each other a lot, it doesn't mean we're dating."

The crook of a smile corners her mouth, she says, "*Daniel*, we see each other almost every day."

Her enunciated –el pierces my eardrum, and my jaw clenches, but I withhold my frustration. "What do we do when we're together?" Chelsea goes quiet. I continue, "We have sex. Nothing more. We never go out. Do we? Tonight…Did Sophie tell you I was going to be there?"

"So? We were hanging out anyway. I wanted to hear you read. I had to convince Sophie to come out, you know. Are you going to be mad at that?"

I go quiet.

"You're ridiculous," Chelsea says. "Why don't you want to try? I think we'd make a cute couple."

"Chelsea," I say, "we can't be together."

"And why's that?" She crosses her arms.

Her hard stare makes me swallow before I say, "I want to love you, I do. But because I love Sophie, I can't love you too."

"Dump her!"

"I can't."

"Why not?"

"We have a history together," I say. "We've dated since college. I'm going to marry her someday."

Chelsea puts her hands up. "So, you're saying for the last year, you've been cheating on a woman you want to spend the rest of your life with?"

"I wouldn't call it cheating."

"What would you call it?" She smiles in exasperation. "Please tell me."

"Why do you do it? You're her best friend!"

"You live with her!"

"Sophie doesn't have what you have," I growl. "When I see you, my animal instinct kicks in and I can't contain myself."

"If you really got to know me, you'd see I'm better than Sophie in every way. I can give you everything you want, *Daniel*. Are you that blind?"

A fireman waves. The crowd around us disperses toward the apartment building. Chelsea and I remain standing together in the middle of the emptying courtyard. The fire truck's flashing lights flick off as it pulls away.

"I want to love you," I say.

"No," she says, "you don't. It's obvious. It all makes sense now. You want to use me. A human sex doll." I attempt to put my arms around her as a new front of tears well in her eyes, but she pushes me away. "I'm a fool. A fucking fool. You don't see me, do you? When you fuck me, you don't see me. You see a pair of tits and your ego. How can I be so naïve?"

"What did you think was going to happen?" I say.

"I don't know *Daniel*," she says. "I thought you and Sophie would realize, finally, that your relationship sucks. It's fucked up. She talks about you all the time. I bite my tongue. I have to. The stories she tells me make me wonder, though. Why are you the way you are and why the does she put up with it? Why the fuck do I?" Chelsea heads for The Empire entrance.

"Chelsea, I love her." I follow her.

"Don't say that."

"I love Sophie. I'm sorry."

We stop in front of the front doors, Chelsea says, "You have no idea what love is."

"Why did you tell me you love me?" I ask.

"I misspoke," Chelsea says. "What I meant to say was fuck you." She lets out a huge breath and throws open the lobby door.

"Chelsea," I say.

She turns to me. "What could you possibly have left to say?"

"Any guy would be lucky to have you."

She rolls her eyes. "You're the biggest asshole I've ever met."

"Wait!" I say. She holds the door. "Do you think my asshole's that big?"

When she glares back at me, I feel everything I hate about myself—the lies, the regrets, the heartache that suffocates me. I wish I could tell her who I was, who I am, where I'm going. I wish I knew the answer to any of those questions.

I love them both. If only I could articulate that to Chelsea. You see, Chelsea fills in the cracks between Sophie and me. Without Chelsea, those holes will be bare, and the truth will shine through. Maybe Sophie isn't my everything, but then again, Chelsea isn't either.

Before I realize it, I'm staring at the empty entryway to The Empire anchored to the sidewalk. I should be sad, I think. I should be happy, I suppose. I should feel something like loss, or anger, or relief. I'm afraid what's left inside of me has no emotion.

FOURTEEN:
inside-out

As I walk home, I think about Givens, about Chelsea, about Sophie. I think I think about other people too much, especially when I'm drunk. But my drunk went out as soon as the fire alarm went off. I need to get some sleep. I've had too much drama for a Friday night. It'll be nice to get to bed. To sleep next to my beautiful woman, my soon-to-be wife. That thought fills me with pride as I swing open the door to our building's casket-sized entryway.

Someone's leaving, so I catch the interior door and head up the stairs to the third floor.

Good riddance to Chelsea, I think with every step. Things will simplify. Only Sophie and I, that's all we need. That's all we had before, and it's all I'll have from now on.

When I get to our front door, I dig into my pocket for my keys. They're empty. The front, the back. No keys anywhere. I never grabbed them off the kitchen counter at Chelsea's.

If I knock on the door, Sophie will answer. She will wonder how I lost my keys. I'd have to get a new set. I can't just find them. What if she asks to help me retrace my steps?

No, no, it will be fine. If I can lie about everything else, this one will certainly be easy. I'm a good liar. She's gullible. We are the perfect couple.

I rap on the door quietly at first. I hope not to startle her with a heavy knock. When no one comes, I hit the wood a bit harder. It's dark beneath the seal, and I realize she may be asleep. I pound it harder, a house-shuddering kind of pound. She should be awake now.

No one comes yet, and there are no lights on inside. It makes me think that Sophie isn't home either.

It can't be true. She's home, I know. She must be. I slam my palm into the door until it bruises. She must be home. "Sophie, open up, it's me," I say with every smack. She's here. I know it.

Tears in my eyes, I attack the wooden door. Still no lights, I kick it. My shoe leaves scuffs. She isn't here. She's with someone else, maybe Givens. She's gone. And I gave up Chelsea to stay with her.

One of my neighbors yells through the wall, behind me, "Shut up!"

I'm out of breath. Inflamed and red, pain scorches across my palm. The base of the door is battered by my shoe. A light appears through the threshold. My heart palpitates with every passing second. A cool sweat collects down my spine as I clear my throat.

The door opens, and Sophie, in her blue pajamas, dark circles beneath her eyes and a sleepy drawl to her voice, asks, "What's going on?"

"Sorry," I say, "I lost my keys."

"You could have called me," she says, stepping away from the entrance to let me pass through. She rubs her eyes as I step inside.

Halfway to our kitchen, I turn back to Sophie, grab

her around the waist and push her against the wall. "I missed you." I lay my tongue into her mouth.

Coming up for air, Sophie pushes me back. "Chill, chill, I'm not awake enough for that."

I suppose it was a bit much. I hug her, saying, "I love you so much. I can't wait to sleep with you tonight." I go to the kitchen.

"Your breath is awful," she says, walking behind me. "Did you stay at the Terrace all night?"

I turn on the light, and over the refrigerator door, I say, "Nothing happened at all after you left. Chelsea and I talked some more. When the show ended, I walked her home." I might get away with this whole thing, and she's none the wiser. "I finally feel good about the writing. You heard? I'm so glad I could share something with everyone."

Pulling out a few cold cuts of ham from the butcher's wrapper, I eat them greedily. Mouthful, I say, "I'm sorry about that thing with that girl. Honestly, there was nothing behind it. I swear. A total and complete misunderstanding, but I can see how you thought I was flirting with her." It's like I haven't eaten in days. Scratching at something at the back of my neck, I grab an extra handful and close the door.

"Givens isn't half bad either," I say with bits of ham still rolling around in my mouth. I notice the look on her face and gulp.

Silence.

Her gaze stirs with a mixture of shock and confusion. Maybe she wants some? I offer the salty meat. "Ham?"

Her stare makes me itch. I scratch the back of my neck again. The tag of my shirt greets my roaming fingers—

Sophie says in a flat tone, "Why's your shirt inside-out?"

Truth, like most things, is negotiable. Sophie wants it. She wants the truth, but she doesn't want it

either. That's where the negotiation lies.

"Are you serious?" I say, feigning laughter. "How embarrassing."

I shovel the ham into my mouth and chew as I grip the bottom of my shirt and lift it over my head. I fumble with turning it outside out. I push my head through again and swallow the ham. It goes down the wrong pipe. I cough. "I spilled beer on my shirt and rinsed it out right away. Here feel. I think it's still damp."

Sophie gives me a discerning stare. It's the kind of stare a poker player gives another player when all the cards are on the table, but the final draw hasn't been revealed. The silence makes me nervous, but I don't show my hand. I'm bluffing and she's betting I'll fold.

I won't, though. I've gotten this far, and there's no use in turning back now. I yawn. "I'm exhausted." I walk toward our room, which lies beyond her, but she is standing in the doorway, guarding it. I say, less than a foot from her, "Let's get to bed." She continues to glare at me, unmoving. I attempt to step around her, but there's not enough room in the doorway to gracefully move passed her. I don't want to knock into her. I'm not a brute. "Come on, babe, let's go to bed."

"What's her name?"

"I think her name is Sophie. So-fee." I put my hands on her shoulders, rubbing them up and down. "Are you alright? Did you have a stroke while I was gone?"

No laugh. Sophie doesn't soften like she normally does. "Tell me the truth. Did you and Chelsea do something after the Terrace?"

"Noooo!" I say. "Chelsea—*blegh*. She's your best friend. I love you, Sophie, but sometimes, you're a little coo-coo."

I step around her. She blocks my way, her arm bracing the door. "Was it that guest at the hotel?" Her stare could pierce glass, but I reflect it with a smile.

"Where is this coming from?"

"Ryan told me he saw you kiss a guest."

"Ever think that Givens is madly in love with you and he'll literally say anything to break us apart?"

"He's not that kind of guy."

Next time I see Givens, I'm going to kill him for having to clean up this mess. I say, sweetly, calmly, innocently, "There's no one else. Only you." That's when a brilliant idea strikes. "You're going to want to see this."

Sophie still blocks my path. I fake left, juke her, and step into the bedroom, heading for the closet. She follows me. "Tell me the truth."

"Just you wait. Just you wait." I look for my suit coat in the closet, pushing aside Sophie's dresses and shirts. "God, you have a lot of clothes." I find the coat.

I reach into the inner pocket. I cup the ring box in my fist so she can't see what it is, at least, not yet.

I half-smile at the timing. It couldn't be any better. This is the moment I've been waiting for. I correct myself: we've been waiting for. Chelsea had been holding me back. That's why I had been hesitant.

Getting down on one knee, I say, "How's this for the truth?" I open the box in front of Sophie. "I love you and," I try to find the poem I folded up in there, but I'm shaking too badly and it's too dark to dig for it, let alone read it. It had something to do with being better because of her, or it had something to do with being a broken man and how she puts me back together, or it had something to do with her being my greatest treasure. It is all jumbled now. Sophie gapes at the ring—it's all she ever wanted.

"You told me to tell you I love you. Well, I want to spend the rest of my life with you. We even got the dream place now. It's time. Please? Marry me."

Sophie doesn't need to know about any of the slew of women that came before or after her. I love her. I always have. I always will. I'm telling her the truth.

And yet, the silence is more deafening than words.

When her expression doesn't change, I nervously break the quiet. "Honest, I love you."

Her green eyes harden into stone. She opens her mouth, then closes it. Her cheek muscles tighten. She shakes her head, sucks in her lower lip, and whispers something I can't hear.

I ask, "Is that yes?"

She snarls. "Get out."

"What?"

"Go!" She howls.

"No," I clamp the box shut. "No way."

"You don't deserve me."

I shudder. "But I love you."

"I'm not stupid."

"Are you sure? Because you're acting like it." I stand.

"Please!" she says. "I loved you, you dumbass. Everything about you. Even when you farted in your sleep. At least, I used to. But you're a loser. You have these grand visions for the future, but when push comes to shove, you're still the same lazy piece of shit I met in college. You haven't changed and let me tell you, I'm sick and fuckin' tired of putting up with your lines, your drunken emotions, your selfish insecurities. This proposal of yours is just another one of your schemes. Tomorrow, you'll forget to text me back, or you'll skip dinner to get some with an old friend, and I'll spend another night wondering what's wrong with me. But it turns out, it was never anything wrong with me at all. You're what's wrong with me."

For the first time in our relationship, I draw a blank.

"If you respect me, tell me the truth," she says. "Who is she?"

"I already told you the truth. There's no one else but you."

"Fine." She backs away. "Fine. If you can't admit it, that's fine. It's over anyway."

"Just like that?" The shock of losing her courses a shiver down my entire body. "Five years for nothing?"

"It was five years for me. Was it even five years for you? Have you ever loved me?" Sophie packs a bag.

"What about the new apartment?"

"Just another one of your messes I need to clean up."

"Where are you going?"

"Chelsea's. She'll tell me the truth."

"She's going to say the same thing. Nothing happened between us."

Sophie zips up the bag and heads for the exit.

I follow her out. "Sophie, if you leave, you'll break my heart."

Before she goes, she turns back, "You have to have a heart for me to break." She slams the door behind her.

I fling open the door. "Sophie, stop!"

Halfway down the hall, she screams, "Leave me alone!"

Victor, the neighbor, a balding, middle-aged shlub in a greasy tank top, opens his door by the steps. "Can you shut up!"

Without pause, Sophie marches up to the man and yells, "Make me!" It's a face of Sophie I've never seen before. I woke the dragon, and she spits fire.

Flabbergasted, the neighbor snorts. "Please, be quiet, h'okay? My mother is trying to sleep." He shuts the door.

Sophie flares her nostrils at me. "I want your stuff gone by the morning."

"But this is my apartment."

"This was our apartment. Now, it's mine." She takes the first step down the stairs.

"Where am I supposed to go?"

"Maybe one of your other girlfriends will take you in." The sound of her footsteps echoes in the empty stairwell of the old building.

I withdraw into our apartment and watch from the balcony. She's in her Civic, parked at the corner, talking to someone as the headlights flick on. She pulls out and drives down the street, disappearing into the night.

A guy and a girl make out on the porch next door—the remnant stragglers of the frat party. His hands slide up her shirt. She rubs his crotch.

Gentleman whiskey calls to me. I sit on the stolen Terrace chair and pour myself a full glass, then another, and another, scanning the horizon for her headlights.

After I don't know how many, I slither my way to the couch inside.

Morning light fights through the foggy windowpanes. I need to get up, but when I get up, I need to get out of here. The time has come for me to go. There is honor in leaving in peace.

I should be happy Sophie's gone. After all this time, this should be what I want: freedom, but the emptiness she leaves behind reminds me that I once was full.

Nestled in its box, the diamond shimmers. I wobble, a raft lost on an endless ocean. I need water to heal this headache. My mouth filled with cobwebs.

I wish I could hold Sophie here and memorize every perfection and imperfection of her again. Have her turn to me, her fingers drawn around my neck, and whisper, "I love you."

At the start of some summer so long ago, we sang love, drunken and lustful. It was not soft. It was not calculated. It was carefree.

When did we start caring? By the end of summer, we were inseparable. We couldn't get enough, but we never had the talk about making us official. With all the college kids coming back, I was out and about. Picked up a wide-eyed sophomore with a decent fake. After that fight, Sophie and I became boyfriend and girlfriend.

When did I stop caring? I don't know. There was never a definite decision. No line in the sand that I crossed out of spite. It was slippage. A forgotten text. A cancelled date. Avoiding her family visits. Things like that that added up over time. Until one day, the right woman comes along and exposes the truth about us. We aren't who we thought we were. We can do things alone and still be happy.

Without Sophie here, though, I'm missing a part of me. She knows me better than anyone else. That's why she called me out. This is a cry for help. I need to do better. That's what she is saying by yelling at me that it's over.

I should leave everything here. Make it my statement of no surrender. I'll abandon it all and fight my way back home. This is only a moment, a blip in time, where we grow. Where our relationship evolves into something bigger, something new and better.

We need this fresh start, a renewal. Sometimes, you need love to go missing to appreciate when it was present.

And yet, what if she doesn't want me to come back? I shudder.

What if Sophie finds bliss in my absence? She couldn't, could she?

The hangover gets the best of me, and I lose my balance. I sit down, shoulders slunk, a boxer in the last round of a losing fight. Beaten, my body aches, but I still have my pride. I'm not giving up.

Where do I go from here? The only friend I have left in this town is Kovski. If he doesn't take me in, I don't know what I'll do.

But why am I thinking so small? Why can't I go even further than that? Leave all this bullshit behind, you know? Try to be something new, somewhere else, a place where no one knows my name. It could be a city like New York or the mountains of Montana. The world is mine to paint black.

Then again, I love Madison. Feels like I grew up here. I can't let that go. Not to mention, Sophie will have me back any day.

I find Kovski's number in my phone and wait for him to answer. Each ring goes by slowly, drawn out by the feeling that he won't pick up, and I'll have to move to Italy to feel like I'm doing something with my life.

The third ring cuts off mid-tone, replaced by the sound of a man's coughing, "Hu-hu-hu—Hullo?" Kovski's voice grovels.

"Kov, it's Danny. What are you doing right now?"

He grumbles, "Sleeping."

"I need to come over."

"For what?" he says.

"Sophie's kicked me out," I choke, "and I don't have anywhere else to go."

Voices muffled through the speaker, Kovski's talking to someone. He says, "Yeah. Come over." The line goes dead.

I groan, pushing myself off the couch and planting my feet on the floor. The room wobbles. I glance at all the things I should take with me: my TV, my nightstand, the pots and pans, the knives. Where am I even going to put them? This is my apartment. Hopefully, Sophie comes to her senses.

I pack the bare necessities plus my work uniform – a few pairs of undies, socks, a couple shirts, and a change of shoes.

There's one last thing. The ring on the coffee table. I thought it was guaranteed to work, but she said no.

I grab it.

On second thought, I leave the ring box open on the coffee table. Tucked in the lid, the poem. It's what I meant to say earlier. I should've memorized it, but what if it's not any good?

I reread it—

Porcelain bathed in evening light
flowers crown the white-dressed tables
our friends and family come to celebrate
how we found each other
in the vast indifference.
They wheel in a cake as big as the sky
I hear the echoes of future generations in your voice
and feel the warmth of the sun nestled in your hands
I belong to you
take me as I am, with a yes
I promise to make every tomorrow
our happiest

I write a note to Sophie at the bottom of the poem: *Love you always.* I sign my name. It's a bit heavy-handed,

but this situation calls for a heavy hand. The heavier the hand, the more meaning. Sophie will understand. She'll probably cry when she reads it. When I come back, she'll forgive me, and we'll be together again.

Looking over my place one more time before I leave, even if I forget anything, I'll be back soon enough. I sling the backpack over my shoulder, take the 12-pack of beer out of the fridge, and head to Kovski's.

On the walk to his place, I realize that I'm single for the first time in five years. This might be the getaway I need.

FIFTEEN:

OVSKI ANSWERS THE DOOR in a pink bathrobe that obviously isn't his, but an acquisition from one of his many escapades with women.

"Wow," he smiles. "Rough night?" He steps aside, pressing his back against his door as I pass lugging my backpack and the 12-pack.

Dropping the bag next to the ottoman, I crumple into his well-worn recliner. It's comfortable enough, except for the smell of old cigarette smoke and cat scratch marks. He told me he found it on the curb years ago.

I wipe the sweat from my forehead and open the beer box. I pull out a can, "Want one?"

Kovski checks his non-existent watch. "Yeah, fuck it."

I toss him one. We crack them open, and I offer a toast, "To fuckin' love."

"Fuckin' love!" Kovski taps my beer.

When the cold beer smacks my dry tongue, I don't stop. I let it pour down my throat. The can glubs and glubs again before it's as light as a feather, and I crush it in my grasp.

On West Mifflin Street, infamous for the Mifflin Street Block Party, Kovski lives alone on the ground level

of a duplex. He promised not to host parties. In exchange, he has a two-bedroom apartment all to himself. He has a bedroom, an office, and a dingy, dine-in kitchen with a sink full of dishes. It's nothing out of magazines, but the rent is cheap.

In the living room, Kovski basks in a meadow of encrusted pizza crumbs, old takeout containers, and bong smoke. He lives a comfortable albeit lazy existence, and he's fine with that.

Kovski chugs his too. He throws the empty at the wooden floor and belches.

The smell is a mixture of Parmesan cheese and beer. I ask, "Did you have pizza for breakfast?"

"Last night. Too busy to brush my teeth." Kovski grabs another beer from the bag and lays back on the couch. He laughs as he cracks the can. "You should've seen this girl. When I unzipped her dress, her ass just kept going. I don't know how she fit it all in there. It was like a sausage casing."

"Is that a good thing?"

"Oh yeah." His guilt-free smile contains what I wish I had done with Sophie and Chelsea. Kovski doesn't want love.

I grab myself another can. It opens with a spitz.

Kovski says, "So, what's going on? You want to talk about it?"

Throwing my head back on his recliner, I take a slug of beer and sit in silence, unsure what to say. It's not like Kovski even knows what I'm going through. He'd never let it get this far. He changes his mind about a woman on a whim, and it doesn't bother him if it inconveniences her—not out of malice; he figures it's mercy. Why waste each other's time? When you're not feeling something, you're not feeling it.

My problem is I feel everything. Each woman leaves their essence behind. That special thing that makes her different from the next woman. For Kovski, it might be a juicy ass. For me, it's the touch, the exchange of looks, and the thrill of the chase. Of knowing, this is something we crave.

Sophie gave me the Earth. Because of her, for the first time, I felt like the world was meant for me. I don't tell Kovski any of that. Instead, I stay stuck in my head and drink more.

Losing interest, Kovski turns off the silence by turning on the TV. Baseball season is in full swing. The only thing ever on during the early afternoon. It's as good of an excuse as any to get day drunk. The commentator's voice soothes the dull pain in my head.

"Chelsea told me she loved me," I finally say. "I told her I didn't."

"Ooof," Kovski says. "Yeah, it's about time one of you said it. I don't know why you keep hanging onto Sophie."

"I proposed to Sophie, and she kicked me out."

Kovski leans forward and narrows his brow, confused. "Hold on. Hold on. What are you saying? Am I missing something?"

"As of last night, they're done," I say with finality. "I'm a free man again." I smile. It comes out crooked.

Kovski puts his hand on my knee. "Now we can finally do this." He glides his fingers up my pant leg to my lips. He leans in to kiss me, his eyes intent and wanting.

"What the fuck?" Surprised, I never knew he had this side to him. I turn my cheek and block him with my forearm.

Kovski falls back onto the couch, laughing, losing his breath, and hollering. "You should've seen your face! You were going to let me do it."

"You're such an asshole." I throw a round pillow at him.

"Go on." He straightens up and wipes away a tear. "I'm listening."

"You already know the story," I say. "There's not much to say."

"You alright?" He's obligated to ask because he's my friend.

I take a drink of my beer and sigh, "I love her."

"Who?"

"Who? Sophie!" I double down. "I love Sophie. It took Chelsea telling me that she loved me for me to fully realize it."

"If I loved a girl," he says, "I wouldn't ever cheat on her."

"Maybe Chelsea was there to prove my love for Sophie."

"Are you trying to justify your reason for fucking Sophie's best friend?"

"You ever think you could be in love with two women at the same time?" I catch my deformed reflection off a used spoon greased with dried vanilla ice cream. It's amazing any woman would want me, let alone two.

"It doesn't work that way, Dan-o." Kovski slaps my knee. "You pick one. That's it. You get one to keep to yourself, or you get all of them to play with. There's no two for one."

"They're best friends." I smile for the first time all day. "What if this is the foreplay before our eventual throuple?"

Kovski leans forward. "You couldn't tell Chelsea you loved her back because you were already in love with Sophie, and you knew you can't love two girls at the same time."

I massage my temples with my index fingers. "Does it matter anymore?"

"You're damn right it matters," Kovski says. "You just lost two girls you 'love,' and you don't think it matters? You're sitting on my couch right now, borderline bawling your eyes out, and you don't think it matters?"

"But if I told Chelsea how I really felt," I say, "put my respect for Sophie aside and really told her, 'Chelsea, I love you too.'"

"What's with you and love, dude?" Kovski says. "I'm talking about telling the truth. Say, 'Hey, I think you're hot. Let's fuck around, but that's it.' As soon as 'love' gets brought up, you've got to drop them or, you know, marry them. How long have you two been sneaking around together?"

"Probably a year," I say.

"Chelsea has been lying to Sophie for a year!" Kovski says. "Twelve months is a long time before saying 'I love you.' I think she's lying."

"She was pretty mad when she found out Sophie and I signed a new lease together somewhere else."

"You signed a new lease with her!"

"This place we always kind of dreamed about came up and we had to jump on it."

Kovski lets out a plume of vape smoke. "Where?"

"Monona Bay."

"Monona Bay? That's the 'burbs, bro. You dodged a bullet."

I say what Sophie always said, "A place where we can swim in May and ice skate in January."

"Listen." Kovski sits up and fixes his gaze on me. "You won't like hearing this, but do your mind, your body, and your dick a favor and start over. Dredging up this love you feel, will only hurt you in the end. Trust me."

"But I should hurt, right?" I say. "I should feel remorse, and pain, and anger, and like it's all my fault. I shouldn't have let it happen. She was the one, Kov."

"Who?"

"Sophie!...or Chelsea."

"Stop chasing your tail." He takes up his beer. "I'm telling you as a friend. Your relationship with Sophie was over as soon as you stuck your dick in her best friend. But let's be real. It was over way before then. You of all people should know there are more women out there. I mean, what about that married woman?" Kovski finishes his beer. "You got another one? Grab one for yourself. We're getting drunk."

I toss him a can. He catches it. I say, "I shouldn't. I've got work."

"That's a damn shame. Broken heart beers hit different." He cracks his can.

The wave of thought hits me that I'll never drink a beer in my old place again. Sophie will never walk in, fresh from a long day of work, hook her purse on our coat rack, click her heels across the room, and kiss me hello.

It's enough inspiration to dig into my bag and pull out another beer. I crack it and drink, long and deep.

"Don't you drive people around?" Kovski asks.

I come up for air. "I'll be fine." It's cold and bubbly. After two or three more sips, a numb feeling replaces the thoughts of Chelsea and Sophie. "You ever been in love, Kov?"

I've known Will Kovski since my freshman year of college. He's never changed. Perpetually single, woman after woman after woman never settling down.

After a long sip, Kovski says, "Chanell."

"Chanell? I've never heard of Chanell."

He shakes his head at the memory. "She was the love of my life the summer of Sophomore year. We were inseparable. Worked together at Whiskey Jack, I was a barback and she was a shot girl. When we weren't working, we were either staying out till sunrise, traveling together, or making sweet, passionate love. My roommates asked her to pay rent because she was over so often. A total screamer, too. Those jealous stoners."

I ask, "What happened?"

"One night, it's always one night, isn't it? We're working together at Whiskey. All I remember is this guy comes in, shaved head and a stupid tribal neck tattoo. He orders shot after shot from Chanell. Getting drunk, but not obnoxious. He scribbles his number on the receipt. I give it a laugh. Not thinking much of it. But I guess she was because she texted him behind my back. After that, we hung out less and less. Desperate, I told her I loved her."

"And? —"

"She said with the new semester coming up that she would be too busy with school to keep seeing me. Three years later, Chanell married that assclown. They already have a kid. And it proves my point. You can't love two people at the same time. Now, I only have one true love." He kisses his beer. "There's no room for anyone else."

I drink my beer too and say, "You'll never love again?"

"I'll know when I know."

We watch the game and drink beer until I go to work. It's enough of a distraction.

SIXTEEN:

DON'T KNOW HOW I GOT HERE. I don't know where I'm headed. The road is a grey conveyor belt, blurry and running too fast. I'm behind the wheel. I want to hit the brakes, but I need to keep going. Going where?

Green circle after green circle. Up ahead, red. I hit the brakes. My neck jerks forward. A horn blasts somewhere in the city. And the Capitol dome paints the windshield. Majestic. Beautiful. A feat of mankind.

"Are you alright?" A voice snaps the air.

"Sure." I turn on the radio. Frank Sinatra's voice fills the van with the qualms of lost love. Fucking Givens loves easy listening. "That better?"

In the rearview mirror, a middle-aged Filipino, in a checkered button-up and glasses, sits next to a child, about five years old, wearing a bowtie. I laugh to myself—what a daddy's boy. The kid's innocent eyes gleam. This is probably the first time he's seeing the Madison state capitol. I remember that feeling. "That's the state capitol," I say to the kid. "Doesn't it make you feel like a bug?"

More honking, people are mad today. Must be something in the air.

"The light is green!" The man snipes in my ear.

"I know. I know. I'm giving you the tour." I hit the accelerator, and we jolt forward. "Don't want the tour. Don't want the tour." I mutter, turning right at the Capitol Square and joining the first of three lanes of traffic that crawls around the corner. I need to cross this large van from the right lane to the far left by the time we get to the Continental—the red brake lights of the car in front of me flash. I stomp the pedal.

We jerk again.

"We'll get out and walk. It's fine." He tries the side door, but it's locked. "Open the door."

I focus on my side mirror. At a dead standstill, I've got to edge. A Hyundai coupe idles in my path to the lane I need. I inch forward and, with no blinker, I slide over and cut off the Hyundai. At some point, you've got to be the bigger man and push your weight around. Perhaps I deserve the honks. I hit the gas hard. The man straps his seat belt as we clear the middle lane. The left lane is still empty, so I keep going. We're golden.

I veer left. Chelsea, on a bike, pedals into view. I smash the break, banging the back of my head against the seat's headrest. Chelsea stops and smacks the hood. It's not Chelsea, but a jacked biker with a thin torso. Glaring at me behind UV-reflective sunglasses, she should feel lucky to be alive. Instead, she rides on. Her spandex shorts hug the curves of her muscle-bound body.

I finish merging into the left lane.

We rev up and turn the final corner before the hotel. A long straightaway. Almost there. My palms sweat and stick to the steering wheel. The van drifts left. We almost clip the mirror of a parked car. I right it again. I've got this. Another honk. The valet spot in front of the hotel is open, but a Jeep blocks a clear path.

As we pass the Jeep, I swerve hard left. Too hard. Givens talks to a sunhat-wearing guest on the sidewalk. They jump back. The van pops up on the curb. I swing the van right, just missing the glass façade of the hotel. I brake to a gentle stop. We sit at an angle on the curb.

I press my forehead against the cold, leather steering wheel. The AC soothes the sirens sounding in my temples. It's enlivening, I think, to survive.

The man jams the side door handle. I feel around and find the unlock switch. "Thank god for seatbelts, am I right?"

The man exits. He turns back for his son. He yells through the gap between the driver's seat and the side door. "Can you open the trunk?"

"I'm not drunk." My tongue sloshes around my mouth. I take a deep inhale and realize what the man actually said. Summoning all my strength, I slip out of the van.

I throw open the trunk and haul out the two suitcases onto the sidewalk, where the guest and his son wait.

"Welcome to the Continental." Givens immediately grabs the luggage and drags them inside. He says to the man, "Follow me."

I stand at the curb waiting, my hand out. Couldn't be more obvious. He looks at it, sniffs, and follows Givens to Dave behind the hotel's front desk.

"Asshole," I say, under my breath.

The man turns around and says, "What did you say?"

"Enjoy the hotel." I smile and suddenly hiccup.

The man narrows his eyes at me.

He walks through the hotel's valet door. I watch him through the hotel's front window. The man says a few words to Dave. They both look at me. I wave. Dave shows a look of concern with the guest, but it's more of a sneer at me. Givens fixes his glasses with his index finger and pushes through the valet exit door.

"Danny, you need to fix this." He points to the van parked crookedly on the curb. "The bell captain is getting off his lunch any minute, and if he sees this van parked like this, he's going to flip out."

I look at the van. "What's wrong with it?"

"What's wrong with you?" Givens bypasses me and hops into the van. He starts the engine and rolls down the window. "Be my eyes."

Cars whiz past. Once there's a gap, I step into the empty road, signaling for the oncoming cars to stop. The van beeps as Givens backs it off the curb. A dark-blue sedan races down the street. I gesture for the driver to change lanes.

Through the windshield, I see it's Sophie driving. Her teeth gritted. Her hands clamped to the steering wheel. The car doesn't slow down, but speeds up, straight at me.

She's less than ten yards away. I blink and brace for impact. There's no point in jumping out of the way. My life is over without her.

The sedan's wheels squeal with black smoke, as the driver lays on the horn at me. Sophie yells behind the glass, but it's not Sophie. It's a woman I've never seen before, raging. I can't hear her as her teeth gnash the air.

The van drops off the curb with a heavy thud. Its rear juts out in front of me as Givens reparks it parallel to the curb.

I stand in the middle of the middle lane between the hotel van and the blue sedan. The heat and buzz rises in my blood. Car horns explode beyond us. I wait for the driver's muted words to hit me, but nothing happens. I stare at the woman, dead in the eyes, and flip up my middle finger.

She clamps her mouth shut.

I turn my back and walk toward the hotel as the sedan's wheels screech against the pavement. She peels off.

Givens waits on the sidewalk with his arms crossed.

"I'm going to organize the luggage," I say to him as I push through the revolving door and enter the cool air of the lobby. My hands shake. I push them into my pockets, but it doesn't stop the tremors. I walk past the front desk, ignoring the man screaming at Dave, his son waves at me. I wave back before I enter the bell closet.

Falling through the blackness, a voice comes to me. "Danny?" He sounds familiar, friendly. "Danny?" A hand prods my shoulder. "Danny?" I open my eyes and I'm flooded with fluorescent light. An outline of someone's round head slowly reveals itself to me. "Come on, wake up."

"Givens? What the fuck? Where am I?" I say, jostling away from his sweaty hands. I hit my head against one of the brass pillars of a bell cart.

"Use this." He uncaps a travel-sized mouthwash. He thrusts it into my mouth.

I choke on it. "Why?"

"That guest complained. He thinks you're drunk." He glances over his shoulder before he whispers, "The captain is going to be coming to talk to you. Sit up straight." Givens stacks my wilted spine. He looks at me square, his whiskered face a few inches from mine, his warm coffee breath wafts through my nostrils. "Talk about how you popped up on the curb for safety purposes, okay?" I nod. He puts his finger into my chest. "And for the last time, my name is *Ryan*, got that?"

I swish the mouthwash and spit it into the trash bin. Givens hides the empty bottle in his pocket just as the bell captain enters.

The captain wears his managerial suit and frown. "Ryan, please give Danny and me a minute."

"Yep." Givens scurries away. The door closes behind him with a decisive slam.

Dizzy in the humid room, I focus on the matter at hand. Repercussions abound for nearly crashing the van into the hotel. Worse, if they make me take a breathalyzer. My heart races. I'll be fired on the spot, potentially put in jail. Why did Givens help me? I think of this morning, my lack of sleep, my sudden move, my loss, all the beer. It's not my fault.

The bell captain kneels before me, his eyes level with mine. I never noticed this before, but he must tweeze his unibrow. He sighs, pushing his shorn brow upward. "Can you tell me what happened?"

I shake my head and let out an exasperated breath. The words come to me. "I slammed the brakes to avoid a fender bender. That was my bad. Then you know how the van sometimes sticks, that happened, which rocked it a bit. It's stupid. He was yelling at me while I was driving. I popped up on the curb because I was worried about his kid scrambling into heavy traffic." I make sure to look the bell captain in the eyes as I say, "If you've got to fire me, go ahead, but I'll say this, I did what I thought was right."

There's an extended silence. The bell captain sizes me up, waiting for me to crack. I hide my shaking hands in my pockets. My crumpled posture says one thing: I tried my best. Not that I'm drunk and don't even remember picking them up from the airport.

"Are you drunk?" he asks.

I crane my head, heat rising to my face. "How could you even ask me that?"

My defensiveness makes him blush. He cups my shoulder. "Guests are nuts sometimes. Next time, don't park the van on the curb."

"Sssorry," I slur. "Sorry," I say again, getting it right.

"Are you okay?" The captain asks.

"The whole everything. I'm a little shaken up. I hit my head pretty hard on the headrest."

The bell captain checks his watch. He thinks. "Why don't you take the rest of the day off?"

"But—" I feign, trying not to sound too eager to leave.

"Danny, go home, get some rest." The bell captain stands. He fixes his belt, knowing he made the correct managerial assessment, something that he'll mention in a job interview in the future.

Givens re-enters the room. "I'll take his shift. Sorry. I was listening."

"Thank you," I say so weakly, you'd think I had Cancer.

"You'll work a double?" The bell captain asks.

"It's Saturday night," Givens says. "I'm not doing anything, and I could use the extra money for marketing my book."

"Well, okay." Satisfied, the bell captain leaves.

Givens lingers by the doorway. He says, "You're welcome."

The only thing I'm thinking about, I ask, "Why Givens? Why'd you tell Sophie?"

Givens stares at me, unsure if he wants to speak. "I'm her friend, and that's what friends do." He shakes his head, not at me, but at the whole situation. He looks like he'll say more, but he holds back. He opens the lobby door. Sunlight pours through the glass façade.

Watching him disappear into the lobby, I call out, "*Ryan!*"

Ryan catches the door.

"She broke up with me last night."

"I'm sorry to hear that," he says, his puppy dog eyes all big and guilty. "I hope you can forgive me." The door shuts behind him.

Left in the quiet room, away from the bustle of the hotel, a heaviness settles between my shoulders, a dull throb in my head, and a longing for my bed, for Sophie, for yesterday to come back. I should be mad at Ryan, but the asshat just saved me from losing my job.

SEVENTEEN:

boys' night

WHEN I WALK THROUGH THE DOOR at quarter past four, Kovski's on his couch, headset on, playing a space shooter video game online. His fingers click the triggers. He notices me standing in the doorway. "Did you get fired?" A swift animated blast kills his character. He pounds the controller into the couch cushion. "Damnit!"

"They sent me home."

"'Cause you're drunk?"

"I told the boss I puked in the lobby bathroom."

"Did he suspect anything?"

I shake my head. Kovski doesn't need to know about my near-crash experience.

His character respawns in the game, but all his attention is on me. "What are you going to do now?"

"I should probably get some rest." It's true. I am exhausted after all these late nights. Yet, in the back of my mind, the loss of Sophie and Chelsea haunts my every thought. I'm an unmoored ship on a rocking ocean. I need something to quell the nightmare. "But it's Saturday night."

Kovski says, "You know what they say about Saturdays?"

"What do you they say?"

"Saturday's for the boys."

"Boys' night?"

Kovski picks up his bottle of beer. "Get some beer out of the fridge."

"I need something stronger."

"Aye, aye captain. The bong and the bourbon are in the office."

Kovski goes back to virtual war. His head bobs to the side as I cross in front of the TV.

Kovski's office is more of a storage locker. He's an adventure guru. Anything you can climb, paddle, or ride, he's got. Keeps him in shape no doubt, but it's a lot of bulky shit. There's no room for anything else. He carved out a small corner where he keeps his electric guitar and amp. Next to that, on a scratched-up end table, an ashtray, a bong, and a bottle.

I take a rip out of the bong, swipe the bottle of whiskey, and think this might end up being the best day ever. From nearly parking the van in the hotel lobby to on my way to a steady drunk and a little high—all with my best friend. Crazy to think the best day ever could happen after the worst day ever.

I'm a man of simple pleasures after all. Today, of all days, I deserve to splurge. I'm obviously depressed. I must take care of myself.

Kovski and I pass the controller and the bourbon back and forth until the sun goes down. Talking bullshit. A nice palette cleanser from the heavy thoughts of love I was dealing with last night. Sports, movies, and inane gossip about our friends. We realize none of our friends

are around anymore. We're the last two from our friend group who haven't moved on to follow some job. I can write anywhere so why bother going someplace I don't know? I guess I should write more stuff too. Better stuff.

Standing at the counter of Whiskey Jack again puts me in the mood. Everybody needs a bar they can call home. I know the staff. They know me. Together, we share stories of wild nights all here at the Whiskey, a prominent establishment that caters to the new adult population. Every night, the bar evolves from an easy-going pool hall into a dancing-on-the-tables kind of party. A little bit country, but mostly rock'n'roll. I wonder where tonight will lead.

The bearded bartender, Jason, pours three shots of whiskey. Kovski and I tap glasses with him and swig. It should burn, but I've been drinking all afternoon. Everything goes down smooth now.

It didn't take much convincing for Kovski to get me to come out. I'd be curled up on his couch in the fetal position right now otherwise. My work practically begged me to get drunk and have fun tonight. You know, sometimes, I hate my job and I think it'll be the death of me, but today, I couldn't be happier with it. The captain said he'd clock me for a full shift. I thank Ryan under my breath. None of this would be possible without him. The knob. I try to hate him, but I can't.

Women mill about the barroom. Some play pool. Others put in songs to be played over the speakers. There's a woman by the front window. She's waiting for someone, probably a date. Her shoulders, bare beneath thin khaki straps, casual, yet sexy for a summer night, makes me swirl my whiskey.

Kovski yammers with one of the waitresses, Cassie. She knows how to work it for tips. Red cowboy boots and hip-hugging jean shorts. Her glossed lips and studded earrings give her an attitude that makes you want to tip her. I've hit on her enough to know that nothing serious will ever happen between us. She goes for tall jocks. Two things no one has ever confused me with.

"I'll be right back," I say to Kovski.

My gaze sets on this woman by the window. I consider all the ways I can start this conversation. Despite her large breasts, I'm assuming everything's natural except the tan. More than that, her tiny geometric tattoos on her arms and neck give her an otherworldly look. The 'manifesting' type who believe in the power of crystals or asks people with confidence to read their birth chart.

As I approach, drink in hand, I smile. It feels so good to be untethered. "Hey—" I say before I even think of anything to say. That's a problem. I go with an age-old line for her type. She turns to me, eyebrow raised. I say, "Let me guess? A Pisces."

She half-smiles, still skeptical. "Scorpio."

"So, you're mysterious. What secrets are you hiding?"

"I'm not even sure what that means. I don't really believe in that stuff." She glances at the exit.

I haven't hooked her yet. "It's too bad," I say, to buy myself some time. "I was going to ask if you wanted your fortune told."

"By a random guy at a bar?"

"Not just any guy. The Grrreat Danny Clark." I give her a pose as if I just threw open my cape in the wind. I bow forward and offer her my hand. "Your palm, my lady."

Her eyes suddenly light up. I think she's into me until a tall man in plaid passes by. They hug. I step back to

give them space. The woman avoids my look as they make their way to the bar. The guy narrows his eyes at me.

I shake my head. 0-1. Any betting man and bedding man knows, it takes a few rolls of the dice before you win big.

At the same time, I don't want to be here all night. Cassie and Jason will hook us up with drinks for so long before this place is overrun. I'm not in the mood to yell over loud music and conversations. It's time for the next spot. Kovski doesn't disagree. We finish our drinks in one gulp and move on.

Across the street from Whiskey Jack, Hawk's Nest boasts the best-kept secret drink specials on State Street. It's an eclectic, and oddly narrow tavern, by no means famous in the Madison bar scene.

Jammed in between the neon beer signs, framed autographed celebrity pictures and old movie posters all over the walls, it's crowded tonight when we walk in. There's a 1980's John Carpenter movie on mute on the TVs. Shoulder to shoulder, men and women stand. A heavy-set couple get up from the bar. Dodging between sorority sisters and a verbose drag queen, I snag the premium empty chairs before anyone else can.

The chalkboard, over the bartender's head, reads "Doubles for Singles Night." I laugh at the irony. I know they mean you get a double shot for the price of a single, but still, it's kind of funny, right? I say it to Kovski. He chuckles.

Kovski rubs the scruff of my neck. "Danny, how ya feeling?" He scans the bar. "There's some talent out there." He means attractive women. I haven't noticed. Usually, I do the moment I walk in, but I didn't this time. I wanted these seats.

This is the kind of place you get tuned up. Everyone knows it. The front of the bar is the only place with tables, all high-tops. They're always full of college kids. Among them, a few women in tank tops and jean shorts. With the number of frat bros milling around, they guard their options. By the bathrooms at the other end of the bar, I spot opportunity.

"How 'bout those two girls?" I nod their way.

"Ready to jump back into the action so quickly?" Kovski checks them out.

One woman in a white shirt and leather shorts scrolls on her phone. Her friend is a farm girl, lost in the big city. Her baby blue cow eyes roam the bar. They meet mine before they flick away. She dives for the straw of her vodka-cranberry.

I say, "Dibs on the farmer."

"Damn you." He shoots back. "I wanted her."

"May the best man win?" I say.

"You know how that will turn out." Kovski humps the air. "*Oh yeah. Oh yeah. Oh yeah.* That's what you'll be hearing all night from my bedroom."

"Because you'll be jerking off to what's happening on your couch."

"Gross," he says. "Save our seats. I'm going to bring them over. Tell the bartender we need the dice box."

There's no easier way to hold a woman's attention than a game of chance. We sweeten it up by making it a drinking game. By passing around the dice, our low-stakes competition leads to an easy way to get to know each other.

Kovski makes his approach. A wide-armed, I haven't seen you in forever to the girl texting on her phone. He

pretends he knows her. They try to remember where from, but it turns out they've never met before. It's a devious way to approach, but with the right level of playfulness, it works almost every time.

"Hey," I get the bartender's attention. "Does the special work on the shots too? If I order one, I get two?"

He fixes his glasses. "Sure, what the hell."

"I'll take two shots of whiskey, which makes 5? Because I can tell you need one." This is the best way to avoid the rail and still pay the rail price.

"Congrats, you're good at math." He smiles and pulls a bottle of whiskey off the rail beneath him. He lays out five shot glasses and pours them to the brim.

I check Kovski. He's still with the farmer. "Might be awhile," I say, I raise a shot glass. The bartender does the same. "To a helluva night."

"I'll say." The bartender slams the shot with a gasp. He grabs my empty.

"Can I get the dice box?"

"No dice."

"Very funny." I laugh.

"I'm serious."

"Why?"

"Too busy." He takes the order of the fat dude in a pink polo hovering behind me.

The three shots wait for Kovski and the women. Judging by their looks, he's working slow. I wave to him to speed things up. He waves back. The women look too. Kovski launches into introducing me, I'm sure. The women don't budge. And still the three shots wait for them, getting warm.

I hate this position. Holding court. A lame duck. I should be out there getting wom—

"Can I have this chair?" This frat guy in a backwards ball cap has the audacity to ask. There's not another open seat in the place. Obviously, this empty one is taken.

"It's taken, fuck off." I turn my back to him.

"Alright, asshole." He slinks back to his friends, a bunch of yawping bros in tall socks, huddled around a high-top. His poor girlfriend is going to have to stand. Boohoo.

The place fills up. People come to the bar, leaning on their elbows, and tap their cards on the bar top as they wait. Someone's going to knock over these shots.

I check Kovski and the women. They're still talking. Laughing. I wish I could laugh like that, happily oblivious to all the hell in the world. Happy to never be stabbed in the heart by love. I've got two fresh wounds that are going to be scars.

Down-up.

Down-up.

Down-up. Each shot goes down smooth. I do all three without thinking in between. The last one makes me cough.

Kovski taps me on the back. "Where's the dice box?"

"No dice," I say. "Where are the girls?"

"Ah. They have to drive home to Sheboygan. No more drinks for them." He sits down. "What's all this?" He points to the empty shots.

"Oh, uh, those frat bros came through."

"I want to be on their level." Kovski glances at them, double takes at that dude's girlfriend. An hourglass Latina in skin-tight jeans. "Shots?"

The thought sends a sour hiccup to my mouth. I cover it with my hand. "Let's do it."

"You good?" he asks, eyes narrowing.

The whiskey rings a bell between my ears, but I ignore the call for moderation. To show my allegiance to the cause, I get the bartender's attention as he walks past. I put up two fingers and point to the shots.

Kovski adds, "And two beers."

The bartender pours out four shots. I curse the deal under my breath. I say to the bartender as he sets them in front of us, "You're going to kill me." The bartender smirks and moves on.

Kovski smiles. He takes up a shot. I hesitate. He hands me one. I can't say no.

"To fuckin' love," Kovski says.

"Fuggin' love," I say and douse my throat. My stomach curdles as soon as the whiskey hits it.

Kovski slams his down. He takes up the next one. "To the fuckin' future."

My mouth tastes of battery acid, but my mind urges me to go forward. When was the last time I got stinking drunk anyway? You must push your limits to find your limits. Sophie limited me so much. I know I have so much more potential. In women, in love, in writing, in drinking. Just let me be, woman.

Fingers shaking, I steady the shot on my lip and lift. The whiskey washes down my throat. It joins the rest pooling in my belly. That should do the trick. The world blurs at the edges. I'm glad I'm sitting down because my foot keeps slipping off the footrest.

"We should get water," I say to Kovski.

Just then, the bartender drops off two pints of beer. I tell him to close my tab after that.

"Better yet." Kovski shoves a beer into my hand. "This should help. See you at the bottom." He bumps the top of my pint glass, challenging me to our chugging game.

"See you at the bottom," I reply. I can't resist. I chug, washing down the burn with the cold, bubbly beer. Finished with his already, Kovski tips up the end of my glass with his finger. I finish the beer, spilling some down my chin.

The mix of hot and cold in my blood injects me with new life.

"Next spot!" I thrust the chair out from under me, knocking it over in the process. I don't bother to pick it up. I announce to Kovski, "It's time to dance."

"Lead the way." Kovski slams his empty on the bar.

Arm in arm, we charge out the door.

When we're on State Street, I trip over a crack in the sidewalk and stumble into some garbage cans. I try to get to my feet, but all the lumpy, stinky, and sticky bags makes it hard to regain my balance. Kovski picks me up and pulls me against the window of a closed barber shop. He asks, "How'd you get so wasted?"

The concern that spreads across his face straightens me up.

I take a steep inhale. An inhale I take when I know I've had a touch too much. It sobers me up. Gets that fresh oxygen to the brain, you know? Of course, you know. We all breathe. It's that kind of breath. And it works. Immediately, I'm thinking clearly.

"Let's fuckin' go!" I shout, charging ahead in the direction of Sloe Gin, a nightclub on West Johnson, a block away.

Rolling up to a club and skipping the line is almost better than sex. There they all are. Behind velvet ropes, the desperate masses huddled together in purgatory. They wait for Lady Luck to let them in. In this case, Lady Luck is a big-bearded, bald meathead named Valance.

When Valance sees Kovski, he unhooks the velvet rope for us. We strut inside. But Valance stops me with an arm barred across my chest. "Whoa, whoa, you good Danny?"

I cackle. "Valance, baby, it's schmee! You know schmee!"

Kovski says, "Schmee needs some water."

"If he pukes, you're cleaning it up," Valance says.

"He's not going to puke," Kovski says. "Come on." He puts his hands on my shoulders and steers me through the door from behind.

In the vestibule, where we get checked for weapons and contraband, the beefy bouncer pats me down. It tickles and I giggle. He grunts and steps aside. We're inside.

Walking the ramp between the entryway and the club, our reflections strut with us in the mirrored corridor. I'm looking damn good tonight. The vanilla and tar smell of hookah smoke beckons us.

Inside the mezzanine, men and women sit around low booths and tables stacked with mountains of glasses and bottles. Champagne pops. Women hoot. The music thumps.

Kovski grabs my shoulder and screams, "We are alive!" We go to the bar. Kovski sidesteps his way through the crowd of people ordering. He's at the front and locks eyes with the scantily clad bartender. She skips him for the woman next to him.

At the railing, I take in Sloe Gin's two levels. Where I'm at, the mezzanine is for the tables, bottle service, and drinks with friends. Down the steps is the pit—the reason the club exists.

The dance floor pulses. The tiles light up in sync with the beat. Smoke blasts. Strobes flash. The DJ spins techno rave music behind a glass partition while a line of people waits to request songs he'll never play.

Kovski brings back two golden cocktails. He hands me one.

"I thought you were gonna get me water?"

"Nah," he says. "Vodka-Red Bulls, boy! Let's get turnt up."

We clink cocktails. When the cold liquid hits my tongue, my energy surges.

My feet kicking with every step as we swagger into the pit. We find a spot by the DJ booth. A nice corner for us to bob our heads to the beat and dance. Kovski is all about the sway of his arms. I'm doing my own thing, a little two-step with a hip thrust and some jabs to the air. Neither of us are going to win any dance competitions, but who cares? It's not pretty, but it feels good.

A pair of brown eyes catch mine—a curly-headed cutie with a big smile. She's with two other women, each with a style that borders on Vogue. Judging by our wrinkled shirts and jeans, Kovski and I might have a chance because no one better has come along. Our eyes meet again.

I tap Kovski and wave him to follow me.

There's nothing subtle about what I do or say in this moment. I'm letting the whiskey do the talking. And what the whiskey says to the women with brown eyes—"You look like my girlfriend if she had curly hair—Sorry, EX! Girlfriend."

"Excuse me?"

I don't mean to, but I lurch into the center of their group. My stare latched onto her. "What do you say? Want to dance?" I do a twirl and trip on something, spilling my drink on the floor.

Brown eyes steps back with an *-eek.* Her friends stop dancing.

I gulp down the rest of my vodka-Red Bull while shaking my hips. I spin around and twerk in front of her,

but I was never good at it. Passion outwits mastery any day. There's no way she can resist.

"What's your problem?" her friend says.

"Go away, dickhead." Another chimes in. I can't really tell what she looks like.

Brown eyes furrows her brow. "I need a drink," she tells her friends.

"Me too." I follow her, but something holds me back. Kovski.

"Dude," he says, "what was that?"

"I dunno. I was trying something."

"It was shit."

"Pssh," I say. "I dunno, man. Sorry, I can't dance."

"You good?" he asks.

I debate telling him that the rising and falling bass rhythms make me dizzy, that the strobe lights blind me, that all the whiskey in my stomach keeps coming back up, but I swallow it down.

I say, "I love Chelsea."

"Are you sure you don't just love whiskey?"

"No. I love her, bro. More than my own soul. I'm going to marry her."

Kovski rolls his eyes. "We need to get you some water." He grabs my forearm and drags me to the pit's bar. It's too crowded for both us to get through. He tells me to wait at the edge of the dance floor for him. He bumps into people as he picks his way to the front. It's going to be a while.

With everything going on and all the strangers swarming around me, I can't stop wishing for Kovski to return. I need someone to hold onto. Pushed out by the party and feeling in the way, I step back further and further. Soon enough, I'm by the stairs. A cold sweat crawls down my back. I don't belong here. The music's mad buzz knocks me off-balance. It's too loud. I beg for the quiet.

Before I know it, I push open the glass doors and stagger out into the hot August night. Cars speed past as I drift down the sidewalk toward my date with destiny.

EIGHTEEN:
911

ETAL-ON-METAL GRINDING makes my eyes creak open. The dark room spins. Beneath the seal, the dizzy light of day. Reaching out for something, anything. My hands find the edge of something hard and cold. I rest my forehead against it. Steadying myself, I breathe as drums kick the middle of my brain.

The black-and-white tile floor looks familiar. What am I leaning against? I feel around with my hand. It's smooth and curved, sticky in some places: a toilet. I slept amongst the toenails and pube hairs.

Head spiraling, I clamber to my feet and catch myself in the mirror. Eyes hollowed out by the whiskey, hair disheveled, still in my clothes from the night before, I splash water on my face, trying to remember. The chill soothes my pounding head. I drink it in. I'm an empty canteen. My mind is a desert.

Drying my hands on the turquoise towel, it hits me—Chelsea. Judging by the amount of used paper towels in the trash can, I puked and missed the toilet.

I wobble to the door. It's locked. I fiddle with it until it unlocks. I fling it open.

In the kitchen, Chelsea's roommate, Haley, either grinds the bones of a hundred dead rats into a fine powder or makes a smoothie. Famously, she hates me. I don't know why. I'm certain it's a delight for her to see me first thing in the morning.

"Thank God. Finally!" Haley sets down a purple smoothie on the counter and sprints into the bathroom, slamming the door.

Actually, this is the first time I've stayed at Chelsea's apartment. Hmmm. I smile to myself. We only tell the truth when we're drunk. All it took was a dozen shots of the serum.

The truth? I love Chelsea. That's why I could never commit to Sophie. It was never meant to be. I'd fallen out of love with Sophie and fallen in love with her best friend. It's a tale as old as time.

This time, I want to dive into Chelsea's love. That cool, calm, and collected ocean she lives in. Being here, looking out her ninth-story window, my gaze on the horizon, the city is at my feet.

Sophie met me first, laid claim, and buried me beneath her love. I was half in the grave until Chelsea revived me, revived Sophie and me too.

There is no doubt that Chelsea and I being together will ruin her friendship with Sophie.

To be someone's best friend is to be their confidante. The one person they can turn to when the going gets tough. They aren't supposed to fuck their partners, especially not after years of mostly steady commitment. But one night, it happened, we finally surrendered to desire and then kept coming back for more.

Sophie will find out eventually. I'm ready to drop to one knee for Chelsea. I gave up Sophie for her. I must be madly in love.

In the kitchen, I open cabinet after cabinet looking for a glass. Not finding one, I duck my head beneath the faucet and drink from the tap, long and deep.

"Glad you're feeling better." Haley emerges, drying her hands on her shorts. "We're going to the lake. You need to get out of here."

"Can you make me one of those?" I ask. The purple drink looks like a hangover cure.

"I'll put half in a to-go cup for you." Haley opens a cabinet and draws out a paper cup from the top of a short stack. "Chelsea was stupid for letting you in last night."

"Sorry about the mess," I say.

Haley dumps half of her glass into the paper cup. "You were so drunk." She hands it to me. "You drank out of the toilet last night." Haley harps. I've never seen anyone sip a smoothie with so much hostility.

I shrug. "Explains the shitty taste in my mouth." I drink, smacking my lips. "Yum. What is that? Dragon fruit?"

I hobble to Chelsea's bedroom door.

"I told you to get out of here!"

"Yeah, yeah, yeah. I'll go as soon as I say goodbye to Chelsea, promise," I say.

"Leave that poor girl alone," Haley relents, knowing she can't stop me.

I push open Chelsea's door slowly and peek in. There she is—my future wife, all cozied up beneath her quilt. I sit at her bedside. Stroking her hair, I murmur, "Good morning, my love." Okay. That was a bit much. She doesn't stir thankfully. I stroke her shoulder and play patterns with my palms on the blanket covering her. Soon, it lifts her eyes.

Chelsea grumbles in the morning light. She turns over, hiding from the sun. I chuckle. "Thanks for taking care of me."

She mumbles into the pillow. "What happened to you?"

"Sophie and I are done."

"I know," Chelsea says, raising her head, hair flopping into her face. "She's not well."

"Did you tell her about us?"

"Hell no. And you didn't?"

"Of course not. God, I don't want to ruin—you know." I don't know how to say it. "You know, you two."

"I think it's a little late for that." She drops her head into the pillow so hard a feather puffs out.

"Listen," I say with a sigh. "I've done a lot of thinking. I—"

"In a day?" She talks into her pillow.

"Can you let me finish?" I jab. "I love you."

She doesn't even lift her head or say anything.

"Did you hear me?"

"Yeah."

"And?"

She turns her head to the side. "Congratulations?"

"I love you," I say again with more power. She has to hear it. The truth has a ring to it. I don't say this to just anyone. Just Sophie—at least used to.

Chelsea rolls to the other edge of the bed and gets up. She closes her bedroom door. When she does, she returns to me. Her eyes set on mine. "Do you?"

"I fuckin' love you," I say. I get up and thrust my body against her. Her body splashes back.

"Are you serious?"

"I'll scream it at the top of my lungs." I holler, "I LOVE YOU CHELSEA!"

"Shhh." She laughs, her finger poking at my lips. "My roommate."

"Haley! I fuckin' love Chelsea. Hear that? I fuckin' love her!"

Through the walls, Haley bellows, "Shut up!"

Chelsea pushes me back onto the bed and lays her head in the crook of my neck. We sleep nestled together, our breaths rising and falling in time.

I wake up to Chelsea shoving a plate into my lap. She kisses me on the cheek. Drizzling a thick layer of maple syrup over the toasted frozen waffles, this is the definition of domestic bliss.

Sophie used to do stuff like this for me. I'd do the same for her. We'd surprise each other. It was the time when *I love you* was a candy we shared, never growing tired of the flavor.

Chelsea slides beneath the covers next to me. I haven't left the bed all morning. Haley must be livid. Serves her right. She's been against me ever since I came over for the first time. So what? I accidentally used her toothbrush. I thought it was Chelsea's. Either way, disgusting, I know, but when you smoked a cigar and you just went down on a girl, tell me how bad you want to brush your teeth. I never apologized. I don't have to. If she doesn't like me because of that, I can't make her.

Haley knocks and yells through the door, wondering if Chelsea's ready to go. Chelsea tells her that she's no longer going and can't be convinced otherwise. I thank the heavens when the hyena finally leaves. We finally have the place to ourselves. Chelsea's bedroom isn't big enough to do much else other than fuck and sleep.

In the living room, I bellyflop onto the couch and turn on the TV like I own the place. Of course, I don't know how the remote works, and I end up turning on her ceiling fan. Chelsea grabs milk from the fridge, so she's no help at all. Staring at the three different remotes before me, I eliminate the ceiling fan one. I take up the one with the most buttons and smash ON. The TV hisses to life. The cooking channel plays. I change it to sports. Except it's too early for anything, the pundits argue over some baseball owner's selfish management of the team.

Chelsea comes over with two mugs of coffee. She hands me one. The foam top is decorated like a flower.

"Is this a cappuccino?"

"When my dad stopped paying for school because I was skipping class. I was a barista for a month."

"I never knew that. I should've stayed over sooner if this is how you treat a guest."

Chelsea sits next to me. Our eyes meet. She smiles and offers a toast. After we clink mugs, we sip our brews.

"Ow!" We both say and laugh, tongues burned by the hot coffee hidden beneath the foam.

When I think about it, the two of us make perfect sense. She's smart, passionate, adventurous, and, like me, a little too cocky for her own good. I savor these quiet hours together free from the burden of our lie. The weight is gone. We can finally fully express ourselves. I was so blind, but now, I see Chelsea. It was always Chelsea. I answered her siren's call and found true love.

We spend the next few hours pretending to watch some new war drama we'd heard about. While the characters fight for their lives, we fight our orgasms, clinging to ecstasy before collapsing, heavy, into the couch. Our tongues glisten with each other's spit. Our bodies bathe in each other's sweat. Our love is an oasis we plunge into again and again.

We undress and redress. Undress and redress. Each time, a little less embarrassed. Each time a little more uninhibited. The room reeks of heat. Of hot breath.

Bent over the couch, Chelsea moans as her butt bounces against my every thrust. There's a knock on the door. It chokes her orgasm.

I pull out. "Is it your roommate?"

"No, it's probably a package."

"A big package," I add.

"Uh-huh." She pulls me back in.

We keep going. She spreads herself further than I ever thought she could. The captain explores the depths of her ocean.

The knock gets louder. Harder. Angrier.

Chelsea squeals, "Leave it at the door."

Thinking we're golden. I smack, pound, and spank her until Heaven swallows me whole and I erupt. Nothing has ever felt better in my entire life.

Chelsea crawls to her feet and tucks her hand between her legs. She kisses me hard on the mouth. "I love you."

"I love you, too." I hook her around the neck and kiss her again.

A soft voice calls from the hallway. "Chelsea? Can you please let me in?"

It hits us both at the same time: Sophie.

Chelsea cringes. Out of instinct, I gather up our clothes in a bundled mess. She sorts through the tangled pile in my arms. She pulls out her shirt and her shorts. She says to the door, "I'll be right there!" Then to me, "Bedroom, now." She slams the door to the bathroom.

Under better circumstances, that would be exactly what I would want to hear. But now, I'm in the middle of the room, lost. How did it come to this?

The knock again. "Chelsea?"

I go to Chelsea's bedroom and shut the door. Hopefully, this is over soon. I have to be at work in two hours.

Sitting on her bed, in purgatory, I listen to the two best friends talk. I can hear every word that they are saying. That's why Haley hates me. She can probably hear every grunt and squeak whenever Chelsea and I fuck.

Sophie cries. Wondering what she did to make me cheat. Why I am such a coward for lying to her. How Ryan saw me kiss Rachel outside the hotel.

Chelsea, her voice high and fast, badmouths me repeatedly. She can't believe that I cheated on Sophie. I think good cover, Chelsea. Her insults fall like kisses. She's protecting us. Then she says something I don't think I hear right. She asks Sophie, "What about that one guy from the Old-Fashioned?"

That tool? If I lose to that competition, shoot me. Chelsea, you should know better. I catch my look in the mirror. Wrinkles crease my brow, I breathe deeply and relax my forehead. This will be alright, but it's taking way too long. I text Chelsea to hurry up.

Sophie can't find out about us. Not now. It's much too soon, but maybe it's meant to be. A smooth hand-off from one lover to the next. I'm the baton. They each love handling my baton, if you know what I mean.

Sophie ponders, "I should've known. All those late nights. His lame ass excuses. I was so naïve." She breaks down in tears. Her timbre makes me shudder. "Could you tell he was cheating on me?"

Chelsea says, "I was suspicious, but I could never prove it. That's why I never told you."

I wish I could explain it to Sophie. Explain that it wasn't about her. It never was. It was about me. It's because I was born with a dick and I want to show it to any woman curious enough to see it. That's all. I loved her. I love her.

The way Sophie says my name always puts me in a trance. "Danny." "Danny." "Danny." In the morning, I often awoke with my arm tucked around her. Dreams never felt closer than with her.

I let her go.

Chelsea cries, "I can't believe anyone would do that to you. He's a monster."

Sophie needs something to drink. I hear a cork pop out of a bottle. It's kind of early for wine. I check my watch. They've been at it for an hour. I lay back in the bed. Sophie and Chelsea clink glasses.

Chelsea asks, "What now? What are you going to do?"

Sophie laughs, "It's funny. With him gone, I'm myself again. That little voice in my head has stopped fucking worrying about where Danny is and what he's doing. Now, she's asking me if I want cupcakes. And I do want cupcakes."

"Did you get cupcakes?"

"No." Sophie deflates.

"We're going to make so many cupcakes you can't possibly eat them all."

"Right now?"

"I might have a mix."

"Should we make cupcakes?"

Fucking cupcakes, Chelsea? Why in the world would you suggest cupcakes? Unless you don't have the mix and you two will have to go to the grocery store to get it. Genius.

Chelsea's voice rings out, "Found some! It's Haley's, but she'll understand."

"We'll save her one." Sophie agrees. Footsteps come toward the door. "Hey, can I borrow a sweatshirt? I'm cold." Sophie twists the bedroom doorknob. I stand back. There's nowhere to hide.

"Let's open the window. Let the summer breeze in. The A/C can be too much. But once the oven's going, you're going to take it off again."

"You're right." The door closes. "You don't mind if we hang out, do you? I really don't want to be alone."

"Of course not," Chelsea says. "Stay as long as you want."

What game is she playing? Chelsea's on a power trip.

But what am I going to do? Should I call in sick to work? Even then, I'm still stuck here, waiting for the inevitable.

That's it. I must be a man and just do it. Face my broken promise and mend it. That's what we all need to move forward.

If I do this, there's no turning back. Sophie will know and she will never forget. Chelsea will lose a friend but gain a lover. Seems worth it.

With all the strength I have, I push open the door. Its hinges groan.

In the living room, Sophie and Chelsea stop chatting.

"Danny?" Sophie looks at Chelsea, then back to me. "Why—why are you here?"

"We—" Chelsea says, "We—we were—"

"I'm having a tough time," I blurt out, putting on the waterworks. "And I wanted to see if there was anything I could do to win you back."

"You were hiding out in her bedroom this whole time?"

"I didn't want you to get the wrong idea," I say. "Like, make you think anything weird was going on."

Sophie takes this in. She lowers her chin and thinks. Truly, she looks dazzling in this light. The view of the Capitol

perfectly frames her. She smirks. "No, nothing weird at all." Sophie grabs her purse from the breakfast bar. "Rain check on the cupcakes."

Chelsea says, "Sophie, please don't go. It's not what you think."

"I was just leaving," I say. "I have to get to work."

"You guys deserve each other." Sophie shuts the apartment door, loud and echoing.

"Cupcakes? Are you kidding me?" I say, "I told you I have work today."

"I was about to tell her we needed to go out to get frosting," she says. "What was she talking about? You kissed a hotel guest?"

"It was nothing," I say. "The other night, I was showing this guest some spots in Madison because she was cool, you know? Well, she got the wrong impression, and she kissed me. I didn't kiss her. Anyway, Ryan should never have told Sophie. It was a total misunderstanding."

I approach Chelsea, a statue in the center of the living room, "Sophie finally seeing us together is a good thing. We can finally stop hiding." I wrap my arms around her.

Chelsea stiffens at my touch, "Have you been sleeping around?"

"Me? Never." Chelsea turns her cheek when I try to kiss her.

"Don't lie to me." She bristles, goosebumps rising across her skin, "Are you seeing other girls?"

"I mean, I was seeing Sophie, obviously," I say. "What? Are you jealous?"

"I want you to tell me the truth." Tears prick the corners of her eyes. "Is there anyone else?"

"You want to know the truth?" Chelsea nods. I say, "Yeah. I sleep around. In the past year, I slept with six other women." Most of them were one-night stands. Two nights at best. What can I say? No one compares to Chelsea or Sophie, except Rachel. "But I keep coming back to you."

A vein fissures down Chelsea's forehead, her face ripens to bright red, and she gasps, "You're a dog!"

"Chelsea, are you really surprised? I mean look at us—and Sophie."

"I'm no different than any of them, am I?" Chelsea says. "I'm just the tramp who stuck around."

"The difference is," I say, "I love you."

"If you loved me, you wouldn't cheat on me. If you truly cared about me, you would've broken up with Sophie a long time ago instead of stringing me along. I'm so stupid."

"Chelsea," I say, hugging her.

Chelsea tries to slip away. "Please leave."

"Come on." I squeeze her tight. "I'm here now. That's all that mat—"

"No!" Chelsea squirms out of my grip and shoves me back. "Go away!" She screams, "You're not welcome here anymore."

"Fine. Be that way." I swipe my keys off the counter, right where I left them the other night. As I go, Chelsea chucks a throw pillow at my head. I slam the door and it thuds against it.

"FUCK!" I yell, loud enough for the whole world to hear.

NINETEEN:

I'T'S BEEN TWO WEEKS SINCE THE BREAKUPS.

Not thinking much, numb really, I pull up to the curb at the airport. Smooth and easy. The Madison airport is a four-terminal outhouse in the middle of Wisconsin. It's a great spot for commuter planes from nearby Midwest cities to fly in. There are a handful of planes daily from New York City, Dallas, or LA. When those planes land, typically the big tippers are on board.

I jumped at my chance for those big tips this afternoon. Hoping that staying in motion would stave off the thoughts of Chelsea, of Sophie, of what happened between us. I've decided to be the vision of utmost corporate brilliance. My shirt starched, my vest and pants dry cleaned, and I polished my shoes twice. I step out of the van and wait on the sidewalk for the arriving guests.

Outside of work, I'm a trainwreck and it's seeping into today. I'm nursing a hangover Hercules would have a tough time handling. Kovski and I have been going through case after case of beer. Every day has been a party with my best friend. When he's not bartending, we're together, hanging out, talking nonsense about women we know or knew, and telling stories from our glory days. The distraction of a steady drunk keeps the blues away.

But this morning, hungover for I don't know how many days in a row, I decided to get my head on straight. Drank an ice-cold glass of water and popped a multivitamin. No more fooling around. I've got to take my life seriously. 30 is much closer than 21 for me. It's time to consider how I present myself to the world and if what I'm doing is the way I want to operate.

Of course, I've had a lot of fun. Too much, some would say. As I tied my tie and tucked in my collared shirt, something new arose in my head—this feeling of professionalism. If I take care of myself, everyone will benefit.

That lasts until now, when I see, backlit by the afternoon sun, an angel. She stalks toward the van, wheeling a large suitcase. On each wing, a man with peppered black hair in a golf polo and a girl, about six, in pigtails and Velcro light-up shoes.

To get some air, I loosen the knot of my tie.

"Rachel Frasier?" I ask, as if meeting her for the first time.

"Right here," she says.

We smile like strangers. A business transaction. Nothing more.

I open the trunk as they drop their luggage on the curb. I hoist the bags into the van, making a neat row.

The man says, "Surprised you don't know her as often as she comes here."

Rachel and I glance at each other. Not sure who should say what they're supposed to say. Rachel takes the lead. "My company recently switched hotels. They have no idea how luxurious this new one is."

"It's a pleasure to have you back then." I say, professionally, a bit too radio voice, I draw it back, "I look forward to getting to know all of you. And who is this?"

The man pats the head of the little girl. She shyly hides her face in his khaki thigh. "Eleanor. Say hi, Ellie."

As quiet as a mouse, Ellie peeps, "Hi."

I'm flabbergasted. She's got Rachel's green eyes. That's all I can notice before she's back to hiding by her dad. I'm surprised she doesn't go to her mother.

"And this is my husband, Tate." Rachel says.

"Welcome to Wisconsin. Name's Danny. I'll be your driver and I'll help you with your luggage when we're back at the hotel. Have you ever been here before?" I slide the last bag into the van.

"First time," he says. "Rachel talks so much about it. I started to worry she moved here without telling me."

"Oh, Tate." Rachel slaps him on the shoulder. Her lips curl into a glamorous smile.

I slam the trunk doors and open the side for them. Ellie clambers aboard first with Tate close behind her in case she stumbles. They head for the far backseats. Children love it back there. Hidden away in their little world. Too bad there's not a lot of leg room for Tate. But as a devoted father, he sits with his daughter.

Rachel meets my gaze. I mouth the words, '*What the fuck?*' She never told me she had a kid!

It's unbelievable that she'd spring this on me without warning. How did she let this go so far without telling me? Why? It reminds me so much of my mom and what she did to my dad. I didn't sign up to be some mom's guilty pleasure. As far as I knew, her marriage was on the rocks. It definitely still is, but there's so much more to it. Rachel has a daughter. What we did will tear their family apart.

Rachel mouths, "*Sorry,*" before she settles into the seat with a view of the driver. I shut the door to the van.

It's a seething silence, as we pass the old Oscar Meyer wiener factory, the Tech College campus, and the multi-family homes on the daffodil-lined road to the Capitol Square. I do my best to swallow the anger roiling in my gut for what Rachel did by starting my tourist routine. My set of questions for newcomers.

I ask, "So, what do you do in the city?"

Rachel smirks, knowing that I know, but Tate suspects nothing, she says, "I'm here to give sales presentations to the doctors at the University Hospital."

"She's a drug dealer," Tate adds.

"Can I have some?" I say. We all politely laugh at my slightly off-color joke.

"Only if you want to get rid of liver disease," Rachel says.

"Might need it, this is Wisconsin after all. Drunkest state in the US."

"It's more like Hep C."

"Ah, not as fun." I cackle again. "And you, sir?"

"I'm an editor." He says it in this behind-the-glasses kind of way, as if being nearsighted somehow makes him more intellectual.

"Like books?" I ask.

"Yep." I might like this guy.

I don't mention my work. It's too forward, but I know where to steer this conversation. "Anything I've read?"

"Oh yes, bestsellers, fiction, non-fiction. Mostly in thrillers and romance," Tate says.

Ellie points out the window at the people in the park. "What are they doing?"

"They're playing frisbee." Tate kisses her head. He asks, "Are we close to campus?"

"You will be," I say, switching lanes through a yellow light. "Here, though, it's residential. A lot of families. Very

few college students out this far. But you'll see the difference as we get closer."

Rachel groans, clenching her stomach. "How much further do you think?"

"Five minutes probably."

Tate asks, "Your tummy again?"

"I told you we shouldn't get the tuna sandwich at the airport."

"What were we going to do? Starve?"

"Order a breakfast sandwich like normal people."

"It looked good! Sorry." Tate says, "Do you want him to pull over?"

Rachel hiccups. "It comes in waves. I think I can make it."

"I'll step on it." I say as I give the van a little extra gas.

"Do you write Danny?" Rachel asks.

"Me?" I say to her face in the rearview. "How did you know?"

"You seem like the type."

Tate says, "What kind of stuff?"

"Poetry. Some call me Madison's Finest Poet."

"Oh yeah? How'd you earn that?" He says.

"It's uh—" I struggle, he's already unmasked me. If I make up a magazine, he'll probably know it and know I'm full of it. "It's uh—it's from college. My poetry professor told me that."

"That's something, I guess. Poetry's hard work." He keeps looking out the window. "Not much money in it either."

"Have you published anything?" Rachel asks me, hinting at one of the first lies I told her.

"In a few online magazines. College newspaper, too. Nothing major. Do you publish much poetry?" I ask him. It's important to know.

"It must be exceptional. A unique voice. Something no one's ever seen before."

"Wow, that's exactly how I write," I say.

Rachel adds, "Maybe you can give Tate a few to look at."

Tate looks at Rachel, wishing she had never said that. He mumbles, "Sure, sure."

We arrive at the hotel, smooth and easy. The beauty of Sunday afternoon traffic. It's lazy. I scamper out of the van. I open the side door for them. They exit. Tate stretches his legs as soon as he hits the street. Rachel walks through the revolving door, following her adventurous daughter.

They check-in as I unload the van. I draw out their luggage and stack it on the bell cart. I meet them at the front desk, where Eva checks them in. Eva? She doesn't work at the front desk. Dave watches over her shoulder as she works. That's right, the boss mentioned she would be training there. Wow, she's moving up. I'm glad to see it.

I have a million questions for Eva, but I stand by because at the rate she's moving, I could smoke a pack of cigarettes. Ellie keeps running off and getting her fingerprints all over the hotel's glass table centerpiece. Tate runs and pulls her back.

Rachel leans against the counter. She taps the corner of her company card on the desk. "Is there—is there any way we can do this later? Can we just get the room key?"

Dave shrugs. "We're almost there. Sorry, we're training today."

Rachel takes a deep breath and clenches her belly again.

Eva focuses on the screen, clicking the mouse through a series of menus. Each click is expected to be the last one, but it goes on and on. She takes Rachel's card and presses it against the machine. "This will go on your room."

Something on the screen catches Eva's eye. Brow furrowed, she moves the mouse.

"No!" Dave yells, reaching for the mouse to stop her.

It's too late, the computer screen goes blank.

"What happened?" Eva asks.

·"The computer asked you to update and restart." Dave says, "We were waiting on the confirmation window, but you hit restart before it was fully loaded. We have to do it over."

Rachel says, "You're kidding me."

"—Stop." Tate yanks Ellie still. Ellie holds still, at least for now.

"Here." Dave moves to the next computer and takes it over.

Eva stands back and watches. Dave goes too quickly for her to understand. Eva notices me looking at her. She glances back at the screen. It's not the time for games. I get it.

Ellie runs off again. Tate yells, "Ellie! Get back here now!" Ellie stops, turns, and weeps. A waterfall of tears cascades down her red cheeks. Her howl shakes the crystals of the chandelier.

Rachel yells at her husband, "Can you please take care of her?"

"What do you think I'm doing?" Tate kneels at Ellie's side. "Shhh. I'm sorry. Daddy didn't mean to yell. It's been a long day of travelling. We're all tired."

Ellie cries. She needs her mother. Rachel knows.

Dave, exhausted, says, "There we go. Your card." Dave takes the card from Rachel.

As Dave charges it, Rachel goes to her daughter. She gets down in front of her. "Hey." She rubs Ellie's hair away from her eyes. "It's okay. It's okay. Mommy's here." Rachel leans her forehead against Ellie's. "Mommy loves you." Ellie sniffles. Rachel hums, and soon enough, Ellie is smiling. "Should we go up to the room? Ooh, then maybe you can have some carrots."

Ellie nods. "Yes!"

Tate takes his daughter's hand and kisses Rachel on the lips. The lucky bastard. She deserves it after those heroics.

Dave calls from the desk, "Your keycards! And credit card."

"I got them," I say, walking to the desk. "I'll meet you by the elevators."

They cross the lobby. Ellie runs ahead.

Tate says, "Hey, hey, slow down!" It's no use. He can't control a six-year-old.

"Remember to give them this." Eva hands me a paper copy of their receipt.

"Thanks." I wink at her.

Dave, his eyes as dead as the moon, says, "Their room is 636."

"Noice." I wink at him, too, to make things equal. He looks away and I join the Frasiers in the elevators. I give them their key cards and receipt before I push the bell cart inside.

The bell cart between us makes the elevator ride feel divided. Rachel, Tate, and their daughter bunched up on the opposite side of me.

Tate asks, "Are you still feeling sick?"

Rachel sighs, "Now that we're on solid ground, I feel better, but I still feel weird."

"Would you like me to bring you antacids?" I ask in a business way.

Rachel peeks at me through the luggage. "No, it's quite alright."

The elevator doors open.

Ellie sprints out first. She heads in the wrong direction. Rachel calls her back, "It's this way." She whirls around and beelines after them.

I bring up the rear, pushing the heavy bell cart. We make our way down the long, carpeted hallway of the sixth floor. Rachel opens the door to their room. Good to see Rachel get it on the first try.

From the hallway, I call out, "Where do you want your bags?" I pull off the heaviest suitcase and set it on the floor.

Tate says, "The closet."

Soon enough, all their suitcases are in a neat row in the closet. As Rachel gets out her laptop and Tate dumps out all the contents of Ellie's backpack onto the bed, I linger, waiting for my tip. "You've got a great view," I announce. It's true. They're face-to-face with the Capitol dome.

Rachel glances out the window, then back to work. "Yes we do."

"Wanna see?" Tate hoists up Ellie so she can see out the window.

"Whoa." Ellie exclaims.

"You should definitely take a walk around the Square after you get settled in." I suggest. "There's also a great Children's Museum a short shuttle ride away."

"That's a good idea. Oh right!" Tate sets Ellie down. "Here." Tate goes to his wallet and digs. He pulls out a business card and hands it to me. "Keep working hard." I take the card from him. It's his contact information with his publishing company. "When you have something ready, send it my way and I'll take a look. No promises."

"I will."

"But only when it's ready," he says.

"Of course."

He puts out his hand. I shake it. His smile is genuine, even hopeful.

I check Rachel. She's too busy with her laptop.

Ellie points to the horse-drawn carriage that makes its rounds of the Capitol Square on Sunday evenings.

"If you need anything, anything at all," I say. "Just call down." I back the cart out of the room.

Before I leave, Rachel calls out, "Thank you."

"You're welcome, Mrs. Frasier."

I close the door behind me. In the hallway, I take the card out of my pocket and look at it. It's embossed with his name in gold lettering. It's heavy too. This is opportunity.

Then again, the cheapskate didn't even tip me.

TWENTY:

copper nickel

SHOTS? SHOTS? SHOTS?" I ASK my co-workers as we arrive at the dive bar. It's Dave's birthday. The whole crew is out: Ryan, Eva, Dave, the bell captain, and the boss, Haseem.

No one says no, so I order us a round at the bar. The Copper Nickel, painted all black, has the vibe of an old western saloon where cowboys go to die. Tired, middle-aged men hang their heads, half-asleep over the bar. At another table, some fellows play sheepshead. Quite the rousing Wednesday night, at least I'm here to liven things up.

The bartender knows Dave by name. If this is Dave's favorite bar, he must hate himself.

That's when I see the dartboard at the center of the back wall. I count our numbers. There are six of us. Too perfect. As the bartender sets down the tequila shots, I say, "Anyone want to do three-on-three darts?"

"Yeah!" Dave creams himself.

Ryan grabs his shot. "It's been a while, but I'm game."

Haseem states, "How 'bout winners get an extra 15 minutes at lunch tomorrow?"

I say, "That settles it, we're playing."

Eva asks, "How do you play?"

The bell captain interjects, "You don't know how to play?"

Dave jumps in on his chance. "I can teach you. It's easy." We all know he's got a thing for Eva. Too bad he won't be getting his birthday kiss tonight. Not with me around.

The only reason why I'm here is that, for the first time since Eva and I met, I am single. Eva is single. Naturally, we'll need to discuss this. It's a common problem, you see, an affliction, really, that we can relieve in each other. Our loneliness has such a simple cure after all—togetherness.

"I call playing with the birthday boy," I say, knowing Dave will want to play with Eva.

As I guessed, Dave says, "Eva, if you want to learn, you should join us."

"Sure." Eva joins our side.

"Let's go!" The bell captain slaps hands with Ryan and Haseem. Dave, Eva, and I take our shots with them. A collective moan carries through the group as the rail tequila burns our throats.

The bartender gives us the steel-tipped darts and a pitcher of beer.

As I follow the crew to the dartboard, I realize that Eva is quite the lucky woman. She's in the company of five men. Five potential suitors. She could pick any of us. Sure, Ryan is a long shot, and Haseem is gay. That leaves the bell captain and Dave, or me.

Not the toughest competition, but it's a delicate situation. The boss can't see us flirting too much, or he'll suggest we fill out one of those stupid HR forms. Paperwork

is not sexy. Before we reach that level, I must seduce Eva first. To do that, I've got to be the best version of myself—respectful and eager to please.

I will show her how good a man I can be. By closing time, we'll sneak off to her home together. I smirk at the thought that I'll finally have a bed to sleep in again.

Dave demands we play 501. A dart game where every number scored is deducted from 501. First team to hit zero wins. Simple enough in theory.

As I pluck the darts from the worn-out corkboard, I imagine how many of us have come through this hall, played these games we're playing, and lived the life I am living. Places don't change. The people do. In a dive like this, I am a guest today and a ghost tomorrow.

Eva's fingertips graze mine as I pass her the blue darts. New electricity shoots through me. For a moment, I forget the past and future, living only in the here and now. Her touch is a supernova to my fluttering heart.

After Haseem makes a few bankable 15s, it's Eva's turn. She steps up to the line. Dave is there, eager to play coach. Haseem and I exchange a glance—we both know the game Dave's playing. I lean against the high top, sipping my beer.

Dave adjusts and readjusts Eva's stance like he's sculpting wet clay. The bell captain finally says, "Let her shoot already."

Dave backs off. "You're right. You're right. You've got this." He crosses his arms and chews his mustache.

Eva flings the dart and narrowly misses the jackalope head hanging in the corner.

"Okay, okay," Dave says. "Straighten the shoulders. Release right at the top. Like this—" He mimes the motion and pauses. "Right at the top. See? Right at the top."

Eva pauses mid-throw and the dart clatters to the floor.

"You still need to follow through," Dave says.

I step in. "Here—do you mind if I touch you?"

She nods.

I stand behind her, far enough not to be creepy. Guiding her shoulder and hand, I say, "Release here, then follow through—like this." I sweep her arm across her body, adding airplane noises. Eva giggles, her entire body vibrating beneath my hands. The other guys just got a masterclass in how to touch a woman.

"Got it?" I say.

"Yep." She lines up and throws. It smacks the upper left corner of the board. No points, but Eva shrieks, "I hit the board!" Who's there to greet her? Me.

We bounce hand-in-hand together, smiling. Dave can only watch.

The game settles into a smooth rhythm. With so many players, chatter fills the downtime. Haseem keeps swiping, convinced the bartender is somewhere on his apps. No luck yet. I tell him to go talk to the guy. He shrugs it off, claiming he isn't really interested, just curious.

Ryan talks about his novel. Eva knows a lot about it. She seems really into it. Or into him? No, that's impossible. Ryan lives in her friend zone. Either way, she suggests Ryan adds a love story between a human and an alien. Ryan lights up, giddy, thumbing notes into his phone as she speaks.

Eva doesn't see when I hit the bullseye. I try to tell her, to tell everyone that I hit it. Dave says, "Good job." We both peek at Eva.

She talks to the bell captain now. As he goes to the line, he tells her to watch how it's done. Steadying his feet, he shakes out his neck and breathes deep. He positions

the dart between his fingers and looks at me, leering. He throws, blind.

Bullseye. Dead center. Eva claps, gushing. "That was incredible."

The bell captain throws again. It smacks the board, and Dave and I groan. Eva asks, "What does the color mean?"

"Triple 20," the bell captain says.

He throws one more time. 14.

Dave gets up and yells. "House rules! You owe us a pitcher."

"Oh, come on, you got to mention it at the beginning of the game!" the bell captain says.

"How many times have we played together?" Dave retorts.

"What do you want, birthday boy?"

"Only the best. Old Milwaukee, of course," Dave takes the darts from him. He's up.

"What happened?" Eva asks.

I shrug.

Dave says, "If you hit the 14, which is hard to hit by accident as a right-handed player. You have to buy a pitcher."

Eva and I watch shoulder to shoulder as Dave shoots. I ask her if she needs more beer. She does. I fill her cup. Thinking there's just enough left for my pint, I pour the rest of the pitcher into mine, too strong and fast. Foam spills over, beer splashing the floor. I ignore it.

"Someone got too excited," Eva says.

"Happens from time to time." I tap her glass. "See you at the bottom." When the beer touches my lips, I don't stop, every gulp more refreshing than the last. I drink it till it's gone.

"Thirsty?" She comments.

I hold back a burp in my throat. "You were supposed to go too. That's what 'see you at the bottom' means."

"Oh, sorry. I don't like to chug."

"It's okay. I don't know what I was thinking. It's been a tough few days. Sophie and I broke up."

"Are you okay?" Eva asks.

Hugging me, her sudden squeeze squeezes out an air bubble lodged deep in my gut, and I burp in her ear. "Sorry." I wipe my mouth after that one. "I asked her to marry me. She said no."

Heads turn.

"You asked Sophie to marry you?" Ryan says.

I nod.

"I didn't hear that part of the story." Ryan hugs me. "I'm sorry."

"You should be." I remind him.

Dave asks, "Is it because you hooked up with that guest?"

The bell captain comes back with a foamy pitcher of beer. "You hooked up with a guest?"

"I didn't hook up with anyone." I lie, irritation creeping in. "Who told you that?"

Dave glances at Eva. Did she gossip about me? I feel betrayed.

"Which guest?" The bell captain asks.

"Dark hair, always dressed in stilettos, New York accent," Dave says.

"You hooked up with Mrs. Fraiser?" The bell captain offers a fist bump. I don't take the bait.

"There's nothing going on between her and me." I insist.

"I actually saw what happened," Ryan says. "Danny hugged her. That's all." I appreciate the backup, but it

confirms that I did, at least, meet her face-to-face.

"No, no," Eva says, "he definitely kissed her right outside the lobby." Heat flares across my cheeks.

"You saw?" The bell captain gasps. Eva nods. "Dude, her family is visiting this week."

Haseem asks, "Why were you even out with her in the first place?"

"That guest you're referring to: Rachel," I say, giving myself some time to come up with a story. "She and I went to the same writing classes together. She lives in New York with her husband now. He and their daughter are visiting with her this week."

Haseem says, "Uh-huh."

"You took writing classes in New York?" Dave says.

"Online writing classes," I say.

"What's the name of the website? Was it helpful?" Givens asks.

"I'll tell you later."

"Hey, boss," the bell captain asks with a sly smile. "Ever slept with a hotel guest?"

"No." Haseem nails a 19 on the dartboard. "Have I wanted to? Hell yeah."

"How about you?" I ask Eva.

"No," Eva says, "They're here today, gone tomorrow."

"That's the point," I say.

"So, you have, Danny?" Dave asks me.

"Have I what?" I say.

"Slept with a guest?" Dave reiterates.

"No, of course not."

Ryan butts in. "I haven't either. Can we go back to the game?"

Haseem admits, "I wanted to fuck this one guy so bad. He was dancing at the Overture. He gave me his number, but

I couldn't, you know."

"Really?" I say.

The bell captain adds, "I think we've all dreamt about it."

I should mention what I did. Bask in the glory.

Eva says, "But to do it, though. It's dirty."

"So dirty," I say to mask my guilt. Taking the chance to change subjects, I offer Eva the darts. "Your turn."

Eva takes them. "Sorry again about Sophie." She rubs my shoulder. It reminds me that someone cares.

We cycle through a few more rounds. Eva hits a double 20 and she's jovial. We inch toward zero. Sadly, no one wants to invest in another pitcher. They complain that they have work in the morning. So do I, but if they're not into it, they're not into it. This will be our only game.

It's down to the wire, so we decide to go dart for dart. We need a clean 15 to win. They need a 17. Good thing, it's my turn.

I step to the line and fire. I hit the 16. Useless. To win, we need exactly zero. The bell captain answers with a 20. Next throw, I hit a one. Now, we need the dreaded 14 to win. He sinks the bullseye. Too bad it doesn't matter.

For me, it's do-or-die. If I hit the 14, I'll be a hero. They'll have to stick around for another drink, and Eva will be so impressed that she'll fall deeply in love with me.

I imagine that life. A rose garden and an endless meadow. She wears a sundress as she picks wine grapes from the vine. Our kids frolic in the grass.

Back in reality, I hurl the game-winning dart. It sails wide and punctures the crotch of a Clint Eastwood movie poster on the back wall.

"Shit."

The bell captain pats me on the back and steps up to the line. Calm, deliberate, he aims. The dart arcs and lands

just outside the 17. He grunts. "So close."

It's Dave versus Ryan now. Dave goes first. He nails the 14 in one shot. Eva leaps into his arms. He's the hero. Game over.

I give him a high-five and announce, "You've got to buy us a round."

"Next time! Gotta work in the morning."

"Rules are rules," I say. "And it's your birthday."

Dave shakes his head. "You of all people know that you can break the rules. I've got to bounce, but it was so awesome hanging with everyone."

"Same. I've got to go," the bell captain says. Ryan and Haseem echo the same sentiment.

"Come on, one more round," I say. "I'm staying out."

"Sorry, Danny," Dave says, "I'll see you tomorrow."

"Eva, are you staying?"

"I can't. I need to get some sleep."

"Fine," I say, wishing for an invitation to her bed.

They all walk out together. I catch up.

Outside The Copper Nickel, like smokers, we hang out and laugh some more. We trade stupid work stories we'll forget and retell the next time we're out. These nothing moments mean more than the words. The camaraderie unites us.

While we linger, I squint at a certain window on the sixth floor of the Continental. There are no lights on, but in there, Rachel and her family sleep.

Rachel hid her kid from me. I should be upset, but instead, I feel closer to her somehow—as if our secret lets me into her world. Watching Ellie in her light-up shoes, so innocent and thrilled for the smallest things, makes everything feel new again.

When we all go our separate ways, Ryan gives me

a back-cracking hug. "Take care of yourself," he says. He walks Eva home. Apparently, they both live off Willy Street. It's a good neighborhood. A bit too far from the action for me.

While I walk back to Kovski's, not really drunk, but not really sober. For the first time in a long time, I feel content. Being out with people without getting obliterated resets something inside me.

A poem drifts into my mind—

Life isn't about winning.
We all lose in the end.
It's how you go about being a person,
big or small, that makes the difference

We all race through well-worn paths
in life dodging death.

Lend a hand.
Kindness turns a cold day warm
and brings back the soft edges
of our unrelenting world.

TWENTY-ONE:

LEAN ON THE VALET STAND. It's a sunny day, but cool enough to be outside with long sleeves and not sweat. The perfect place to avoid Dave and the lot of them. Everyone except Ryan is here today. Somehow, none of them are hungover, not even Dave, and it was his birthday.

Pissing and moaning won't do a damn thing. I chugged a bottle of water and a vat of electrolytes before work this morning. Never saw Kovski last night. Got home after he went to bed, and I got out before he woke up. He should appreciate that.

The radio at the valet stand crackles. It's Eva. "We've got Rachel Frasier coming down for a ride to the University Hospital."

I reply, professional, concise, no funny business, "I'll pull the van out front."

"Thank you."

The only time this tone comes out is at work. I am a different man here than I am anywhere else. Or at least, that's what the hotel expects me to be. In that expectation, I treat every guest with the highest of white glove service. I might as well jerk them off with a smile plastered across my expressionless face. The guest must be happy, by any means necessary.

It's business, you say. Without me, some other poor college kid would have to polish the bell carts. I'm expendable. My whole life, a story I repeat daily—

Sorry, I am so hungover. I can tell when I start over-philosophizing.

As I bring the van up to the curb, Rachel, in an open-back blue dress, crosses the lobby. Her briefcase slung around her shoulder. She hides her gaze behind big black sunglasses.

Dave points her out to the curb, where I stand by the van. Her smile fades as soon as our eyes meet.

Like the professional I am, I open the van door for her. She climbs in. I swagger to the driver's seat.

Adjusting the rearview so I can see her better, I ask Rachel, "University Hospital?"

"Yeah." Rachel sighs, looking out the window.

There's something off about her today. Usually, she's at least feisty.

"How's your family enjoying Madison?" I ask.

"Ellie loves it. Tate goes on and on about finding a place to live around here."

"It's not a bad place to raise a kid."

"Are you from around here?"

"Me? No." I say, "I grew up in a farm town in the north that no one's ever heard of."

"Do your parents still live there?"

"One of them does."

"Divorced?" Rachel arches her brow.

"Yep."

She frowns. "That's rough."

"I turned out alright." I don't tell Rachel how she's

helped me understand my mom's reason for cheating better than ever before.

"You think that's where Tate and I are headed? Divorce?"

"Yea," I say. "Yea, I do. Why'd you invite your family to the hotel?"

"They surprised me with tickets to Madison. Wish they would've told me because it's stressful enough having to work here, let alone having to show them around." Her mouth folds into a frown. "Can we—can we take the scenic route?" She digs into her purse and pulls out a pack of cigarettes.

"Of course," I make the turn into the university campus. The sophomore move-in is happening. Much more life fills these once deserted hills. Professors' cars park behind the academic buildings. Summer vacation nears its end.

"Did you tell your husband?"

"God, no. Could you imagine?"

"Yeah," I say, "I don't think he would've given me his card if you did."

"You're welcome by the way," she says. "Seriously follow up with him."

"Isn't it in bad taste? I mean you and me fucked."

"Listen. We made a mistake. That's all. We can't let it affect the rest of our lives."

I say, "It was a beautiful mistake."

Rachel doesn't say she agrees, but her silent smile says it all.

I bypass the hilltop where we stopped last time. The dorm parking lot is crowded with parents and their kids. Rachel doesn't notice the change in course. I take her somewhere I haven't been since my freshman year. Along the way, I point out my old college dorm, a three-story brick building built in the 1920s, standing amongst a cluster of sleek new steel-and-glass dorms.

"I broke up with Sophie," I say.

"You did?" Rachel asks.

"I had to," I say. "I can't possibly cheat on someone and still be in love with them."

"Where are we going?" She looks around. We're on a back road headed to the Lakeshore Nature Preserve. If you know where to look, you can still see the chimneys of the University Hospital above the parking garages nearby.

"This is a Madison secret," I say.

I turn into a small grove, where a gravel parking lot meets the cattail shore of the lake. "We used to come here to smoke pot and drink," I tell her. I cut the engine and hop out.

I get the door for her.

She says, "I don't know Danny. Maybe you should just drop me off."

"We're already out here. Come on. I need a smoke as much as you do."

I lead her down a thin, dirt path. Pushing aside the cattails, I reveal an ancient log and a makeshift fire pit on the shoreline. The water laps against the pebbles.

"Okay," she says. "We can hang out here for a minute."

"That's what I thought."

Rachel sits on the log and pulls out two cigs. Both in her mouth, she flicks her lighter. It doesn't catch. I try to block the wind with my hands. When that doesn't work, I shield Rachel with my body. We edge closer together. The flame wavers, teasing the tip, almost catching, almost catching.

Smoke escapes the cigs as she puffs.

I sit back down beside her. She hands me one. I put it to my mouth. It's wet with her saliva. I savor it and breathe in a silver haze.

The water laps against the shoreline. Frogs chirp amongst the lily pads. The nicotine buzz sends a shiver down my spine. I can't believe my luck. This exquisite woman beside me, all mine. Not even her husband got this much time with her this morning.

Rachel lets out a deep fog. She flicks the ash off her cigarette. "You think I should leave my husband?"

I inhale too much and cough. "Woof. You've got a kid together. You still love him?" I tap my cig.

"I can't imagine my life without him. He's part of my everything," she says. "How could I possibly let him go? And what about Ellie?"

"But do you love him?"

"It's different now. Or I'm different. I have to accept he's the one."

"You should tell him you want to sleep with other people but always come home to him."

"That's not love." Rachel blows out a hail of smoke.

"You think he ever cheated on you?"

"No, never. He's so good with Ellie and talking things out with me, I don't even think he's looked at other women since he met me. The other night, I was drunk," she says. "You took advantage of me."

"Is that also what you think happened the night we kissed again?" I say, recalling the headache I went through afterwards with Ryan. "I know you weren't drunk."

"What do you want me to say?" Rachel asks me, her eyes wide and her voice pleading. She's not mad. She wants me to stop reminding her of all the wrongs she's done.

I say. "Tell me what you want from me."

"What really happened between you and your girlfriend?"

I puff my cig. I let out a smoky sigh. "She found out about our kiss and that was that. Five years gone." I don't mention Chelsea. Rachel doesn't need the whole truth, just enough to know we ruined each other's lives, perhaps for some greater purpose. "Your turn."

"That's awful. I'm so sorry." She considers her words. "It doesn't feel real anymore. My life. My family. What happened between us. It's like I'm wearing someone else's clothes. Like I put on this mommy costume whenever Ellie's around, and when she's not, I tear it off and I'm myself. I'm young and untethered again in this big, beautiful world. With them here, I'm really, really stressed out. I want to be the best mom, and I want to work hard, but I want to have my own thoughts sometimes."

Rachel stomps out her cigarette and kisses me.

Our tongues meet heavy and wet. Tobacco smoke lingering on our breaths. Rachel pulls away and wipes her mouth. "I'm sorry. We should go." She gets up and walks through the cattails back to the van.

I toss my cig into the lapping water and follow her.

Rachel left the side door wide open. I go to close it. Inside, Rachel sits, her dress slipping up to reveal the cream of her thigh. "I don't know what's the matter with me." She says, running her fingertips down her neck and into her cleavage. "I'm just so hot. Feel me. I'm sweating." She reaches for my hand and pulls me beside her. She wraps my palm around her knee.

"I can help you cool down." I open the center console between the front seats and pull out an ice-cold bottle of water. I roll the cool, sweating plastic along Rachel's neck and watch as goosebumps prickle her skin.

"That feels so good," She lays her head back. Unmistakable scent wafts through the air. Weakly, Rachel whispers, "Are we bad people?"

"Not at all," I say. "Bad people don't care, and we care."

"And yet, we do it anyway." She lifts her head to me. Her eyes glazed by the orange of the sunlight.

"Sometimes the worst things are the best things. Where would you be if you never met me?" I say.

"Trapped in a sexless marriage," she says. "Oh wait, I still am."

Eager to make her forget, I rise, and I kiss her on the lips. As I pull away, she yanks me down by my tie and kisses me harder. When she lets go, she says, "Can you tell me a poem?"

"You want to hear a poem right now?"

"Tate used to write poetry all the time. I miss it. Those spontaneous moments. He always called me his muse."

"Are you going to be my muse?" I trace the line of her jaw with my gaze.

A smirk pricks her cheeks. "If you can handle me."

"What should the poem be about?" I ask.

"Whatever you're thinking."

My mind races through all the possibilities of what I could say. I could talk about the van, her eyes, the shore, how we're chained to earth for eternity. That we're born screaming and we've been screaming since our birth. But those words carry no heat. She needs something sexy to light her up. I say, "Nothing's coming to me."

"I thought you were a poet?"

"I am. I need a spark of inspiration." I glance at her lips. She knows.

Rachel bites her lip in anticipation. Our mouths connect and we lock our tongues, wet with a cool mixture of longing and sadness. Her hands find my crotch.

I say between breaths, a poem—

Your love dies quick
unless I feed the flames
reignite a spark
stoke your heart
as night burns away.
From the ashes,
the rose sun rises
greeting the new day.
As you take me higher,
our wings set ablaze
we tumble into the fire
I'm lost in your gaze
The words keep repeating
how lucky are we
how lucky are we

"How lucky are we?" Rachel says, her green eyes smoldering. Her fingers slide below my waist and unzip my fly. The captain greets her at the door.

Eva's voice crackles over the dispatch radio. "Danny, we have two guests that—"

Clicking off the dispatch, I pull Rachel into the far backseat, where we can lie down. It's still cramped. She manages to rustle down her panties and toss them away while I put on a condom. She slides beneath me, her hand gripping the captain.

"Are you sure?" I dare to ask.

For a moment, she considers the question. We could stop now with our relative innocence still intact.

Her grip tightens around the captain. Then again, we already committed the original sin.

Rachel pulls me inside her. The addiction to our lust pours out of us. Rachel groans until she can't breathe. The press of her skin sends shockwaves through my fingers as I grope her. My pulse races. I've never felt more alive.

When she's on top, the low ceiling forces her to lean over me. Her breasts slap against my face. She rides me up and down. Letting the heat of the moment grow between us.

She's excited to be taking action, to be doing something for herself, and to show the world she didn't get old, the love got old. Her breath gets hotter, faster, and heavier. The windows fog. I can feel her betrayal, her anger, and the frustration as she pounds herself into me. Even if it's wrong, she won't stop doing it. She lets out a painful howl as she thrusts hard, taking everything I have inside her.

And I give her everything, I give her my soul, my body, and what's left of my love. She takes it all. She takes everything until she's full. She winces from deep inside herself and collapses against me.

I bask in my glorious release—in disbelief that I just had sex in the hotel van.

The cold drip of tears runs down my chest. Her mouth fills with air, but her lungs don't. She lets out a long sob. Her body quakes. Slowly, she peels her body off me and crawls to the seat behind the driver. Shivering, she curls up against the van window.

She shuts her eyes. "Danny," she whimpers. "Take me to the hospital."

It is a short, silent drive. She sleeps the entire way. I don't turn on the radio. I don't disturb her. When I pull up to the hospital curb and open the door for her, Rachel jolts upright. Her body language hardens. Back to business—there are sales to be made.

On the sidewalk, I hope for her to kiss me goodbye. Instead, Rachel takes me by my hands, and she looks at me as if about to say something. She blinks heavily as she takes a deep breath. When she opens them again, they're big, watery, and sorry. Her forehead creases with the fine lines of the years that divide us.

I want to say something too, but I don't know what to say.

Rachel shakes her head as she lets go of my hands. There's nothing left to say. It was fun while it lasted. She turns away and fixes the bunched-up hem of her dress with a tug of her fingers.

Through the glass, she checks in with security. I wait for her to look back at me, but she never does. She disappears down some infinite hall I'll never know. Whatever we had is over. She put the fire out.

I forget about the emptiness the moment after brings, when we get what we craved, and there is nothing to feel now except the feeling of knowing. And once we know, we miss when we once didn't.

TWENTY-TWO:

ON THE WAY BACK, I ANSWER the frantic hotel dispatch calls. Eva's upset that I haven't been responding. Apparently, two guests are waiting for me to give them a ride. I blame traffic and the sophomore move-in day. That's the simplest response. Weekdays are always unpredictable anyway.

When I pull up to the curb, waiting for me is Tate and Ellie. I'm getting the full family treatment today. I adjust my collar, fix my tie, and straighten my nametag. As far as anyone is concerned, it was a routine commute to the University Hospital.

"What a great day," I announce. "I get to take care of the whole Frasier fam. Sorry for the delay. Traffic was horrendous. So where are we going?"

Opening the side door for them, Ellie dives in first. She heads straight to the far backseat. Part of me fears it's still warm with her mother's heat, but it's preposterous. Just the tendrils of guilt I need to cut off before they choke me.

"Children's Museum," Tate says.

"That's fun," I say, in the direction of Ellie.

Before Tate gets in, he stops and digs in his pocket. "I've got to apologize. I was so distracted the other day. I forgot to tip." He shoves a twenty into my palm. "I get so caught up in what I do now that I forget how it was when I was younger. Keep hustling, Danny. That's what you've got to do to be a poet. Shit like this. Opening doors for people and whatnot. But take it from me, never, never stop writing."

"Thank you," I say, as sincerely as any man can say after fucking another man's wife. I slide the bill into my back pocket.

"Ew, Daddy! Look underpants!" Ellie squeals. She holds up a pair of rumpled-up pink women's panties.

Out of parental instinct, Tate grabs the underwear without hesitation. He drops them. "They're wet!"

Splayed out, we all stare at the pink panties on the black top. A car honks past the van.

"These look like—" Tate picks them up again. His fingers pinch a small pink flower embroidered into the satin. Trembling, he turns to me his eyes the size of a knife point.

I try to salvage the realization. "I'm so sorry, sir. This is embarrassing. Guests sometimes forget things in the van. I'll take them and dispose of them." I hold out my palm, hoping to take away the evidence.

Tate calls into the van, "Come on Ellie."

"But Dad, I thought we were going to the Children's Museum?"

"Get out of the van!" Tate demands.

Tate balls up his wife's panties and grabs his daughter's hand to help her out of the van. On the street, he yanks her along as he heads back into the lobby. Ellie looks back at me, unsure why I can't drive them wherever they want to go.

I shut the doors to the van and hang around the van's bumper to peer into the glass lobby.

Through the glass, Tate waves his arms wildly at Eva. Dave stands by rubbing his chin in disbelief. Together, they hear out Rachel's cuckolded husband. He pulls out the pink panties. The proof of our indiscretion, still wet with her desire.

His story draws the attention of the bell captain. Soon, Haseem. Everyone listens, shocked.

The Oscar-winning moment: Tate drops his elbows on the counter, thrusts his face into his hands, and weeps. Eva gives him a box of tissues.

Somehow, they all know where I'm hiding. Their eyes find mine. Haseem curls his finger at me, his lip stern.

As I enter the lobby through the valet door, the bell captain helps Tate and Ellie find their way to the elevator. Haseem leads me down the hallway beneath the grand staircase.

On the velvet carpet, I follow Haseem's muffled steps to the corporate wing of the hotel. This is where the Continental managerial offices reside. Haseem leads me into the conference room where I usually pilfer bagels and cream cheese from guest business seminars. Hopefully, it's about that.

I can hope, but we all know the truth.

"Explain." The hotel owner, Vincent Flores, asks me from the other end of the conference table. His arms crossed over his Armani suit. It's rare to see him in the flesh. He usually enters and exits through a different entrance on the alley side of the hotel.

Haseem and the head of HR, Brenda, sit by each of Mr. Flores' shoulders. His years as the boss chiseled the leather of his face. He is clean-cut on all the details down to the close crop of his hair. His impeccable suit is decorated with a single breast pocket pin: a sapphire set in gold. It's piercing like his eyes.

Beneath the fluorescent glow of the office boardroom, I'm guilty as charged. I should come clean. But if I come clean, I know I'm out of a job. I'm not going to incriminate myself in this court of law. Too bad this situation is a crime of passion that yields no jail sentence. I deflect. "What do you think happened?"

"A guest reported his 6-year-old daughter finding his wife's underwear in the back of your van. The guest accuses you of committing sexual acts with his wife inside of hotel property. What do you say to that?"

"It's preposterous. Do you have any idea of how crazy that sounds?" When in doubt, question the accuser.

Brenda crosses her arms and leans back. My argument makes her reconsider. In truth, this kind of thing has never happened before at this hotel. What can I say? I'm a Renaissance man.

Haseem asks, "Why did your drive to the University Hospital take so long?"

"Traffic," I shake my head. "The guest asked to take the scenic route, which I thought would be faster than the normal way. But no, it's Sophomore move-in day on campus, and well, we got caught." I even believe what I'm saying at this point.

"And your failure to respond when we called?" Haseem presses.

"I had turned down the radio to listen to the guest tell me a story. I forgot to turn it back up until after I dropped her off. Once again, my fault."

"At what point do you think she took off her underwear?" Mr. Flores asks.

"You want me to answer that?" I say. "I highly doubt she took her panties off in my van without me noticing. Maybe they fell out of her briefcase. Or somehow got scrunched up in her clothes?"

The bell captain charges in. "They're all settled in. I gave them a gift card for room service." He takes a seat at the table. "Where are we?"

Mr. Flores says, "We're trying to determine how the pant—women's underwear were found in the van."

I say, "Hey, maybe it is my fault. I didn't do a van check this morning. Could've been left over from Ryan's shift last night."

This draws a few chuckles from the bell captain and Haseem.

The bell captain pipes in, "Did he mention how him and the guest have been seen kissing?"

"She has a husband!" I snipe.

"He was bragging about it the other night."

"I was not," I say. "I was squashing the rumor."

Haseem states, "We should call Eva in here. She saw it happen."

"Do it," I say, sweat snaking down my back. "She'll tell the truth." By that, I mean, she'll lie for me. At least, that's what I hope.

Mr. Flores asks the bell captain to bring in Eva. He runs out of the room. While he's gone, it's quiet. Mr. Flores stares straight ahead. Not at me. But over me. I check what he's looking at. It's one of those inspirational posters that reads, '*Courage*,' and has an eagle soaring over a jagged mountain.

Brenda reads emails on her phone. Haseem twiddles his thumbs. I flip a pen over and over on the tabletop and think about what I'd do without this job. I'll be fully and completely untethered. No job, no house, no woman, nothing. That's why I won't let them take away the only thing I have left.

The door swings open. The bell captain steps in, followed by Eva. She stops at the middle of the table, all eyes on her.

"Thank you for joining us, Eva," Brenda says. "We need to ask you one thing. Did you see Daniel kiss the hotel guest's wife?"

Eva plays with her bracelet, rotating it as she considers what to say.

Haseem adds, "This is a safe place, Eva. You will not be in trouble no matter your answer."

Eva's eyes search mine. They glisten and her lip trembles as if apologizing. She turns to Mr. Flores and admits, "Danny kissed her outside of the hotel entrance a few weeks back. It was late and he wasn't wearing his work uniform, but I recognized both of them."

I scowl at Eva. Traitor. She buries her gaze in the floor.

Yet, her answer makes the situation more confusing. Technically, I wasn't on hotel property, and there was no identification linking me to the hotel.

"See? I did nothing wrong." If they can't determine an answer, I'll stake my claim of victory.

"So, it's true? You did engage with the guest's wife prior?"

My overconfidence got to me. I backtrack. "As soon as I discovered she had a husband and child, I cut off all ties to her."

"Except you took her to the University Hospital this morning, in fact volunteered when her identity was revealed," Mr. Flores says.

"I'm just doing my job. The bell captain needs to be at his post, right?"

"With the length of time you were gone, it's clear to me that someone is not telling the truth. Which

keeps coming back to you. So, I'm going to ask you one more time, did you or did you not engage in a sexual relationship with the hotel guest?"

"If I tell you no, you won't believe me. If I admit that I fucked her, you'll fire me. What reason do I have to answer your question?"

"Very smart, Mr. Clark," Mr. Flores says. "But guilt finds its way to truth by other means. We can check security footage and I'm sure we'll find the proof we need. Why bother with all that? Because you're right. No matter what you say, you and I know the truth."

"That I fucked her?" I say and Brenda gasps. "Is that what you need to hear?" I say with finality.

"Watch your language," Mr. Flores says. "Now, is that true?"

"I did. Ask anyone. It's the dream. And I did it. I fucked her in her hotel room. I fucked her in the van. She wanted it, and it felt so fuckin' good."

Ripping off my nametag, I say, "Don't bother firing me—I quit." I toss it on the table. I undo my tie. "I don't know what the big deal is. It's just sex. We all do it." I strip the vest from my shoulders and unbutton my shirt.

"Daniel, please," Mr. Flores says. "Leave with dignity."

I unzip my pants and drop them to the floor. "This job took my dignity." They catch on my shoes, but I yank them off anyway.

The bell captain grabs my arm. "Come on, let's go." He drags me out of there in my undershirt, white boxers, and tall black socks.

"Thanks a lot, Eva," I say as I pass her. Her eyes examine the floor.

My black patent leather shoes echo across the marble lobby. Loud enough for everyone to notice. I glance over to Dave on my way out. He pretends not to see me.

The bell captain leads me through the revolving door. The same door, a new guy, who looks just like me, will be entering for his first day on the job soon.

On the sidewalk, the bell captain leans his elbow on the valet stand. "Dude, you're something else. Between you and me, I would've done the same thing." He sticks out his hand. "If I ever see you out, I'm going to buy you a drink."

I should be happy for the kinship. I shake his hand, my own cold and clammy. A BMW rolls up to the curb. The bell captain turns to me. "Now, get the fuck out of here. You're making us look like shit." He waits, perfect posture, hands behind his back, for the driver's door to open.

Unsure what to do, I walk back to Kovski's. A car honks past. The driver catcalls me. The summer wind nips at my naked thighs.

TWENTY-THREE:

OVSKI'S IN THE KITCHEN, EATING a banana when I tell him the news. He shrugs. "It's about fuckin' time. That job was eating your soul." He stuffs the rest in his mouth and garbles, "You can finally show the world what a great writer you are."

That thought knocks me off my feet. I sit at the dinner table. It's covered in his old mail, empty glasses with sticky purple residue at the bottom, and the crumbs of a hundred breakfast sandwiches. I brush off the top with a swipe of my hand before I hide my head between my elbows.

"You're really surprised?" Kovski asks. He tosses the banana peel over his shoulder and into the sink for no other reason than he can. "What were you thinking?"

"I couldn't help myself. How do you say no when a woman has her legs wide open?"

Kovski cackles. "That's a good question. Lesson learned. Now you know why you should say no."

"I'll never forget that look in her husband's eyes," I say, pointing at my own. "All the veins turned bright red. I've never heard a grown man sob like that."

"Oh, he cried!" Kovski lights his bong. "That poor guy." He rips it. A grey plume curls through the pipe and into his mouth. He lets out a gust of smoke.

"Give me that," I say. "I've got to live a little."

"That's what I'm talking about!" Kovski says, handing over the bong.

I put my mouth to the hole and flick the lighter. Kovski pinches the plug. "Allow me."

I breathe deep, the bong filling with smoke. The bowl burns orange. Kovski smiles. "Keep breathing." A thundercloud of smoke awaits release. He lifts the bowl and the rush of fog hits my lungs. I take it all in, hold it for as long as I can, and let out a silver haze.

My sobriety disappears. I fall languid onto his couch. The checkered floors of the house skew. Kovski walks tilted across the living room, calling through a megaphone, "So, what are you going to do now?"

"If I knew, I would tell you." I lay back into my pillow and close my eyes letting the marijuana high set in. A technicolor tapestry plays against my eyelids.

"Rest up, buddy," Kovski says. "Maybe start looking at apartments."

"Sure. Sure," I murmur, dissolving into chemical nirvana.

The days pass and I turn into a shell of a human being. Because I said I quit, I can't get unemployment. I dig into my savings. At the same time, I don't have the strength to do much else other than play video games and watch movies. Kovski and I get along great though. When he's home, he joins in whatever reverie I'm in.

Besides the daily hangovers, it's so good, I even

consider asking Kovski if he could clean out his office so I could get a proper bedroom. We're best friends. He could never say no to that.

When we're good and drunk, I'll ask him. He begged me to come out. It's the start of Labor Day weekend. Which means, it's the first weekend when all the college students have moved in. Also, it's the last weekend before school starts. The swagger and gravitas of youth invades State Street. Bars host lines out the door. Music blasts from the balconies of twelve-story high-rises. Everywhere, new co-eds breathe life into the city.

At Paradise, known by locals as The Dice, we order two double Long Islands. The old bar, a Wisconsin shack that hasn't been redecorated since your grandpa went to college, makes the meanest Long Island.

Experienced drinkers, like Kovski and I, laugh at our decision. Any night that begins at The Dice ends up a little fuzzy.

We clank our pints together. We swirl the straw—they never mix it all the way, usually there's a thick layer of vodka on top. Then we drink, it's cold and refreshing with the burn I crave. I'm about to pull away when Kovski tips the bottom of my cup. He keeps drinking with a smile at the corner of his mouth. I chug the Long Island.

Dry slurps strike the air. Time for another drink. He pushes me to the bartender. "Get me another one," he says. "I'll grab us a table."

Drinks in hand, I find him in the backroom, where a group of frat guys shoot pool. Kovski sits at a cigarette-scorched laminate table, holding a whiskey shot, a tray of empty shot glasses in front of him. He leans toward a raven-haired woman with dark lips and a tight black tank top that makes her cleavage pop. They tap glasses and toss them back in unison.

I set his Long Island between them on the slick and sticky tabletop and pull up a chair next to Kovski.

"Howdy," I say, settling into my seat.

They ignore me. Kovski stammers, "No, no, no, women lure men in and use marriage to keep us around."

Her golden eyes brighten with anger. "You think women are the aggressors?"

"All men want to do is fuck and move on."

"Some women are like that too," the woman says.

"I second that," I say, sipping my Long Island. I forgot to stir it, and the rail vodka makes me cough.

"I remember my first drink." She laughs at me.

"Ha-ha," I say, catching my breath. "Where'd you learn that one? A high schooler?"

"As a matter of fact, I did."

"Nanny?" Kovski quips.

"In another life, I am a teacher," she decrees.

Maybe it's the all-black fingernails or the spiked bracelet, but something tells me she's lying about what she does. But why? Looking at Kovski, I can tell it doesn't matter. He's staring opportunity in the face. He knows it, and she knows he knows it. She's the type of woman who strikes up a conversation with handsome men at bars.

As any good wingman, I keep the dialogue flowing. "So, this is your last weekend of freedom before school begins?"

"Yep."

"What's your name?" I ask.

"Sid," she says. "Short for Sidney."

"Sid—that's a pretty name." Stupid thing to say.

"Is it?" She says.

"In the right context," I say. "In a room full of Karens, Sid would be a sigh of relief."

"I'm fucking with you. It's alright. I know my name sucks." Her self-importance pisses me off. Sid has that kind of smug smile that makes you hate-fuck them. "What are you boys doing tonight?"

"Celebrating," Kovski says. "Danny, here, retired."

"Oh yeah?" She says. "What did you do? Strike it rich in crypto or something?"

"Got fired from my job," I admit. Maybe it's the Long Islands making me lazy because I'm not hiding anything anymore.

"You must not be too broken up about it if you're out here partying," Sid says. "What'd you do anyway?"

"I was a bellboy at the Continental," I say.

"No shit. My parents stay there when they visit. You ever get to stay in the rooms?"

"That's what caused the whole mess, Danny got too curious." Kovski slaps my shoulder.

"It's nothing. I don't want to talk about it." My sudden shyness is brought on by her intense hazel eyes.

"I have to know," Sid says. "What'd you do? I'll get the next round if you tell me."

"What if I tell you?" Kovski leans in and sucks his straw.

"Nope. Danny has to say what happened. I need to hear from the donkey's mouth."

"Come on, Dan-o," Kovski says to me. "It's funny, if nothing else."

"It's my life, Kov."

"And you did something stupid, man. Now go on, spill it or I will."

"I fucked one of the guests."

"Dude! That's incredible," Sid says, offering a high-five. "How was it?"

"Best sex of my life."

Kovski can't help himself. "It's not just that—they got caught fucking in the hotel van by her husband."

"Holy shit. That's fuckin' nuts." Sid gets up. "What are you drinking?"

"Double Long Island," I say.

"Same for me," Kovski adds.

"I like you guys already." She runs her fingertips over Kovski's arm.

Sid walks through the throngs of co-eds that have entered since we sat down. When she gets to the mob of people waiting to order drinks, she glances over to Kovski.

He's busy watching the pool table. Unbeknownst to the pudgy guy with the pool stick, Kovski holds the butt end. When the guy tries to shoot, the stick doesn't budge. "What the hell?" The guy tugs.

Kovski lets go, giggling. The guy's stick flings forward, and he rams the cue ball into the eight ball. It rolls into the corner felt of the middle pocket.

"Do over. Do over." The guy fixes his backwards hat. "Keep your hands to yourself."

The guy resets the cue ball. Kovski does it again.

"Are you fucking serious, bro?"

"Bro, bro, bro," Kovski mockingly surrenders. "I'll keep my hands to myself." He sits on his hands to demonstrate. The guy lines up his shot. He glances at Kovski, who remains still. He shoots, misses wide, and scratches.

"Thanks a lot," he says.

"I think you did better with my help," Kovski retorts.

"Get control of your friend or I'll take care of him myself." The guy stands over Kovski, fists clenched. It's the kind of thing a man says because he doesn't want to seem like a bitch.

The empty threat makes me smile. "If you can figure out how to control him, please show me."

Not getting the reaction he was hoping for, the guy returns to his table, pouting. He takes a slug of his Long Island and hands off his pool stick to his partner. He pretends to forget about us, but I catch him looking our way.

Kovski downs the rest of his Long Island. He takes a deep breath. "Danny, tonight's the night. Tonight's the night. I'm a hot-blooded sex machine and I'm looking for one thing: satisfaction." Kovski rubs his hands together. "What do you think of Sid, huh? She's got this like weird, gothic hot girl thing going on. I bet she has pierced nipples."

"I don't think she's a teacher."

"Nah, me either." Kovski smiles, eying her.

"Can we go to the next bar?"

"Now?" Kovski says.

"I'm not feeling the vibe here."

Kovski sucks down his drink, not realizing he already finished it. "Bro, the night is young! Live it up. You just wish she had a friend for you to mack on."

"Isn't it too soon?"

"Danny, we're already out. You're already drunk. Enjoy it. You obviously wanted to be here and that's why you're here with me."

"Can we please go to Hawk's or something? There's a lot of dicks here."

Kovski looks around. I'm not lying. We're surrounded by guys in jeans, in short shorts, in lame ass t-shirts, and everywhere in between. Sid slices through the forest of dicks with three drinks in her hands.

She sets the three Long Islands in a triangle between us all and offers a toast. "To new beginnings." Kovski raises his glass, sloshing. I pick up mine. It's ice to the touch.

We toast and I drink half of it in a gulp.

Kovski says, "What do you think of leaving this place and going somewhere else?"

"Like your place?" Sid says.

Kovski giggles. "And why would we do that?"

Sid leans over and whispers something in Kovski's ear. Kovski grins at me. "Danny, I'm sorry. But we must cut the night short. Sid isn't feeling well, and I need to take her home."

"Seriously?" I say. "You're ditching me?"

"Do you mind if I talk to my friend real quick?" Kovski says.

"I'll be by the exit." Sid makes out with Kovski, their tongues tangling and untangling as I stand by. Disgusting. Sid strolls through the crowd, sipping her Long Island through the straw. We both watch her butt sway as she goes.

"You're too drunk to fuck," I say. "You know that, right? You've had how many Long Islands and shots already?"

Kovski shushes me. "I'm not worried about that. I have to ask you a huge, mega favor."

"What?" I already know what it is before he asks.

"Can you please find somewhere else to stay tonight?"

I say, "No. I can't. I need to stay at your place. I have nowhere else to go."

"I love you, brother. I love you to death. But since you showed up at my door, my balls are black and blue."

"Go back to her place."

"She's got roommates!"

"So do you."

"Danny, please. It's one night. There's got to be somewhere you can go. Hell, treat yourself to a hotel."

"Everybody moved away, Kovski. All my friends are gone. You're all I've got, and you don't want me to stay with

you? Honestly, honestly, I wanted to ask you something. Can we clean out your office and I move in there? We can be roommates for real."

"Oh," Kovski says. "Uhhh—I don't know if I gave you the wrong impression. This thing with you staying at my place is temporary. It's nothing more than that. No offense, I don't want roommates anymore."

What he says strikes me so hard in the gut that I can't speak. My best friend doesn't even want me around.

Kovski says, "Are we good?"

"Yeah. Kovski. Yeah. We're good."

"Alright." Kovski slaps me on the back. "Because I'm stamping my ticket to Poontown." He sets down his Long Island and walks away, but before he goes, he turns back. "Hey, feel free to come back tomorrow. I've got to work anyway."

I nod my head. "Remember to wrap your tool."

"Always." Kovski smiles. He walks through the crowded barroom, not a care in the world. Through all the heads, I see Sid. Kovski comes up to her. They make out against the front window. The bouncer tells them to move along. They exit.

I'm alone in this crowded bar. Everyone is a stranger. It's a different reality when all your friends leave you. Any one of these people I could talk to, but I don't want to talk to anyone. I just want my life back. The life that was going so well for so long.

"Hey, could you move?" The frat guy wants to shoot and I'm in the way.

I move alright. I finish my Long Island. And I finish the rest of Kovski's Long Island. I'm finished with this place. Finished with everything.

As I walk away, the frat guy lines up his shot. I swat the cue ball into the corner pocket.

"Dude, what the fuck?" erupts from the table, but I'm too far into the crowd for them to chase me.

Back on the street, I'm struck with the question: Where do you go when you have nowhere to go?

TWENTY-FOUR:

Tonight, I'm writing the perfect chapter in the beautiful love story we tell our kids. I'll leave out some details. Every story is messy in real life, but to our kids, what I'm doing now will sound like divine intervention. I show up out of the blue and promise Sophie the world.

This time, I have my keys when I step up to the apartment building. That's the thing about life, you know? It has a plan. Why else was I at Chelsea's the other week—to get my keys. Sophie catching us together was the universe reminding me that Sophie is drawn to me, even when we're apart. That's called true love.

Back in front of our banged-up apartment door, I could cry. I'm back. I really am. As soon as I walk through this door, I'm going to be the man of Sophie's dreams. The devoted boyfriend, the ideal husband, hell, tomorrow we should go out and find us a dog. I'm serious.

I hold my hand in front of my mouth to check my breath. I sniff. Mildly alcoholic, but Sophie won't notice because she'll be so excited to see me. I rap my knuckles on the front door and wait. I don't want to surprise her by opening the door. No, I'll stand here and show her respect.

There's no answer, no shuffling, nothing at all. I check the time on my watch. It's closing in on midnight. It's early enough for her to still be awake.

Sophie won't like hearing that I lost my job. I'll say that I quit because I'm going to get a real job. Not writing. A job with a salary and benefits. No more waiting for my writing to get discovered. I've got to be realistic if I'm going to marry this girl. She has to know that I'm thinking ahead. So yeah, I'll apply for a sales job at an insurance company or something. They're always hiring, and it pays decently. I'm sure I could wheel and deal.

It's taking her a long time to answer the door.

All the love stories preach about being bold in the face of adversity. I check the doorknob to see if it's locked.

It is.

I take out my keys and find the right one. Nervous, my hands shake as I push the key into the lock. When the key doesn't fit in, I think she changed the locks. My key is upside down, so I turn it over. It slides in. I turn it and the jamb releases. The hallway light illuminates the dark entrance as I step inside.

I can tell some things have changed since I left. The smell of a recently blown-out candle. There's a new painting sitting on an easel by our balcony. A vase of flowers she painted. In our time apart, her sadness rekindled her passion for art, and this, this is her expression. I am the vase and she is the flowers. Or, our apartment is the vase and we are the flowers. I'll ask her.

Two wine glasses stand on the kitchen counter—one empty, probably from yesterday, and the other half-full. I take a sip. It tastes good, not from a box. She always had better taste in wine than me. She has no taste for whiskey. That's love for you. You find someone who has the parts you're missing.

From the kitchen, I can tell the ring box isn't where I left it. I suppose she didn't want the daily reminders. If I

had to venture a guess where she put it, I think of the junk drawer. The one drawer filled with all the things that have no other place to go: scissors, a protractor, lighters, her old paint tray, and an assortment of keys, all of which don't belong to anything in this place.

There, wedged between the overflowing drawer and the counter top. I yank out the ring box. I open it. Despite the soft light, the diamond glows. The poem I kept under the lid and left out for her is gone. Did she throw it out?

Music wafts across the air, a distant beat and harmonized drumming—the frat house next door must be having a party.

I stuff the ring box into my back pocket.

In the living room, a brown flannel drapes over the arm of the couch. That's strange, I think, but maybe she's gotten a new one.

With wine glass in my fingers, I approach the closed door of our room. Inside, my damsel slumbers awaiting true love's kiss. Everything's that's ever happened to us will be our past. After today, everything is in front of us, our entire future intertwined. I sip the wine and clear my throat.

The last time I saw this door, I was leaving. It looks different now. Like it's not even mine, like this whole house isn't mine anymore, like I'm trespassing onto a life I'm not a part of. I have to see Sophie in our bed again to know there's still room left for me in her heart. I twist the knob and push open the door. Its hinges squeak.

And for a moment, I'm suspended in time and space.

A man's skinny, hairy ass thrusts back and forth between the spread legs of Sophie. The bed thuds and bounces with their bodies. She groans.

The glass of wine falls from my grip and crashes to the floor, bursting. Sophie's head raises from the pillow.

Her voice breaks the air. "Danny?"

The man's curly brown hair swishes to the side as his eyes discover mine. His face I've seen before, but I don't know where. He backs off from Sophie, his hard dick pointing straight at me. "Who the hell are you?"

I say, "I'm her boyfriend."

"Boyfriend?" The man looks at Sophie for answers.

"We broke up," Sophie cries. "Believe me. It's over."

"Get away from her." I shove the guy. He topples backwards and bumps his head on the dresser. I won't back down. No, I must protect my bride.

"Danny, stop!" Sophie screams from the bed. She covers herself with our comforter.

"Leave or I'll make you." My fists clench.

He puts his hands up and stands. "It's alright, dude. Be chill. She says she doesn't have a boyfriend; she doesn't have a boyfriend. How am I supposed to know?"

My voice grovels through my teeth. "Get your fuckin' clothes on and fuck off or I'll kill you." He doesn't move. "3-2—" I swing my fist at his jaw.

My face whips to the side in pain. I crumple to the ground.

Wriggling to my knees, I try to stop the room from spinning by pressing my hands into the floor, shards of glass tear into my palms. I spit out blood into the pool of red wine. My right eye swells shut.

The man's flaccid dick hangs over me. "Should we call the police?"

Sophie asks, "Technically, he lives here. His name is on the lease. But I kicked him out."

"Why did you come back?" The man taps me with his foot.

I crawl through the glass, glowering at the man, my voice trembling. "Do you love her? Because I love her. Love her more than the air I breathe. More than

the songs that birds sing. More than the sun in the afternoon sky. Do you love her that much? Do you? Do you even know what love is?"

The man drags me to my feet, "Get yourself together and get out of here."

I shove him away. "I'm not going anywhere." I get down on my knee and pull out the ring. "I love you, Sophie. I know I've been a shithead. I know I cheated on you with your best friend and a married woman and like a hundred other girls. But know that I love you more than any of them. I don't know how to live without you in my life. I'm broken in so many places; I need you to put me back together. That's the only way I can face tomorrow. Next week. The life ahead. Please. Marry me."

The man glances between Sophie and me in silence. I stare into Sophie's soul. She must see how shattered I am without her. How every piece of me aches for her. How I thought breaking everything might put us back together.

Her lower lip quivers. In the grey-black light, her jade eyes are hollow, black circles. She clutches our blanket over her naked chest. A frown tugs at her mouth; she shakes her head. "I loved you, I did. You were my everything. But it's too late, nothing you ever say or do will ever make up for what you've already done."

Maybe it's the late hour or the crash of adrenaline, but a wave of exhaustion hits me. After sleeping on a couch for so long, I long for our bed. Here, Sophie lies with another man.

Putting the ring back in my pocket, I slink out of the room, out of the apartment, out of her life.

I realize who the guy is. I can't believe she fucked the waiter from the Old-Fashioned.

TWENTY-FIVE:

lady liberty

STUMBLE THROUGH THE DOOR of the Empire behind a couple that's too stoned to care. Following them into the elevators, they kiss beneath the sizzling light, blinded by love.

The girl sees that I'm watching them. She stops kissing.

"No, go ahead. Pretend like I'm not here." As soon as it comes out of my mouth, I wish I hadn't said anything. Thankfully, the elevator door opens and I'm back on the ninth floor. I tell them, "Savor it."

I head down the hallway toward 911. Over my shoulder, I hear the guy ask, "Are you okay, man?"

Never better, I think, never better. That punch cleared up cobwebs in my head. Sure, I can't see out of one of my eyes, but for some reason, the whole world feels more vibrant than ever. This is what it's like when you decide.

What decision, you might ask? Chelsea. We left on a bad note last time. I haven't heard from her since, but that's what happens between two people who love each other. They fight. They break up. They come back together stronger. It's the natural cycle of a relationship. Sophie and I did that a couple times. Once about some woman I was flirting with. Another time about our future together. It's amazing what a bouquet of roses can fix.

Tonight, I don't have flowers per se but I have the desire of ten thousand roses. For Chelsea and me, we're in the sweet spot, the growth spot. We're coming back stronger than ever. We must. I don't know where else to go.

Knocking on her door, I'm reminded of how naïve I was last time, how naïve we both were. I'll admit when I said I loved her, that it was too soon after the fallout between Sophie and me. What did Chelsea expect? She told me she loved me the night before. What changed?

To my 16-year-old tender heart, a girl confessing her love would've been a dream come true. Now, though, after being with Sophie for so long, love feels dangerous, an unstable emotion shaking me down to my core and it's got me crumbling. Partially, my fault, but I'm here again to repeat what I've known all along—Chelsea is the one. Why else do I keep coming back for more?

Some might call it insanity, but I call it love.

I knock again. I check my phone for the time. In doing so, I notice the blood on my hands. I wipe them on my pants. I'm bloodier than I remember and my shirt is soaked in red wine. No wonder that girl on the elevator looked at me so strangely.

What a night.

From inside the apartment, footsteps approach the door. I step back and push a smile between my cheeks. I can tell by the shadow that cuts across the pinhole glass that she's looking at me.

"Go away." It's not Chelsea. It's her roommate, Haley. Goddamnit.

"Let me in, Haley," I say.

She says, "What's going on with your face?"

"I'll tell you if you let me in," I say. "I really need a bandage." I try the doorknob, but it's locked.

"No."

"Please?" I say. "Get Chelsea. She'll help me."

"She doesn't want to see you."

"We love each other and you're keeping us apart." I plead.

"Booty calls don't equal love," she declares.

"What if it does in this case?" I say to the steel door. "What if we can't keep our hands off each other? What does that mean?"

"You're fuckin' drunk and horny."

"No. Not with us. Chelsea and I are different." I lay my forehead against the cool metal door. It soothes my throbbing cheek.

"No texts, no calls, and you show up at her door covered in blood or wine or whatever the hell that is after midnight?"

I hear Chelsea's voice inside, "Who is it?"

"Who do you think?" Haley says.

"Go home, Daniel." Chelsea says through the door.

"Chelsea! Please?" I say. "I'm injured."

"Injured?" Her shadow moves to the pinhole. Now's my chance.

"I love you," I say to the door. "If you'd open the door, you'd see my face and you'd know it's true. I love you. I always have. That's why I can't let you go."

Chelsea pushes Haley aside and peers through the peephole. "Oh my god, what the fuck happened to your face?"

"It doesn't matter. What matters is that I am here." I clasp my hands together, begging. "Please, please, let me in."

"Don't do it." Haley says.

"But he's hurt?"

I bang on the door. "I love you Chelsea." Tears blur my vision. "If you love me, you'll let me in."

There's more whispering. The deadbolt clinks. I step back waiting for the door to open. Ready to throw my arms around Chelsea and hold her there for the rest of my life.

Nothing happens. It's silent.

I yank the knob, rattling the door like a cage. I explode. "Chelsea! Come on, open up." The tears turn to sweat as I slam my palm against the steel. "Chelsea! Please! Chelsea!"

A scrawny Indian man in plaid pajamas peers out his door holding a golf club. He looks at me, his eyes wide and worried. It's enough to make me head to the elevators.

That's it? That's all? No goodbye? After a year of sneaking around, I deserve more than this.

When I'm outside the Empire, I pull my phone out. I have two missed calls from Rachel. She left a message that reads—*Call me when you get the chance.*

It's nice to know someone's thinking about me. Wanting to bask in that feeling, I wait to call her back.

Not thinking much of where I'm going and it's not like I have anywhere to be. I head down State Street to the Capitol. I bypass bar after bar. College kids laughing and yelling about how it's the greatest night of their lives.

The thing about State Street is there's always someone somewhere doing something. It's a street that breathes with life. Being on it always gives me toxic nostalgia.

Against that coffee shop glass, I kissed a woman studying acting. I never knew if she faked her orgasms.

On this park bench, Grey strummed the guitar and I played the harmonica. We'd sing folk songs. Made enough money to buy burritos and beer afterward. The women who'd hang with us. They craved our creative, fearless passion. Our stupid, loud music paid well in phone numbers.

Passing State Street Brats, we used to hang out by the three laughing monkey statues out front for hours after the bar closed. Those were the days.

I get to the Capitol Square and sit on the granite block beneath Lady Liberty's feet. Her torch lit toward the campus at the other end of the road.

I call Rachel. As the phone rings, I notice the people moving through the city. Everyone walks with a different purpose, some fast, some slow, some go the long way, and others go straight there. For me, I have no purpose or place to go. I am truly free.

Rachel answers on the third ring. "Just a sec." In her background I hear the shuffling of feet, the sliding of a screen door, and the silence after it's shut. "Hey—how are you?"

"Still dreaming about you." I say, a smile to my voice—the first time all night.

"Oh god, you're one of those guys that like to cuddle after sex, aren't you?"

"I never got to show you. It's my trademark."

"You do have nice arms."

"I'm listening," I say. "Where are you right now?"

"On our balcony. Ellie's asleep and Tate's reading."

"Domestic life."

"You'll get there someday. Let me guess, you're outside some bar trying to score some hottie."

Looking at Lady Liberty, I smirk. "You know me too well. Wish you were here."

"Stop it. You're not supposed to say things like that to me."

"I can't help it. You can't either, obviously, texting me on a Saturday night."

Rachel clears her throat and speaks low. "There's no other way to tell you this, but I thought you should know."

"Whoa, why so serious all of a sudden? Are you going to tell me what happened with your husband?"

"Tate was angry, but he knows, he knows how much we need each other, especially with Ellie. There's nothing that will ever change that. But it's not that, it's something else. After we had sex the first time, I was feeling strange after. I know you wore a condom and whatever, but—"

"No way, I got tested. I'm squeaky clean."

"It's not an STD."

"You're pregnant?" I recoil, my gut knotting. "It's your husband's."

"It couldn't possibly be his because we'd have to have sex to do that. It was yours."

"Was?"

"I thought it was best for you to know that it happened and I took care of it."

The words sink beneath my skin. Goosebumps crawl from my neck to my toes. "You took care of it? You had an abortion? Why—why didn't you tell me? We could've—could've—"

"Could've raised the baby together? We made a mistake, Danny. That's all."

"Does Tate know about the abortion?"

"Yes," Rachel says.

"You told him?"

She says, "We made the decision together."

"He didn't force you, did he?"

"He asked that I get an STD test. They did a pregnancy test just to be sure. That's how we found out. But no, he said his opinion. This was my decision."

"And you're still together?"

"This was something we needed."

My chest thumps and I can't breathe. "He forgave you?"

"We're working toward it, but yes."

Holding the phone against my ear, I stare at the ground, where an ant crawls along a crushed cigarette butt.

"Danny?"

The hopeful way she says my name snaps me out of it. "Yeah?"

"Please don't ever contact me again."

I say, "I'm sor—" The line goes dead.

An abortion? An abortion? She took care of it without even asking if I wanted to keep the baby. I was the father, but it was her choice. We recklessly brought life into this world, and it had to be destroyed.

The pangs of regret mix with the acid in my stomach. In nine months, I could've been holding my son. My son—gone before he ever had a chance. A life erased by my mistakes.

I clench my belly and groan. I can't change what I've done. I'm going to remember this forever. Desperate to escape, I wobble to my feet. My thoughts rage on and on about the pain I caused, the lives I've wasted, and the time I spent chasing fantasies instead of facing reality.

Turning my back on Lady Liberty, on State Street, I head for somewhere no one will find me. Cast in the Capitol Lawn light, my shadow creeps along the white marble columns. Above the dome, the full blood moon looms.

TWENTY-SIX:

STAGGERING ACROSS THE MONONA TERRACE promenade, a whiskey bottle smashes against the cement. The shadow of a man, slouched, legs crossed beneath him, fiddling with change in his palm. The stench of piss-soaked nights spent in the heat clings to the air. He croons to himself. I glance at him as I pass. Beneath his grey hood, yellow eyes meet mine. He spits at me.

I quicken my pace. If he knew the night I've been through, he wouldn't do that. No one would. He doesn't care. He's only worried about himself.

Unlike the buzzing Memorial Union, you can hear crickets at the Monona Terrace. This is where galas, corporate events, and ceremonies congregate. The night Rachel met me, she was here.

From this solitary height, Lake Monona swirls below. At night, the terrace lights reach only so far. Each wave glitters as it breaks against the rocky shore. Beyond them, the black lake stretches over the earth, dotted with houses and the glow of their docks on the farther bank.

Unbeknownst to most, there's a spot where you can hop the railing and land on the sun-burnt grass on the other side. A sandy trail leads to a fenceless overlook. I used to come here in college whenever classes, or women, or parties got me down.

Carefully, I sit, letting my feet dangle over the ledge. On this perch, alone. Finally, alone. I can think. There's no one to judge me. There's no pretending to be somebody I'm not. It's me. Just me.

The water whirls and recedes into itself. Breathing in and out.

It's hard for me to breathe.

Rachel, to make that decision, to know so deeply the weight of a mistake, and to end it. I don't think I could've done the same. I would've moved to New York City for her. For us, for our child. At least, I think I would. I never genuinely sat down and thought what it'd be like to have a kid. In the past, it was an easy no, but now, I'm not so sure. Obviously, I would need to clean up my act a bit, but I think I could settle down and be a good father.

Rachel never even asked?

Mercy. She showed the child mercy. I have no right to claim it was ever my choice. She's the one who has to carry the kid. A fling turns into a family. It almost happened—the thing I only ever hear about. Almost happened to me. She showed mercy. Sweet mercy. I should thank her.

Rachel had to explain to her daughter why her father deserved to be so upset. Ellie's going to think I'm a bad guy. I'm sorry.

I'm not a bad guy. I didn't rob a bank, hold up a gas station, or kill anyone—I killed a baby. *My baby.*

What the fuck am I doing with my life?

I steal hearts, carry them all in my chest, make them believe they're the one, then break them one by one until there's no one left.

Right here, this is the result of everything I've ever done. This is me. A man soaked in red wine and blood, filled with regret.

The ring. I dig it out of my back pocket. The shimmering piece of earth haunts me. Pinching it between my thumb and index, I round the red moon within its circle. What the hell is this? This ring—a promise forged in metal and stone, two elements that endure forever. A gift and a curse. Heaven and hell. You can give all your love to someone, and they can snap you in half in a single moment.

Why did I even try?

I gave myself to Chelsea, but honestly, I never felt anything real for her. When she's back in school, she studies all the time too. It's not like we'll see each other much. Sure, we can have long conversations because we adore books and music, but I never wanted to meet her family. If I dated her for real, I'd have to attend garden parties, sip Aperol spritzes and pretend to laugh while listening to bland stories told by rich people. I doubt she'd want me there. She never bothered to ask if I'd join her for one of her family's soirées. We dragged on together because the sex was exhilarating. Neither of us imagined that as soon as Sophie was gone, the allure would vanish too.

Dating two women at the same time is too much trouble. If I'm going to be single, I'm going to be single. If I got a girl, I got a girl, no fooling around. It's not worth it anymore. It hurt seeing the waiter and Sophie, but I suppose I deserved it.

I gave Sophie my love, but when she wanted to double down, I folded and ran away. Went to the bar and got too drunk to function, thinking that was the solution.

I'd pass out next to Sophie, thinking it was the same as passing out in her arms.

It worked for a few years. Sophie welcomed me into her world, and I showed her around mine. As we pushed our worlds together, gaps shone through in a few spots, but we accepted these cracks as we accepted each other. No one's perfect. Our life together went on.

We were so good for so long, except for one thing: the future. As our shared world expanded, these cracks that we once tolerated grew, eventually becoming the only things we ever noticed. Still, we believed tomorrow would fix them.

So when those questions about what I wanted arose, I lied. I told her I wanted to marry her. That we'd live in the suburbs together. That we would make great parents. I told myself that tomorrow I'd want to change the things I didn't want to change today. But as the years passed, those lies I believed remained lies— and nothing changed.

Out of nowhere, that night with Chelsea, someone I never dared to try. Those differences between Sophie and me, Chelsea filled in the cracks. Everything changed. Because we were happy again, and Chelsea and I discovered that we could get away with it.

The first months after our initial indiscretion, Chelsea and I went at it like starving dogs. Sophie, Chelsea and I would hit the bars three or four nights a week. When Sophie left early, Chelsea and I found excuses to stay out longer and all hell would break loose. As long as I arrived home before sunrise, Sophie never suspected a thing.

Love makes you naïve. Sad, but true.

Who am I to judge? I bought this stupid ring. The woman behind the counter wore a low-cut blouse over a pair of sandbags that could stop a hurricane. When she

leaned into the case, I stared too long at her and not enough at the price tag. She begged the question, 'Do I want my love to be small or extravagant?' I chose extravagant and emptied my bank account to make up for all the wrongs I'd done.

Staring at the ring, of course, it wouldn't work. You can lie so much that nothing's real anymore. I'm a poet. That's what I tell people. What have you written? That's the question. I make up a story. It's my specialty. I am always the hero. Publishers or agents or my day job are the villains. But the truth? I'm too scared to even submit anything. My work rots in the bowels of my notebooks. Too afraid to let the world see who I am.

Afraid I will never be good enough. So why bother?

I am the real villain, not anyone else. By keeping the truth hostage, I torture myself in the shadows. It's why everyone left. They never got the truth. Sophie's gone. Chelsea's gone. Rachel's gone. My job's gone. Hell, Kovski's gone. I'm bleeding out tonight.

Getting to my feet, I head up the path, back to reality. If I get a drink somewhere, I can find a bed to sleep in.

Who am I kidding? Look at me. I'm a disfigured clown.

For no other reason than I can, I cock my arm back and launch the ring at the moon. The diamond flickers all the way down until it's swallowed by the dark waters beneath me. It doesn't make a splash like I thought it should.

I could throw myself off this cliff. That'd make a splash.

I'd be in the news tomorrow: 'Danny Clark, Madison's Finest Poet, Dies by Suicide.' It'd be a poetic death—something to give my writing meaning. Sophie would have to sort through it all because my work is still at our old place. Who'd get my royalties? My mom and dad, I guess. That'd be a surprise. Neither ever thought I should be a writer. We haven't talked much since I turned 18, but they'd be sad if I was gone. Hopefully, they'd figure out how to split the royalties without killing each other.

The next day, I'd be old news. As if I never existed at all.

I feel empty. Empty of everything. Empty of the past, of the present, of the future. If I could write a poem to capture these feelings, I'd call it something beautiful, but the words won't come to me. I don't know how to write anymore.

Wet, hot tears sting my swollen eye. I should jump. Not just for myself, not just for my situation, but for everything, for everyone. We're all stuck here, churning our legs, running out the clock. Everyone else can run on without me—let me drown.

Sophie was right. Carrying on won't change all these things that I've done. Nothing will. I've inked pain into my memory. From here on out, I'll live with the knowledge of abandoning lovers, of midnight mascara soaking cold pillowcases, of a lonely man believing none of his broken promises would ever leave a scar.

It's too much. I take a deep, shuddering breath. I could've done better. I should've done better. I can't change anything. There is no tomorrow.

I float on this terrace while the rippling shore below beckons me.

The blood moon paints a red coffin upon the black, shimmering wake. It's a fine enough target. Jagged rocks probably lie hidden beneath the tide, eager to shatter me into a thousand pieces. With one step, I am undone.

The waves call, louder now, to join them.

I lift my left foot, feeling the open air. I wobble, my arms flailing. I almost topple into the abyss. A sharp gust licks my heel as it sings *Hallelujah*—

"Hey! —"

A woman's voice cuts through the dark. "What are you doing?" I glance over my shoulder. Her silhouette hops the railing and lands lightly. I don't know why, but seeing her, makes me break down in tears.

"Come on," she says, descending the trail. "Come with me. We can sit and chat awhile. The moon's beautiful tonight, isn't it?"

The familiar voice sparks a memory of something someone once told me she did every full moon. I cry out, "Eva?"

Eva freezes, eyes wide. "Danny?"

"I'm glad you're here." I step away from the edge and fall into her arms. The water crashes and hisses against the shore below.

"You're okay," she murmurs, like Rachel to Ellie. "You're okay." Her hands rub my back, grounding me.

A new wave of darkness sets in and I can't muster any words. A sob gushes out.

She repeats. "It's okay." Holding me to her shoulder, she says, "it's okay." Her body warms my cold heart.

It won't stop the flood. "I killed a baby."

"You did what?"

"The guest. Rachel. She got pregnant. And she—" Hiding my head in my hands, I weep.

Eva says, "Let's sit on the terrace, huh?"

Trembling, I nod. Unable to walk on my own, she puts her hands around my waist and guides me back up the trail.

On the bench, we sit side by side. Our shoulders touching, it makes me feel better resting against her. Safe knowing she's there.

We look up together under the same spell. The crimson moon floats above us now.

Words would only ruin this moment. Our hands find each other and embrace. This night is nothing in the grand scheme of the universe, but somehow, this moment, I know, I'll remember forever.

"I love the full moon." Eva slides down until her head rests on the back of the bench. I do the same. We stare straight up at the red moon, sparse clouds, and the pinhole light of the stars. Not looking at me, Eva says, "Close your eyes."

"Why?" I ask.

"Just do it."

So, I close my eyes. "Now wha—"

"Shh," she says. "Listen."

"To what?"

"Listen."

In that blackness, I listen. First, I hear the hum of the building's ventilation system. The freshwater sighs against the shoreline. Long-lost crickets play their small fiddles. Underneath it all, a soft, steady beat thumps low. My heart.

Eva says, "On nights like this, I like to close my eyes and listen for as long as I can to the world. So, when I open them, I forget I'm anything at all, and all I see before me is the moon and the stars, and it feels like I'm flying through space. Free."

"Does it work?"

"Only if you don't try."

"Don't try?"

"Shh..."

Minutes or hours pass. Blind, I hear the cacophony of Earth, an orchestra always playing. Rippling thoughts rise to the surface again. Heartache and pain, I swallow my loneliness. I'm going to do better, I swear.

Eva whispers in my ear, "Open your eyes."

Deep, far, and wide, I see beyond the moon, the galaxy, and dare to fly into the black mask of the universe. In that great distance, I realize we are all lost in space—riding on a rock stuck around a star destined to explode. Nothing we do truly matters. That's why we toodle around down here together: to give each other purpose. It could be living on the shore with a view of the city, or becoming a lawyer who believes the guilty can change or being a great parent. The answer is different for everyone. Perhaps mine is to remind others to push their limits every once in awhile.

Eva and I drift through the depths of space together, suspended in silent awe. Silent in knowing we don't understand what's out there any more than our ancestors did a millennium ago. The only meaning we have is the meaning we make.

I peek at Eva again. She doesn't return my gaze, the distance between us wider than the galaxies. I'm left pondering what if. What if I told her how I felt? What if I took her home? What if she says no? The questions rage in my mind, but it's all wrong.

Because in these questions, Eva is missing. Who is Eva really? What does she want? Am I even the one for her? I don't want to pick her up. I don't want to take her home. I don't want to pretend I love her for one night, then never see her again.

I want to love her. I want her to love me. I want us to love each other the way lovers do. I want my world to revolve around hers, and when our worlds collide, we create a grander existence—a universe filled with us. And when we stare up at the stars, it is us seeing us drawn across the cosmos.

I can't say that. This moment would buckle beneath such grandeur. All I want to say is we should forget about ourselves. Maybe by forgetting, I'll remember what love is supposed to be. It's not this grand gesture, but a simple promise to be there.

"Thanks for being here." I squeeze Eva's hand.

"I can say the same thing," She squeezes back and we lean our heads together.

I say, "Are you going to ask me what happened?"

"No," she says. "I have a good feeling I know."

"Is it that obvious?"

"Yeah," Eva answers without looking at me.

I watch a car cross the bridge to Monona Bay. "Why'd you tell the bosses about the kiss with Rachel?"

"Because it was the truth."

"But if you didn't say anything, I'd probably still have a job."

"I told them what I saw. That's all. You not wanting me to, doesn't mean I didn't have to tell the truth."

"But you could've saved me."

"You wanted to get caught."

"Why would I want to get caught?"

"Because, deep down, you knew. You were trying to see what you could get away with. Because you're bored."

"Bored? I'm not bored." I snap. "I'm the least boring person I know."

"It's not about being boring," Eva says. "It's about why. All you ever tell me is you got drinks here, ate dinner there, scored some hottie outside of that bar and *oh my god, I'm so hungover.*"

"That's an exciting life to me," I say. I don't have a clue what she's talking about.

"But you never tell me you're happy," Eva replies. "You live in this whirlwind, but it goes nowhere. And when it almost did, like with that guest's husband, you

know, the publisher? You blew your shot before you could even take one."

I slump my head against her shoulder. The weight of the night hits me, she's right. I'm out here because I lost my job, which stemmed from Rachel, who I met because I wanted to escape Sophie, even though Sophie did nothing wrong. It was just a quiet Tuesday.

"I am bored." I admit, "Nothing's new here anymore. I even recycle the same tired lines on the women I meet. But what can I do now? How do I pretend that I never hurt anyone?"

"All you can do is learn from it," Eva says, rubbing my arm. It feels nice. Friendly. Loving. "And do better."

"I'll do better. I promise."

We bask in the hopeful moonlight, its glow soon to fade.

I clear my throat. "Can I ask you a favor?"

Eva tilts her head, her lips inches from mine.

"Can I crash at your place? My friend Kovski kicked me out so he could bang a goth chick tonight."

She blinks. "What is your life?"

"I told you it's not boring."

Eva considers me. "Let me guess you don't have a change of clothes?"

I shake my head.

"Figures." Eva sighs and stands. "You're the male equivalent of a hot mess."

As we leave the promenade, the broken whiskey bottle crunches beneath our feet. The man on the bench lies curled up, sleeping. I slip my arm around Eva's waist. She pushes it away. We walk on side by side.

TWENTY-SEVEN:
songs for beginners

BEFORE EVA FLICKS ON THE LIGHT, she apologizes for the clutter. I barely hear her, lost in how often I dreamed of this place. Standing on her threshold, it's not what I imagined.

It's an eclectic mishmash of old and new furniture, woven rugs, and photos of her with her friends and family. Eva makes do with the tiny living room that opens to her kitchen. On the breakfast bar, a small TV and stacks of books. Her bohemian lifestyle is on full display. A vinyl record player, a bean bag chair, and a keyboard are tucked beneath a handwoven tapestry.

"I knew it," I say.

"Knew what?"

"You're secretly a hippie."

"Pshh. What can I say? I dig music and nature."

"Including natural substances?"

"I haven't smoked pot in years."

"Damn," I say. "I'm kind of fiending. Would love to lay back in that bean bag and listen to vinyls all night."

"Go for it. I've got to go to bed. I've got work in the morning," She says, heading into her bedroom. I follow her. She turns back at the door. "Excuse me!"

"Sorry," I say. "I thought you were going to show me something." I return to the living room. It was an honest mistake. I've never been here before.

Looking around, I collapse into the bean bag. I flick through her records. A mix of new and old pop, RNB, soul, some funk, and a lot of classic rock'n'roll. I take out a record with the cover of a man walking out of the woods.

Turning on the player, I set the needle in the groove. I turn up the volume. The lonely voice croons about remembering better days. Those words never rang so true.

"*Songs for Beginners* by Graham Nash," Eva says. "Solid choice."

"I like the cover."

"It's simple like that. Here." Eva tosses a large women's volleyball hoody and a pair of grey sweatpants at me. "These should fit."

"Someone was a big girl in high school."

"Shut up. I like my sweatshirts baggy."

I pull off my wine-stained, still-damp shirt.

"Hello?" Eva says, her voice sharp.

"Hi?" I wonder.

"The bathroom's on the left."

I glance down at my bare chest. "Oh right. Good call." I step to the bathroom, surprised that she cares. It's just skin, but I respect her wishes.

"Thank you," Eva says as I close the door behind me.

As I drop my jeans to the tile floor, I figure she doesn't want to give me the wrong impression.

When I open the bathroom door, Eva, now in a matching set of silk cami and shorts that make her legs look incredible, comes in. She dabs at the dried blood and dirt with a wet towel, cleaning the scrape below my eye with a cotton pad and rubbing alcohol.

I wince.

"It's not so bad," Eva says.

While she's focused on me, I watch her in the mirror. Her soft breath skims my cheek as she dabs the bruise. I risk it. "You're remarkable, you know that?"

"And you're done." Eva steps back, rolling her eyes. She grabs her toothbrush, presses toothpaste onto it, and walks out of the room, brushing her teeth.

"What?" I dry my face with a hand towel. She's a tough one.

Searching for mouthwash, I open her mirror medicine cabinet. A few pill bottles in there. Seems like she struggles with dry skin. Poor girl. I'll ask if she wants me to rub lotion on—

"What the hell are you doing?" She says with her mouth full of toothpaste. She spits into the sink.

"Do you have any mouthwash?"

Eva closes the medicine cabinet and opens the cabinet below the sink. She pulls out a bottle of the blue stuff. "Knock yourself out." She walks out of the room.

"If you need help with putting on lotion before bed, let me know." I swish the mouthwash and spit in the sink. "We could do tradesies. I do you and you do me. No one wants to wake up with dry skin!"

I walk into the living room. Her door is closed and shut. I crossed a line, I get it, but what if she were in love with me too? I say, loud enough for her to hear, "Sweet dreams, Eva."

"Goodnight, Danny," she says through the door.

On her couch, I unfold the blanket and sit a while with it on my lap, listening to the music. Everything here is hers. I'm living in her life. Even if it's just for tonight, I know Eva better than I've ever known her before and I want to know more.

The needle finds the end, lifts and returns home, leaving the record spinning in the dark.

In the morning, I wish I could say we spilled our hearts out like syrup over blueberry pancakes. Instead, I wake up to an empty apartment.

Eva left without saying goodbye. I feel like a one-night stand. After all this time knowing each other, there's no true love between us. She was looking out for me. That's it. That's all we are. That's all we've ever been—friends.

To thank Eva for what she did last night, I write her a poem on the cartoon hamburger-shaped notepad sitting on her coffee table—

> *There's a place beyond the stars*
> *hidden by the sun and moon*
> *where dreamers go in secret*
> *to live their truth.*
> *In that sacred space,*
> *the boundaries of reality change.*
> *Our atoms spread across infinity*
> *and we piece ourselves together*
> *from the chemistry in the galaxies,*
> *forever shifting.*

I lie back on the couch, picturing this place as my home. Eva's taste is nothing like Sophie's or Chelsea's. Not elegant, not stylish, it's independent of all that. As if everything here appeared alongside its own story. The lack of aesthetic is her aesthetic. Eva trusts herself—her tastes and desires. She doesn't need to impress anyone.

I try to impress everyone. With men, it's my ability to drink and carouse women. With women, it's to say something clever to entice their curiosity. Everyone, I try to make believe I'm worthy of their time. Make believe. It's all lies. My entire life. When was the last time I believed in something?

Coming up blank, a book on her shelf catches my eye. It's a travel guide to the best spots in the U.S. I forget sometimes there's a whole land out there I haven't explored. Thousands and thousands of miles of open road filled with towns that only postal workers have heard of.

What am I doing here? Stuck in Madison.

Flipping to a random page, there is a glossy photo of an Oregon coastline, the sunset casts the boulders and endless tide in periwinkle. If I had a car, I'd drive there right now to breathe the kind of air that lives there.

Why can't I? I just need a car and some gas.

A drunken memory closes the book. Last night, I threw the ring into Lake Monona.

TWENTY-EIGHT

Wading beneath the Monona Terrace, my pant legs rolled up over my knees, I search for the ring amongst the sand in crevices of large scum-covered rocks. The hangover, hot between my ears, cools with every passing rush of waves.

Kovski sits on the stony shore smoking a fat joint. The lake laps at his bare feet. He gave up a while ago. Ryan and I haven't though.

Ryan asks, "Why did you throw the ring off the terrace?"

I roped him into this. The poor sap still feels bad about telling Sophie about Rachel and me.

"I was drunk," I say. "Thought it was a good idea at the time." It's days like today that make me wonder why I drink. If I were sober, this never would've happened.

"I get that, brotha." Kovski blows out a silver cloud. "That's why I believe people should use bigger things than a ring to propose. You know how hard it is to lose an engagement jet ski?"

"I know it was stupid. But it's here somewhere."

"How long are we going to be here?" Kovski says. "I'm getting thirsty."

"As long as it takes," I say. "This is partially your fault. If I could've wandered to your place instead of off into the city, this wouldn't've happened."

"Don't blame me! Blame God. He gave Sid amazing tits. I had to do what I had to do to see them."

"Since when do you believe in God?" I ask.

"Since last night, Sid turned me into a believer." Kovski giggles, ripping his joint. He won't take the blame. At the end of the day, I'm still the idiot who chucked the ring into the lake.

Ryan pushes up his glasses. "There's a real possibility it's gone for good. I mean, it could be anywhere."

"Water is a fickle mistress," Kovski says deeply, smoke coloring his breath.

"We've got to find it," I say.

"What I'm trying to say is, what if we don't?" Givens digs into a small, sandy pool.

I take a moment to think it over, wondering if I should say it. It's about as good a time as any. "I'm leaving Madison."

Kovski says, "Because of all the shit that's happened to you recently? Listen, man, it's temporary."

"No, Kov, it's a sign. It's time for me to go."

Ryan asks, "Where are you going to go?"

"Nowhere, if we don't find this ring. I need to pawn it to buy a car unless, of course, Kovski, you let me borrow your car."

"For your new life? Hell nah." He kicks water at me to emphasize his point.

"You said you always wanted a Vespa."

"No means no. Sorry. You want a fresh start? Go find yourself your own shag-mobile."

"We've got to find this ring." I thrash about in the water searching. If I don't get a car, I'll never get out of this town. The muck clouds everything. This is impossible.

But we keep looking.

"Hey Danny," Ryan says, "I've been meaning to ask you."

I already know what he's going to ask. "Of course. Yes, of course, I'll read your book and give you notes."

"Thanks for the offer. I'll remember that. But no, it's not that. It's…" Ryan adjusts his collar. Beads of sweat collect along his temples. He inhales. "It's more like I'm going to tell you. I'm going to ask Sophie out."

I laugh. "Seriously?"

"I don't want it to be weird if you see us together."

"Did you hear? I'm leaving Madison. I don't care what happens to Sophie. I hope she has a happy fucking life. Because it's over between us." Secretly and honestly? It hurts to think about her with another man. The punch flashes in my memory and the apologetic gaze she gave me afterward. Yet, she did nothing to help me. I add, "You really think she wants to date you? I mean, look at you. And she's—she's gorgeous."

"I have to try."

"I'm not going to stop you," I say. "But maybe cut back on the bagels and cream cheese."

Kovski gets up and stretches his back. "You mind if I have a go at her?"

"Fuck you, Kov!" I say. My blood boils. "Sophie isn't some throwaway. At least I know that Ryan likes her."

"Just messing with you, dude," Kovski says, touching his toes. "But I'm happy to hear you care about her a little bit."

Something shimmers among a cluster of rocks to the far right of Kovski's feet. I pad out of the water and go to it. In the fissure of a massive black stone, the lake laps over the diamond ring, basking in the sun. I reach in and pick it up.

"I found it."

"Huh?" Kovski turns.

"I found it!" I shout, leaping into Kovski's chest. He catches me.

"No way!" Ryan exclaims. He stumbles out of the water and throws his arms around both of us.

Together, we splash around the tide pools, laughing and jumping for joy.

Back at Kovski's, I stuff my clothes into my backpack as he stands by and watches. His hands on his hips, like how my dad would stand when he supervised me in the yard as a child. Present, but not fully there.

Ryan excused himself to go home. I guess my story with the ring inspired him to write.

I sniff a pair of underwear to see if I'd worn them. I had. I stuff them in the duffel bag.

"You know," Kovski mutters, at first like he's talking to himself. "I've been thinking of upgrading. Maybe, get a pick-up truck to haul my gear."

"Oh yeah?" I say, folding Eva's sweatshirt.

"Way easier to load and way more space for a kayak."

"Are you trying to tell me something?" I press the last shirt into the backpack and zip it. I keep Eva's sweatshirt and pants out.

"Are you serious about buying my car?"

"Are you serious about selling it?" I sit on the couch.

"I think so." Kovski crosses his arms. "I'm also pretty stoned."

"How much?"

"I want to support you, buddy," Kovski says. "Give me what you got from selling that ring. It can be symbolic or something."

"It was a nice ring, but it wasn't worth as much as your car," I say.

"I saw how much cash he put in that envelope. I'm comfortable with it."

"Are you sure?" I take the envelope of cash I got from the jeweler out of my back pocket. He offered to give me a third of the price at first, but after hearing my story, he gave me half.

"Better do it before the high wears off," Kovski says. "You never know what I'll be thinking."

"Exactly, I don't want to take advantage of you."

"Damnit, Danny, take the car!" Kovski gets up and finds the keys. He tosses them into my lap and holds out his palm.

I flick through the thousands in cash and sigh. It's better to keep money moving than letting it collect dust. I give him the envelope. Kovski doesn't count it.

He hugs me and whispers in my ear, "Let's get beers to celebrate."

"I can't," I say. "I think I'm going to take a break from drinking for awhile."

"I was hoping you'd say that." He steps back.

I hitch the backpack over my shoulder and carry Eva's clothes under my arm.

Kovski smiles. "If you ever need someone to talk to out on the lonesome road, I'll be here. And I want some crazy stories when you visit because you have to visit."

"Yeah, yeah, yeah…I love you, man."

"Love you too, dude."

The screen door slams behind me. I hop off his porch and click the key fob. An all-white Altima beeps a few houses down. I stroll Mifflin Street, knowing this is the last time.

A woman in a cocktail dress, carrying heels, trips into the grass. Her friend drunkenly helps her up, their voices slurring.

I slide into the worn-out leather seat of my 'new' car. I've been in the passenger seat a thousand times, but never behind the wheel. I adjust the mirrors, turn on the ignition, and my racing heartbeat matches the engine. Pride washes over me, and I smile at my reflection in the rearview. Beyond me, the two women wobble across the street, holding each other on their long walk home.

Their story is the kind I used to live. With the upcoming semester, the town will explode again with energy. Fresh faces will set out to discover new limits. I used to be one of the characters, and for the first time in nine years, I won't be.

I hook the first left off Mifflin Street and make one last stop before I say goodbye to Madison forever.

TWENTY-NINE:

ashes

OPHIE OPENS OUR OLD APARTMENT DOOR and lets me in. A month ago, I would've kissed her hello. We walk the short hallway into the kitchen. On the counter, two overflowing boxes hold my stuff.

Sad to say, there isn't much. We'd talked about it over the phone. She's keeping anything that can't fit in a car, which leaves these boxes filled with my clothes and the odds and ends. My beer sign has finally come down.

"Is this everything?" I ask.

"I think so," Sophie says, her hand in her back pocket, leaning against the counter.

Our awkward, silent treatment opens all the hums, clicks, and hisses in our home. The oven, the laundry, the coffee maker, the TV, and the bathroom fan next door. It's all so loud when nothing distracts you from it.

I shuffle through one of the boxes. "Where are all my notebooks?"

"Shoot. You know it's out of my reach."

"It's alright," I say. "I'll grab it. You mind if I look around for anything else?"

"Of course." She stays in the kitchen, busy on her phone.

"I'm going to miss this place," I say, stepping into our old bedroom. Already renovated with a new bedspread and pillows.

I open my old end table that I've had since I was a kid. It once held my harmonica, condoms, notebooks, pens, and other random things. Closing it, it's empty now. I run my fingers down the notches on the corner.

At the closet, I stand on my tiptoes and pull the cardboard box off the top shelf. Having to lean against Sophie's tops and dresses, I inhale deeply and savor her smell.

Setting the box on the bed, I open it. Inside, it's stacked with old Moleskin notebooks, loose-leaf, cocktail napkins, and whatever else I used to write stuff down. It's all here. The story of my life lives in this box.

Looking at the end table, I think about what I'm going to set my stuff on at my next place. When I'm done traveling, I'll need something. "You mind if I take back my end table?"

"Go right ahead." She says through the wall.

I move the lamp to the bed and hoist the end table onto my shoulders. It's much lighter than I remember. Carrying it into the living room, I say, "You did good."

Sophie stacks the two boxes on the counter and carries them. I take the end table and the beer sign, leaving the writing for now. We head down to my car, hazard lights blinking at the hydrant. I fold the backseat down and load the boxes from Sophie. The end table doesn't fit.

"On second thought, maybe you should keep it."

"Now that it's out here," Sophie says, "maybe it's better to leave it on the curb."

So, I leave it.

Seeing Eva's folded sweatshirt and pants in the passenger seat, an idea hits me. I grab them.

My feet fall heavy on the steps as I make the final trip into my old apartment.

Sophie's waiting in the kitchen. "I need you to initial something real quick." She slides over a stack of paper with a pen on top.

"The divorce papers?" I quip.

Sophie shakes her head, not amused. "The lease. We got the place."

"You're moving?" I say.

"Thinking about it."

"You didn't think about asking if I wanted to stay here?"

"Shit. Sorry. I just figured—" Sophie says, catching herself. "Do you want to stay here?"

I can tell it was an honest mistake. I've been so gone from her life that she forgot I was still part of it.

Looking over the place, every nook and cranny still carries Sophie. There's no way to start over here. On the balcony, there's the Terrace chair. I should take it with me too, but it won't fit in the car either. She must want it if she didn't offer to give it back. It can be something to remember me by. Sophie can set it on the end of her new pier, and when she sits there, maybe she'll think of me.

The language on the lease says something about relinquishing all rights and responsibilities for the new apartment. As I read, I imagine Sophie living on Monona Bay. How one morning when the world is one big snow globe, she'll walk to the shore with her skates slung over her shoulder. She'll brush aside the snow to make a rink. Wind in her hair, rosy cheeks, she'll smile as she glides across the ice.

I suppose it was never our dream. It's easy to believe in someone else's vision when you don't have one of your own. What's mine? I don't know. I'm going to figure it out.

"No. I'm out of here." I take the blue pen and initial the line.

Sophie hands me my box of writing. Our fingertips graze as I take it in my arms. She says, "I think you've got it from here."

"Are you sure you don't want my work? Most of it's about you. It could be worth something someday." I linger in the hallway, knowing this is our last time.

"You've got to publish something to make it worth anything."

"I write in the pursuit of truth, and there's nothing more worthless than that." I wait for her laugh, but it doesn't come. "It's funny because how worthless and priceless don't mean the same thing?"

"I'm sorry," Sophie says, "but I made lunch plans."

"With what's his dick?"

"No, Tyler and I are done."

"Oh."

Sophie breaks down in tears. "Can you please go?"

"Wait, before I go, do you mind giving these to Ryan for me?" I grab Eva's folded sweatshirt and pants off the counter.

"Women's volleyball?"

"I stayed at Eva's place. Don't worry, nothing happened. She let me wear this since I was covered in blood. Anyway, I can't exactly drop it off because I got fired from my job."

"You got fired too?"

I nod.

Sophie hears the truth in my voice and accepts the folded clothing. "I'll make sure he gets it."

"You know," I say, "Ryan is actually a good guy. Like maybe the best dude I've ever met."

"I told you. Too bad you never gave him a chance."

"Yeah, I really should've." I put my arms around her. "Hey, did you ever get that promotion?"

"Yes." Sophie nods, her face twists, and she collapses into me. Her tears soak my chest. My own fall down my cheek and disappear into her hair. It's *Unmistakable.*

"Congrats. You deserve it." Sophie wriggles away, but I hold her close. "I love you," I whisper, letting go.

Sophie chokes out, "Bye." Her jade eyes linger on me. Perfect in her plain white tee. Nothing else to say—except she can't say she loves me too.

Angry at the world, angry at myself, I wander onto the frat house lawn next door where a circular grill catches my eye. Taking off the grate, I stuff my box of writing into the charcoal pit. Old smoke from the coal dust puffs into the air. The cardboard crunches against the burnt-out metal. I pick up the long-stem lighter, forlorn in the grass. Testing it, a flame flickers in the wind.

Paper needs nothing more than a single spark and I have a whole box of kindling.

I don't have to be a writer anymore. No more opening the vein and letting it drain out until I'm a cesspool. If I stop believing I am one, I can make all this aching go away.

I press the lighter along the edge of all the loose poems and notebooks in there. The napkins flare first, gone in seconds, but igniting the rest. Soon enough, the notebooks smolder, the ink melting together. On top of the pile, a poem called *Two Caterpillars* turns to ash as I read—

There is bliss in the wrinkled
sheets, a womb that intoxicates,
at the same time, suffocates.
Bright light hangs over the trees,
the fresh air calls to us.
Leaves cackle together in the soft breeze.

We exist separate, more so now than ever,
held together by an olive branch,
which vibrates in the sunshine,
but gnarls in the passing storms.
We've changed, better, innocently quivering,
two cocooned caterpillars discovering new life.

The wind, like truth, has a way of changing things,
all the innocence we thought we knew,
we don't know now.
Where the secrets dried, we push away.
The time has come to let the world see
so does love soar at our new wings
so does heartache remain
when only one of us breaks free

Finding a red Solo cup on the porch stairs, I dash the fire with what I think is water. Turns out, it's Everclear. Fucking college kids. The blaze roars bigger and wilder.

I grab the half-empty bottle of Gentleman from my car. Twisting the cap, the cork pops, and for a second, I think about taking a swig. Instead, I pour it into the inferno. The flames lap up the whiskey and consume my writing until everything I've ever known curls into smoke.

THIRTY:
anywhere

HE THING ABOUT THE ROAD is it gives you time to think.

White lines crawl mile after mile. Farmhouses and grain silos dot the horizon. Within the next few weeks, the leaves will change to reds and oranges before their somber death at the feet of the trees where they were born. Winter looms heavier as the days drift toward the new year.

I'm thinking too far ahead.

Instead, I should focus on the here and now. Where I've come from and where I'm going. I don't know where I'm going. I'm a modern pioneer discovering new land alone. My manifest destiny lies somewhere out there. I'm going to find it.

In between, there's a lot of land to cross and there's me, only me. I check my gaze in the rearview mirror. The swelling beneath my eye swirls with purple and yellow bruising. *I killed a baby.*

Shifting lanes on a deserted highway, I try to outrun the pain. This pain buried deep. My hands tremble as I tighten my grip on the steering wheel. My foot stomps the accelerator.

Trees and electric wires blur. The speedometer needle climbs to 90…100…110. The Altima shudders. Every bump in the road reverberates through the metal cage.

My pulse rattles through me. A tear drips down my cheek. I wipe it away, but another comes. I breathe deep, trying to hold back the flood. It's no use. The storm of everything I've done wrong crashes into me, thought after thought repeating.

I let off the gas and drift down the next exit. My vision is too fuzzy to keep going. I pull off at a gas station, tucked into the rocky bluffs—an oasis in the melancholy plains of the Midwest.

Head heavy, I peel myself off the driver's seat and fill the tank.

Alone in the middle of America, I stare at the road. The highway bridge stretches across the fading day. An oil tanker screams past, headed West. Between here and the Rockies, a thousand miles of rolling fields.

I've got nowhere to go, but I'm going. With nothing left to lose, I might as well see what's out there. Those friends I went to college with did it. Now, I'm doing it, but it's harder than it looks.

Everyone seems to know what they want all the time. As if the world isn't filled with a trillion options. Part of me wonders what I'd be like if I didn't take the journey I took. All the different choices I made and didn't make. How all of this would be different if I did one or two things differently. How I'd be different, likely better, likely happy, not bitter, not sad.

Yet, where am I in all this? In Madison? In the mountains? In a new city? What is it that I want?

People want. We yearn and burn for the things that make us happy. I love women and whiskey. Yet happiness lies deeper than these surface cravings.

When I think about the happiest moment of my life, whiskey isn't in it. The woman isn't naked beneath me. It's Sophie and me holding hands on that pier of some rich snob's mansion overlooking Monona Bay. When we saw no lights on and snuck through their gate. Not even drunk or anything, we sat there and dreamt together of owning a house where we could swim in May and ice skate in January. Our heads leaning on each other, the fireworks boomed on the 4th of July after hours of anticipation.

Everything was us, us, us. A couple eager to take on life together. We almost had it.

But I was scared, like I'm scared now. Scared that when the dream finally comes true, it won't be all that it's cracked up to be. It'll be real and I'll have it, and my life will go on. Soon enough, I'll be wishing for something new again.

Some dreams take longer than others. Like writing a book takes forever. There's far more pleasure at the bottom of a bottle of whiskey than in writing a novel. Then again, I never really gave it a try. So caught up with women and drinking, poems were all I had time for. What's it like to commit to something like that? To obsess over hundreds of pages of words. It's a lot like love in a way.

A pick-up truck swings into the next bay, and a portly man in a cowboy hat hops out. His stare checks mine. I look down at my silent pump—the gas long since stopped. I rerack it.

I get back into my car, turn on the engine, and let it idle. With the highway before me, I see two lives.

If I go left, I'll head East. Back toward Madison, back toward the life I've always known, but I could be different. I could take over Sophie and I's apartment and get a new job, maybe at Whiskey Jack's. Kovski's always hiring barbacks. But if I want to give drinking a rest, a place like that is filled with too much temptation and not just behind the bar. I could find work more aligned with my creativity, and, like Ryan, write a book on the side. I could see Eva again and ask her on a real date. She's seen me through enough to know me. It's my turn to get to know her, the real her. Not the dollhouse version of Eva that I tried to fondle and sleep with.

If I go right, I start over. I can even change my name. Be the version of myself I never let myself be. But who even is that? I don't want to go down the same paths in a different place. I've seen how that story goes. A new town doesn't fix the biggest problem and that's me.

Churning and churning, I never know if I'm ever making the right choice, but I have to choose anyway and live with it. That's what life is: decision after decision after decision and all the revisions that come later.

So why should I bother believing that I can't change my mind after I already decided? There really are no rules to anything—we just make them up as we go along.

A minivan pulls behind my idling car and waits for me to move. I suppose I must carry on. I rumble forward, loose gravel crackling beneath my tires. My headlights trace the dark road ahead.

ERIC MAUS IS A POET, SCREENWRITER AND AUTHOR in New York City. He grew up in a small town in Wisconsin and studied poetry at the University of Wisconsin-Madison. *Women and Whiskey* is his debut novel, published under his imprint Highball Press.

For more of Eric's work, visit his website: www.ericmaus.com.

ERIC MAUS in 2013 when
he first started
WOMEN AND WHISKEY

a brief history of women and whiskey

On October 4th, 2013, I was fired from my bellboy job at a hotel in Madison, Wisconsin. When I signed my release, they misspelled my last name as Muse. I took it as a sign. A week later, I began *Women and Whiskey*. I finished the first draft December 18th, 2013. I was 23.

It was originally third person for the first three drafts including an entirely handwritten manuscript, which culminated in the 2015 version. Based on a reader suggestion, I switched to first-person and rewrote the whole book for the fourth time.

In 2017, while working as a Realtor in Milwaukee, I queried 50 literary agents and received only rejections. Later that year, I moved to New York City in search of better inspiration.

Living in Brooklyn, I put the book in the drawer. My writing evolved from novel to screenplays. From there, I began filmmaking and studying comedic writing, including stand-up and sketch comedy. I wrote five features, two comedy pilots, and shot a dozen short films.

All the while, Women and Whiskey lived in a box below my desk. I pulled it out in 2018, 2021, and 2024. Each time, I created an outline, rewrote a few scenes in the first 100 pages, realized the monumental task of rewriting it once again, and put it back in storage.

Why the drawer? I was never satisfied with the end. That's why I could never publish it.

In 2025, ankle surgery sent me to the desk. In my solitude, the ending came to me. Knowing I finally had it, I dusted off the old manuscript of *Women and Whiskey*. I rewrote the whole book in May 2025, finishing a chapter a day.

Funny thing is, I gave the new version with the new ending to eight readers. None of them liked the last chapter. Laughing at life's comedy, I rewrote the end one more time. As much as this is my story, no great art exists without feedback.

Women and Whiskey aged in the barrel of my heart for twelve years. It is yours now. I hope it was worth the wait.

acknowledgments

First and foremost, thank <u>you</u> for reading my work.

Before anyone else, I have to thank my brother, Adam Maus. He read versions of this book that did not deserve to see the light of day. His support has allowed my writing to flourish, and I cannot be more thankful for that. He's writing his own book now and I hope you read that when it's published.

Thank you to the following readers:

-2015 Version: Annie Greengoss, Tom Schneider, Chloe N. Clark

-2017 Version: Kenny Bontempo, Amanda ReCupido

-2025 July Version: Brandon Collins, Sarah Roth Jones, and Kathy Manning

Special thank you for the loving support and patience of Julie Landin.

Thank you to Joni Wildman for the cover art and being there during many whiskey-soaked nights. *@joniwildart*

Thank you to Drew Kopmeier for listening to me ramble on and on about this book for 12 years.

Finally, thank you to my parents, Ray and Lynne, for supplying me with pens. Without their support through the twists and turns of a creative career, this book may have never existed.

Cheers to you all and see you at the bottom...